"ARE YOU—GOING TO BE STAYING HERE IN COLORADO FOR A WHILE?"

The question hung in the air. She almost felt like someone else had asked it.

"Maybe," he replied.

With a flash of chagrin, Annie guessed from the amused gleam in his eyes and her own sentimental rush of emotion that she had to be looking up at him as wistfully as a lovelorn teenager. Which was so not like her. And she certainly didn't want to give him the impression that she'd dragged him into a doorway with the intention of kissing him. Still and all, it had been way too long since she'd kissed anyone. And there he was. Everything she wanted in a man and then some.

Stone closed the distance between them with one long step and took her in his arms.

More Christmas Romance from Janet Dailey

JANET DAILEY

Christmas in Cowboy Country

ZEBRA BOOKS
KENSINGTON PUBLISHING CORP.
http://www.kensingtonbooks.com

Christmas in
Cowboy Country

Chapter 1

"Move it."

Annie smiled to herself. She knew the gruff male voice very well, even though she couldn't see her dad. Tyrell Bennett had to be just over the low ridge that separated the road from the ranch's back acres. She'd pulled up behind his pickup in her own, a slightly newer vehicle, red to his dark blue.

But who was he talking to and why did he sound so cross? Couldn't be one of the hired hands. They had all been let go when autumn turned into an early winter. The Bennetts were more or less on their own in the Colorado backcountry until spring.

She walked to the top of the ridge in bounding strides and looked down at the two men below her. Tyrell's gnarled fists were squarely placed on his belt, his wiry arms bent at the elbow. The unzipped down jacket he wore against the biting wind lent some fullness to his tall frame, but it seemed to her that her dad was thinner with every year that passed.

The man he'd spoken to looked up at her. He was a stranger, though clearly a westerner by his stance. He was taller than Tyrell, lean and muscular, wearing a fleece vest over a checked flannel shirt and heavy jeans with work boots. Annie couldn't see much of his face besides the strong jaw and deep grooves that framed masculine lips somewhere between a scowl and a smile. Dark brown hair curled over his collar, controlled by a ball cap that he'd pulled down over his eyes, no doubt to keep from squinting.

Distracted by her presence, he stood with one hand resting on a surveyor's tripod. The thing looked new; it was bright yellow with pointed red feet jammed deep into the dry land for stability.

He didn't flinch under Tyrell's fierce glare when the older man spoke again. "If Chuck Pfeffer is looking for an argument about property lines, he can speak to me directly."

Annie sighed inwardly and made her way down the ridge, stepping carefully so as not to trip on the clumps of dry brown grass. Their troublesome neighbor generally was looking for an argument about one thing or another. Pfeffer had been disputing the precise placement of the boundary between the two ranches since he'd moved in several years ago.

"Mr. Bennett, I—"

Tyrell cut off the surveyor with a curt wave of his hand. "Pack up and git. And you tell that son-of-a-gun Pfeffer that you can't take a shortcut through my land to his."

"That was my idea."

Tyrell glowered. "Is that right? My ranch is posted. No trespassing."

"I apologize. Must have missed the signs."

They really weren't easy to see. Only a couple were left on distant fence posts, small squares of painted metal nailed up decades ago, dotted with rust and BB holes. But if you were from the area, you knew the signs were there and respected them.

"Hmph. Where's your truck, anyway?"

"I walked."

Annie glanced at the stranger's long legs. The jeans had bits of grass clinging to them and his work boots were good and dusty, so maybe he had. Couldn't have been easy with the tripod slung over his shoulder and a heavy bag of surveyor's gear to lug.

"From where?" Tyrell's tone was a fraction less angry as curiosity got the better of him.

The stranger nodded in the direction of the neighboring ranch. The Pfeffers' house was more than a mile away, a small white box set on flat land dotted with scrub trees. Behind it towered a mountain, shadowed with the deep green of pines and the tattered remains of the aspens' golden glory.

"Oh. I thought you had crossed my land to get to his. So it was the other way around, huh? Either way, I'd like to know what Chuck Pfeffer's up to this time—"

"Dad." Annie ran the last few steps, hoping to

forestall a pointless argument. It was certainly possible that the stranger was only doing his job and meant no harm.

Tyrell turned to her, a look of surprise creasing his weather-beaten face.

"You're back early, girl. I thought you and your mother were going to stay in town for the day."

"Mom met Cilla at Jelly Jam Café and decided to stay. She told me to run along so I came back. Cilla will drive her home."

"Oh." Tyrell Bennett seemed satisfied with that explanation. Annie suppressed a smile. Her dad had never lost his lifelong habit of watching out for his womenfolk. So long as he had some idea of approximately where they were, he was fine.

It had taken a bit of adjusting for Annie to get used to not going wherever she wanted without a second thought. She'd moved back home several months ago to help her parents—and herself. A skiing accident in early spring had broken her leg, and complete healing was taking months longer than anyone had expected.

At least she wasn't limping anymore.

The stranger looked at her with renewed interest. Annie never had been one to obsess over her appearance, but she was glad she'd brushed her long dark hair to gleaming smoothness before she'd come out and that she had on new jeans that fit her just right.

Politely, he touched a finger to the brim of the ball cap, just as if it were a Stetson. The old-fashioned courtesy pleased her. And besides, it gave her a better look at his eyes.

Calm and crinkly at the corners. Very deep brown with long lashes and thick dark brows. He studied her face for a few moments, stopping there and skipping the usual head-to-toe sweep she got from guys checking her out. Probably because of her father's presence. But Annie felt herself flush faintly under his serious gaze.

"Never mind the introductions. I don't know this feller's name," Tyrell informed her. "And I can't say that I want to know it. I believe you were just leaving," he said to the man.

Annie felt a little sorry for the surveyor. He couldn't know how strongly her dad felt about his land. The Bennetts had owned it for several generations.

The surveyor only nodded in response to Tyrell's pointed comment as he packed up quickly, removing the electronic theodolite from the top of the tripod and putting it into an equipment bag. In another few seconds the tripod was folded and slung across his broad shoulder with a carrying strap.

"Yes, sir. That's correct."

Tyrell narrowed his gaze and looked to the horizon, refusing to acknowledge the *sir.* Or the fact that the stranger was cooperating. Her dad had always been tough to butter up.

"Good-bye." The surveyor saved his last nod for her. And . . . a ghost of a wink, while her father still wasn't looking at him.

Annie watched him walk away until he went over the crest of a low rise, and then down. Then he was gone.

"Have you eaten lunch?" she asked her father.

Tyrell's annoyed expression faded away. "Not yet. I'd be happy to sit down with you and have a bite."

"Deal. Let's go." She put her arm through his and they walked back to the trucks.

"How about a tuna fish sandwich?"

It wasn't her dad's favorite meal, but he would eat it if there was nothing else. Annie rummaged through the pantry shelves.

Besides the lone can of tuna, they were overstocked with a sale brand of chili that no one seemed to like much and the kind of lunch meat that tended to be saved for blizzards. Lately, what with one thing and another, she hadn't had a chance to do much shopping.

"If God wanted ranchers to eat tuna fish, there would be horns on the can. But okay," Tyrell said, grinning at his daughter as he settled himself in a kitchen chair to watch her prepare his lunch.

"You know, I thought you and that surveyor might get into a fight," she said, vigorously mashing the tuna and mayonnaise in a glass bowl. She chopped a stalk of celery into tiny bits and added it for crunch, then got out the bread.

"I was kinda steamed," Tyrell said. "But I wouldn't go that far. Even if I am an old cuss."

"No, you're not." She cut the sandwich in half and set it in front of him. "Go ahead and eat, Dad. Don't wait for me."

"I'll wait for you if I feel like waiting for you," he said firmly.

Annie shook her head, smiling, and quickly made a second sandwich.

After eating lunch Tyrell settled into his favorite armchair with a book while Annie started to tidy up the kitchen of the old ranch house. She went out to the hall and woke him up, not on purpose, when the closet door squeaked. He turned his head to see her putting on a denim jacket with a warm plaid lining.

"You going out again?" he asked.

"Yeah. Thought I'd make a run to the big supermarket. We need more canned goods and fresh stuff too. And cold cuts. It's a long drive, but the prices are great. The cupboards are bare," she joked. "Almost, anyway."

He looked outside at the fading sky. "Drive safe. I wonder where your mother is. Think I oughta call her?"

"She just texted me." Louisa Bennett, known to all as Lou, believed in staying in touch. "She should be home in about fifteen minutes."

"Okay then. Have fun at the store." His fond gaze took her in as she wound a hand-knit scarf around her neck. "Now when exactly did you get so tall and grown up? Doesn't seem that long ago when you were trying to climb out of the shopping cart, not pushing one around."

Annie laughed. "Young and wild, that was me. Those were the days."

"How old are you again?"

She knew that he knew perfectly well how old she was. She was the baby of the family, though. Her two older brothers, Sam and Zach, never let her forget it. But she answered him anyway. "Twenty-eight."

"Hell," he sighed. "Then I am an old cuss. And you are definitely grown up."

Bouncing over ruts in the ranch road in her pickup, Annie soon reached the turnoff to the county road to Velde. Out of habit, she stopped the truck to check the mailbox, something she'd meant to do before lunch and hadn't. She unlocked the box with a key on her ring and felt around inside. Nothing. Not even one of her mother's catalogues. She closed the small arched door with a soft bang and locked it again.

The county road was empty when she swung out onto it, looking down toward the small town of Velde below, nestled in the valley. There had been a number of new houses built in the last several months on subdivided land. The town limits, which had always been so clearly marked, were slowly spreading out, moving toward the foothills of the Rockies, in the general direction of the Bennett ranch and others.

She sighed. Progress was good and it created jobs, but it still felt odd that the distant lights of town seemed to get closer every year. Home was where she liked to get away from all that, even though, working in Vail and then Aspen as a ski instructor, she'd loved the bright lights and the glamour of expensive resorts with an international clientele.

Just not all the time.

Velde was Colorado the way it used to be. She rolled down her window, not minding the chilly air, enjoying the evening hush and the cold fragrance of the woods in winter.

Annie drove on. The slight change in altitude was still enough to make her ears pop. She swallowed and looked around, spotting the frame of a new house through aspens that had lost their leaves.

Had that been there last week? Probably. Ranches were being bought up and subdivided into ranchettes. Of course, everyone was entitled to live where they chose if they could afford it, but she wasn't the only one who would miss the openness of the land. Once that was gone, it didn't come back.

Her dad had told her grumpily that Pfeffer's land wasn't zoned for subdividing, which was only one reason he'd made a stink about it. He wasn't able to tell her exactly why the surveyor had been there, but she could guess.

Annie couldn't help thinking about the banked fire in the stranger's dark eyes when he'd turned his thoughtful gaze on her. It had been a while since she'd been looked at that way. He probably was only a few years older than anyone she'd dated from around here, but he sure seemed a lot more manly.

It wasn't like living in Vail and Aspen had spoiled her; there hadn't been that much choice in either place. Between hard-partying ski bums wanting to crash at the condos she'd shared with roommates and rich guys looking for temporary flings, dating was no big thrill.

After the cast on her leg came off and she was able to venture out on her own into Velde and nearby towns, she'd run through the local possibilities one by one. And then pretty much retreated to the ranch, where there was always work to do.

An oncoming car blinked its headlights. Annie checked—hers were on. Then she realized Priscilla Rivers was behind the wheel. She waved and Cilla waved back without rolling down the windows or stopping to say hi. You never knew these days when a semi might be coming in either direction.

Annie looked in her rearview mirror. As she'd expected, her mother had turned to watch her go around the curve ahead, even though she knew her daughter had taken the road to town and back ten thousand times in the last ten years. Annie didn't really mind.

She knew her mother liked having at least one of her grown kids at home to fuss over.

Now that her oldest brother, Sam, was married to Nicole, a window designer for major fashion retailers, they traveled a lot. As of September, Zach had been in Oregon with his wife, Paula, who'd taken a leave of absence from the Denver police force while they looked at land in the Pacific Northwest.

In a way, it was Annie's turn to hold down the fort. She missed skiing, but she knew she'd get back to it. The blinking red light at the intersection of county roads had her slowing down.

Yowch. Annie felt a sharp twinge in her healing

leg as her foot pressed down on the brake. She distracted herself until the pain went away by making a mental list of what they needed from the market.

Annie saw her mother through the kitchen window as she hauled shopping bags filled with food out of the pickup's cab. Lou had the side door open before Annie reached for the knob.

"There you are. Thanks so much for doing the shopping."

"No problem."

Working quickly, they got everything put away. Her mother boiled water for herb tea while Annie opened a package of cookies and rinsed some grapes, which she put into a bowl on the table, along with mugs and small plates.

She looked up. "Where's Dad?" Normally her father came into the kitchen when he heard someone pull into the drive.

"He's gone up to bed."

"Already? It's only eight."

"I guess he was tired after giving that surveyor a hard time." Lou laughed as she sat down. "What was Chuck Pfeffer thinking? But to hear your dad tell it, the fellow won't come back."

Annie wouldn't mind if he did come back—just not here. She gave a shrug. "Maybe not onto our property. But he'll show up someplace else, that's for sure. There's a lot of new construction going on."

Her mother shook her head with mild concern. "Tell me about it. I don't know anything about Chuck's plans, though. But other folks are thinking of selling up and moving out. It's a shame, really. Still, you can't stop change." She nibbled thoughtfully on a grape.

"True enough." The subject was depressing, so Annie changed it. "How's Cilla?"

"Same sweet tooth. Jelly Jam had those wonderful crumb-top muffins just out of the oven, so we ordered some and started talking. We kind of forgot about the time."

"Dad didn't."

"He had nothing to worry about." Lou rolled her eyes. "It's not like I get into town that often. Anyway, Cilla is coping fairly well, under the circumstances."

Annie gave her mother a questioning look over the rim of her mug. "What's up?"

"Well, you know she took in her cousin Bree's girls," Lou began.

"You mentioned that." Annie dunked a cookie and ate it. "How old are they again?"

"Three and six. Full of fun, but so mischievous. They turn her house upside down. Cilla loves them to pieces, but there are days when she feels a little upside down herself. She and Ed never had children, so of course she's not used to it."

Annie let her mother ramble on about her best friend, whose kind heart meant people sometimes took advantage of her.

"Bree is divorced, right?"

"Yes. Her ex is totally out of the picture. He doesn't see the kids and doesn't pay a nickel of child support. Right now Bree is making good money, but she earns it the hard way." Lou shook her head. "Fourteen-hour shifts at an oil field camp in North Dakota, cooking for hundreds of roughnecks. That's a tough job."

"Yikes. I bet." Annie had helped her mother cook for the ranch hands at haying time while she was growing up. But they were courteous and appreciative, and there had never been more than six or seven of them.

"Cilla says a camp like that is no place for children."

"I'm sure she's right."

"So she has the girls until January. Then their mom comes back. Bree's saving every penny so they can start a new life, just the three of them." True to her nature, Lou finished the story with a happy ending.

Annie hoped it came true. "Good for her. And good for Cilla."

"Just so long as she doesn't lose her mind," Lou said wryly. "Of course, Ed helps. He got dinner on the table by five and Cilla took home a pie for dessert. So she got a break."

"I'm glad you both escaped."

Lou Bennett's blue eyes sparkled as she smoothed her pixie cut. "The hairdresser's next. That salon is full of runaway women."

Annie laughed as she finished her tea, then took the mug to the sink, washing it and the few dishes that had been left from lunch. Her mother got busy with some paperwork she'd left on the kitchen table.

"Oh, here's my Christmas card list," Lou said absently. "Shoot. I'm going to need at least two boxes this year. I like to get them mailed by December first."

"That's four weeks away." Annie concentrated on her task. "You could send out e-cards," she said.

"I just can't. It's not the same. Some of the animated ones are cute, though. Hmm. Maybe I'll send e-cards to the kids and real cards to the grown-ups."

Lou paused as Annie racked the plates in the dish drainer.

"I hope Sam and Zach come home for Christmas," Lou said softly. "With them here plus Nicole and Paula, the house will be filled to bursting. Just thinking about it makes me happy."

Annie suppressed a smile. "Wait until grandchildren are in the works. You might feel differently then."

"I'd be even happier. But don't tell those four I said so. They're still newlyweds, after all. Well, Zach and Paula are. Not Sam and Nicole. They've been married for two years. Imagine that."

Annie didn't respond. It was a lot harder to imagine herself in a relationship, let alone being married.

Her mother reached into her tote bag for a file folder. "Oh, no," Lou groaned.

Annie turned, flipping the dish towel over her shoulder. "What's the matter?"

"I promised Nell Dighton that I'd bring her these forms for the Christmas fund-raiser and I completely forgot. She needs them tonight."

"I'll take them to her," Annie offered.

"But you already drove to the big supermarket and back."

"It felt good to get out. Besides, Velde is a lot closer. And I don't feel like watching TV or reading."

"Are you sure?"

Annie hung up the dish towel neatly. "Hand 'em over. Be back in a flash."

Annie switched off the radio in the truck before the sad song was over and clambered out as soon as she'd parked. The neon sign that marked the town's vintage saloon glowed a cheerful red. The odd mood she'd fallen into on the short drive vanished.

Annie pushed open the swinging doors, enjoying the authentic creak. Her boot heels clunked pleasantly on the old plank floor of the entryway, which led to the saloon's real doors. Handsomely framed and made of weatherized glass, they offered a glimpse of the climate-controlled interior, which she knew was nice and cozy.

Old and new. That was her little hometown all over. The proprietress, Nell Dighton, had been her high-school English teacher before she'd retired and bought the saloon several years ago. Which was why Annie never met any of her dates here. But she loved the place.

Annie still hesitated to call Nell by her first name. In Annie's mind, she was still Mrs. Dighton and would always be Mrs. Dighton, a widow and pillar of the community, plus a real stickler for good grammar and proper language. Though that seemed to be changing. Maybe the influence of her grown son Harold had done that. The two of them were close and he liked to tease her when she lost her temper in public and burst out in not-so-proper language.

Like right now.

Nell seemed to be locked in the storage closet, judging by the unladylike curses issuing from behind its closed door.

Annie walked that way and put a hand on the doorknob, noticing the door wasn't really shut just as Nell backed out of it, her arms piled high with miscellaneous boxes marked *Xmas* and *Fragile* and *Don't Peek*. On the very top of the pile was a small box with a big question mark on the side.

"Let me help you," Annie said, laughing.

"Oh, goodness. Thanks." Nell blew the dust off the top box. "There's just so much stuff. Decorations, garlands, ornaments—I didn't sort it out before I put it away in January. But I do know that bottom one has the lights. I wanted to test them."

"Good idea to get an early start." Annie relieved Nell of some of her burden, settling several boxes on a round table by the piano.

"Well, yes. Whew. But if I don't have everything I need and have to shop for something, the sales start before Thanksgiving nowadays. I do want to be ready." Nell looked curiously at her, as if she'd just realized that Annie didn't often come in at night. "What brings you here at this hour?"

"My mom forgot to give you the fund-raising forms. And—oh, heck. I just forgot to bring them in. They're out in my truck."

Annie wasn't usually so absentminded. Brooding about her nonexistent love life on a lonely road with country music on the radio was never a good idea. But Nell Dighton was the forgiving type.

"That's great. I was about to call her."

"Well, before I bring them home again, let me go get 'em."

"You do that. Thanks, honey."

When Annie came back in, Nell was still checking out the various boxes. She lifted a half-crushed lid and peered inside. "There are the lights. Got a minute to help me straighten them out?"

"Sure."

Annie reached in and drew out a complicated tangle of dark green wires and big fat Christmas bulbs, the traditional kind. The bulbs' colors were flat and dull. She smiled at Nell. "I always love it when they're all laid out in a dark room and get plugged in. Can we close the blinds?"

Even though it was dark out, the street lamps poured golden light in through the windows.

Nell chuckled, looking into some other boxes without removing them. "Go right ahead. Just so long as I don't have to get down on my knees. You don't even have to untangle them."

Annie set the tangle of bulbs and wire on a table, and went to the windows, letting the wooden-slat blinds rattle down. Then she switched off all the interior lights. There was enough light coming in from the street for her to find her way back.

"Show time," she said to Nell, grinning like a kid as the older woman handed her the plug to the string of lights.

Annie kneeled by the outlet, positioning the prongs, then turning her head as she pushed in the plug. All of the bulbs blazed with glorious color in the darkened saloon.

"Yeah!" she said happily.

"Looks like they're all working," Nell said on a more practical note.

Annie rose, dusting off her knees and walking back to the table. She stopped in her tracks when the saloon door swung open.

It framed a broad-shouldered, lean man in a checked flannel shirt and denim jacket. No ball cap this time. Just a lot of thick, dark hair, ruffled by the wind. She recognized him immediately. The glowing light from the tangle of Christmas bulbs didn't soften his rugged features that much.

"Hello again," said the stranger.

Chapter 2

Annie stared at him. "Ah—hello."

There was no reason he shouldn't be in the saloon, but seeing him there took her aback. He looked taller indoors.

She managed an awkward smile and went back toward the table where the Christmas boxes were haphazardly piled, stopping for a second to flip the wall switch. Then she bent to unplug the lights and picked them up, stuffing them back into their container.

Nell bustled over and moved behind the bar as the stranger stepped inside the saloon and took a stool. "Welcome. What'll you have?"

"A beer, thanks. Anything on draft is fine."

She offered him a choice of three and he selected the darker ale. Nell chatted him up as she filled the tall glass, setting it carefully in front of him.

He didn't drink it right away, half glancing at Annie.

She caught his gaze for a second, then looked down, into a clear plastic container that held pinecone birds. They seemed to be stuck together. They could use organizing. She popped off the lid and reached in, then put the lid back on when she realized that they were glued to each other. So much for that big idea.

"Would you like some peanuts?" Nell wiped her hands on a bar towel, smiling at him.

"Sure."

She took a small bowl from under the counter and poured shelled peanuts from a paper sack into it, sliding it over to him.

Hmm. *His very own bowl,* Annie thought. And fresh peanuts. Nothing was too good. Nell's brown eyes looked awfully bright.

"Mind if I ask why you said hello *again* to Annie?"

As a lifelong resident of a small town, Nell had pretty good instincts for sizing up outsiders. Clearly, she had decided on the spot that this one could be trusted. It didn't hurt that he was chiseled and handsome.

"Not at all," the man replied.

A bit belatedly, Nell thought to look Annie's way to make sure that she didn't mind the question either and received an almost invisible nod in reply.

Let the stranger do the explaining, Annie thought. She was interested to hear how he would describe the encounter on their ranch.

He took a long swallow of his beer. Nell forged on with an even brighter smile. "Have you two met?"

"Yes indeed. Not long ago. Today, in fact. I would say it was around noon."

"Oh my. High noon?"

Annie knew her former English teacher was being a little flirty, but only because she was interested in extracting information.

"Could have been."

"Sounds like a showdown," Nell teased.

"You might say that." He was nice enough to flirt right back at a plump, graying lady who was old enough to be his mother, Annie thought.

He took another sip of his beer. "By the way, thank you for telling me her name. Mr. Bennett didn't seem inclined to introduce us."

"Oh." Nell clink-clanked the glassware that was upside down on a draining rack, just for something to do. Annie gave her a *please-shut-up* look, but the older woman didn't seem to pick up on it. "So what's your name? I'm Nell Dighton."

"Marshall Stone. Pleased to meet you."

"Likewise. Now, I know you're not from around here," she continued. "So let me take an educated guess—"

"Wyoming," came the laconic answer.

"And what brings you to Colorado?"

"I'm a surveyor. As to how I met Annie"—he seemed a little reluctant to get into it—"I was out on Chuck Pfeffer's property when I ran into Mr. Bennett. Apparently I went a step too far. He didn't take kindly to my presence on his land."

"Hmm," Nell said pleasantly.

Annie knew her ex-teacher would have the whole story out of her mother before Annie got home, unless Marshall Stone stayed at the bar longer than that. There wasn't anyone to keep him company and Annie wasn't going to linger. She did want to talk to him. But she didn't like the idea of looking like she was waiting for him to ask if he could buy her a beer.

And if he did, her mother would hear about that too. And her father. There were definite drawbacks to moving home, and the lack of privacy was one.

Not that she'd cared about it particularly until now.

Nell walked around the bar and over to the free jukebox. "How about a musical interlude?"

Annie caught the flicker of amusement in Stone's dark gaze. "Okay."

The older woman took a small metal disc out of a dish next to the jukebox and awaited his reply.

"Whatever you like, ma'am," he said gravely.

"All right." Nell popped the disc into the slot and chose a few tunes, then sauntered back to Annie, who was trying not to look at the way Stone sat on the bar stool. He was now surveying himself in the antique mirror behind the stacked rows of liquor bottles.

He had changed into clean dark jeans and traded his dusty work boots for black cowboy boots, the hand-tooled, expensively simple kind.

The real deal, she thought. They looked like he'd had them since forever. One heel was hooked over the bottom rung of the stool and one was set solidly on the floor. Since he wasn't looking at her, she studied the rest of him discreetly while Nell re-stocked the lemon and lime wedges in a compart-mented holder, slicing the fruits with a sharp knife and humming along with the jukebox.

Those legs were long and lean, but muscled through the thigh. No showy buckle for him. His was just plain silver—probably real silver, she thought suddenly—and the belt was simple black leather with a chased silver tip.

Nice butt. Narrow. He shifted, getting comfort-able on the bar stool. He had serious shoulders that filled out the back yoke of his flannel shirt. His dark hair just reached his collar, where a few locks curled. As if he sensed her gaze, he ran his right hand over his hair in back.

Whoa, she told herself. *Time for a ring check.* Try-ing to be invisible, Annie craned her neck to peek at his other hand, the left, which he'd just rested on the bar. He seemed to be about to use it to pivot himself around.

She saw nothing, not even the white shadow of a ring. She smiled to herself, then pressed her lips together hard when his eyes met hers in the an-tique mirror.

A long, lazy, mocking look made heat come into her cheeks.

"Oh, dear. I cut myself. Not too badly."

Saved by the Nell. Annie jumped up to go help her.

"Now don't get excited, everyone," the older woman admonished them both. "It's just a tiny cut."

Marshall Stone slid off his seat and stood. "Ma'am—"

"I don't need rescuing," Nell said with a wink. "You stay there."

"But—"

She already had a paper towel wrapped around her finger when Annie got behind the bar.

"Where's the first aid kit?" Annie bent to look under the bar, not familiar with the layout of items.

"In the corner. Next to the baseball bat." Nell pointed.

Chatting to Marshall Stone the whole time, Nell unwrapped the paper towel and let Annie dab the cut with disinfectant and bandage it. He looked on, seeming to approve of Annie's technique while fielding a few more personal questions from Nell.

"There. That should heal up quickly." Annie crumpled the bandage wrapper and tossed it and the paper towel away.

"Thanks, honey." Nell patted her cheek.

Which, Annie realized, was still flaming. Marshall Stone's steady gaze on her had a lot to do with that.

A mixed group of young guys and their girlfriends came through the door, calling out hellos to Nell and Annie while they slung their jackets and down vests over the hooks on the booth posts, sliding into two adjoining booths.

"Here comes everybody. Can you manage?" Annie asked.

"Yes. My son should be here in five minutes."

"All right. Then if you're okay, I guess I'll run on home," Annie said quickly.

"Of course I'm okay. I appreciate you bringing in those forms. You tell your mother I said hello."

"I sure will."

Marshall Stone stepped aside as Annie went around the bar. His expression didn't change from neutral friendliness as she made every effort not to brush against his sleeve. In fact, she went in a half circle around him.

"So long," she murmured.

He inclined his head in a polite nod. "Nice to see you again. Take care now." His reply was deep voiced and unexpectedly intimate.

At least Nell hadn't heard the exchange. The saloon owner was taking orders from the first booth as the second booth began to swap stories of the day's jaunt on a scenic mountain railroad.

Annie headed for the door.

Nell hurried over with her order pad in hand. "Wait. I almost forgot." She flipped through the pages until she got to a blank one and jotted down a note. "Would you give this to Lou? Just in case I don't get a chance to call her tonight."

Annie looked down at the piece of paper when Nell tore it off and gave it to her. "Town meeting tomorrow. Eight P.M.," she read. "Oh, okay. Will do."

"You should come too," Nell said.

Annie shook her head. "No, thanks. Not my thing."

"It's your civic duty."

Annie only smiled as she pushed the door open. She could think of about a thousand other things she'd rather do than sit through a long, dull meeting.

Like go out on a date with Marshall Stone. But at the moment, she couldn't think of a way to make that happen.

Chapter 3

"Why do you have to go to the meeting? Because you and your brothers are gonna inherit this ranch someday."

Tyrell Bennett's far-seeing gaze swept over the rolling acres of the ranch, lightly frosted with the first snowfall of the season, then moved back to his daughter's pensive face. He chucked her under the chin. "I said *someday*, Annie girl. Not soon."

He strode to the blue truck where his wife, Lou, waited behind the wheel as Annie hurried to catch up to him.

"Did Zach and Sam attend town meetings?" she asked.

"Once in a while. Not if they could help it," he said dryly. "But the time has come for you to listen and learn. Take notes," he added.

"I was planning to." Annie followed her father and got into the bench seat ahead of him. She thought it best not to offer an argument. Her dad generally won the important ones.

"Is this your first town meeting, honey?" her mother asked. "Somehow I thought you'd been to one before."

"I have. You took me with you when I was six. I remember falling asleep on a pile of coats."

"Oh, that's right."

"I expect you to keep your eyes and ears open," her father informed her.

"This could be important."

"Really? Mom says the mayor's not even going to be there."

"He oughta be," Tyrell grumbled. "Maybe we should stop by his hangout and tell him we're not going to vote for him again. Go to the Grizzly Bar and Grill first."

"Oh, Ty," his wife said soothingly. "Let him be. Annie's right. There will be other meetings."

Lou backed up the truck and swung out onto the ranch road. They reached the main road in minutes and were on their way. Annie slid a sideways look at her dad. He frowned at the sight of the small city's lights below, gleaming in the dusk.

She wondered if he was thinking what she'd thought: that Velde looked different lately. More spread out, but not in a coherent way. Far below, toward the east, there were two rows of cold white lights revealing a new street that seemed to go nowhere.

Those definitely hadn't been there yesterday. She strained to see. There weren't any houses. It was just a street waiting for houses to be built. Someone had turned on the street lamps, that was all.

Annie sat back. The new development, if it was one, was still a long, long way from where they lived. The ranch was very much theirs and probably always would be. Her parents were about the least likely to ever sell their land.

But some would and they had the right to do so. Like her mother said, they couldn't stop change.

The Bennetts entered in time to help themselves to coffee from an urn, and sat down in the back row holding their foam cups. Annie looked around. She recognized a lot of the people in attendance without being able to put a name to every face. There were newcomers, but that was to be expected.

Her father turned his head and spotted someone he didn't like, judging by the way his eyes narrowed. Annie looked in that direction.

Chuck Pfeffer was leaning against the wall under the exit sign. He was a rangy man in late middle age with light brown hair cropped close to his head, wearing khakis, not jeans, and a nylon windbreaker.

"Will you look at him standing there. Great spot for a quick getaway," Tyrell muttered.

"Dad, shh. I know you don't like him, but he's not a criminal. What if he hears you?"

"I don't care." But Tyrell settled down for the roll call and the minutes of the last meeting. Annie took out a notebook and a pen and slipped on tortoise-frame glasses. She hadn't heard anything worth writing down yet. She simply listened.

Then Lou, who had moved forward to talk with Nell Dighton, turned around to gesture to her husband to come forward when someone abandoned the folding chair next to hers.

"All right, all right," he said to her as he rose. He looked down at his daughter. "Annie, no sneaking out."

"I'm not going anywhere," was her indignant response. She leaned back and hugged her notebook to her as he edged past.

The procedural details continued at a snail's pace. Annie took a few notes, but she could feel her eyes glazing over already. The meeting could take hours.

A deep voice that was oddly familiar spoke from behind her, as if its owner was bending low. "Is your dad coming back?"

Annie whirled around. Marshall Stone's face was inches from hers, his mouth curved at the corners in a faint smile. This close, she could see how unfairly thick his eyelashes were and the rough trace of stubble along his jawline. His strong hand rested on the metal chair that Tyrell had just vacated.

She glanced toward the front row where her father was now ensconced between his wife and Nell. "Doesn't look like it."

"Would you mind if I sat with you?"

"No." That was the truth. The one-word reply didn't sound too eager. He couldn't read anything into it.

Stone stepped between the rows of chairs in the

back, excusing himself without much need to. Lean as he was, he didn't bump into anyone.

"I wasn't expecting to see you here," he murmured, easing down next to her in the confined space.

"My parents' idea. I'm supposed to be learning something."

"Any luck?" He gave the appearance of paying attention to the speakers, but his profile showed a real smile this time.

"Not yet. So why did you come?"

"Chuck Pfeffer asked me to attend," was Stone's reply.

"Oh." His reply made her uneasy. He didn't offer any more information.

The rangy man was still leaning against the wall, his hands now jammed in his pants pockets. Pfeffer was never going to be pals with her dad, but they shared a property boundary and it would be best if they resolved their differences on that subject peaceably.

Where Marshall Stone fit into that issue was something that puzzled her. His presence at the meeting was a surprise. Why Stone was hanging around Velde after completing the surveying assignment for their neighbor was a mystery.

She hadn't spotted him out their way since Tyrell had ordered him off their land yesterday. Annie made an idle note or two. She wasn't going to tell him that she'd been looking for the bright yellow gizmo atop the tall tripod, something that would be pretty easy to spot in open fields. So was he.

It occurred to her that he must be staying somewhere in town, since it was now the second day since his arrival. No doubt Nell had obtained some information on that, or tried to.

The council members spoke into microphones with the volume cranked high enough to cover her low-pitched exchange with the man at her side. No one complained or even looked at them. Annie kept half an ear on the proceedings.

Stone's presence distracted her.

If he were any closer, she'd be in his lap. The folding chair was simply too small for him. Cautiously, he extended one long leg under the seat in front of him, trying to get comfortable.

As if he were trying to minimize his bulk, he folded his arms across his chest. Different shirt, she noticed. Same muscles. Holy cow. He radiated masculinity. And heat. It was warm enough already in here.

The council members droned on for a long while and then took questions from the audience. Annie checked her watch. It was past nine.

The questions turned to zoning issues and then someone asked about a new ordinance requiring residents to prove title and have property lines redrawn for land some families had owned for generations.

Up front, Tyrell Bennett sat straight up, listening closely, and so did her mother. The atmosphere in the hall began to crackle with tension.

She noticed that Chuck Pfeffer was no longer holding up the wall under the exit sign. He had walked to the front to join the council members and face the townspeople. Someone handed him a wireless microphone.

"It's getting late, so we won't keep you much longer," Chuck began.

We? Chuck wasn't an elected official, Annie thought. He wasn't even an appointee.

"I'd like to introduce a consultant to the town council who has the expertise to help us all," Chuck continued. "This is Shep Connally. Shep, would you like to say a few words?"

A thickset man in a rumpled suit stood up and walked the few steps from the front row to Chuck to take the mike. He gave the audience a jowly grin and straightened his colorful tie. The rest of his attire was sober and dull, but it did kind of look like he'd slept in that suit.

His short speech sounded rehearsed, but people listened attentively. Connally presented himself as the man to see about property problems, which he promised to resolve.

"To the best of my abilities and the fullest extent of my knowledge," he added in a booming voice.

Heads were turning, as if the homeowners and ranchers in attendance were asking each other who this guy was. Annie didn't remember his name mentioned in the local newspaper. Then Connally answered the question that everyone seemed about to ask.

"If you're wondering what makes me an expert, let me reassure you. I have over twenty years of experience with property issues and law. Chuck talked me into doing some consulting for you folks and the town council."

Shep turned and pointed to a council member on his right. "Joe Gitterson here can give you my bona fides. I understand he's Chuck's right hand."

Not a glowing recommendation. Tyrell Bennett turned around and frowned for Annie's benefit. She didn't know Gitterson or any of the other council members, but she had a feeling this wasn't how the town was supposed to be run. She made a note. *Who pays Connally? Follow the money.*

"Joe is actually the one who hired me just a month ago," Connally added, talking faster. "Chuck doesn't have that authority, if any of you were wondering about that."

Annie distinctly heard someone mutter, "Damn straight." Not her father, though.

"So. Moving on. I just want you all to know that I got up here to Colorado as soon as I could."

There was a pause for dramatic effect. He could have been a carnival pitchman or a tinhorn politician, Annie thought.

"And I'm ready to knuckle down and work."

Like this so-called consultant was doing the people of Velde a huge favor, she thought. And he hadn't said where he was from.

"It's clear that many of you have important questions," Connally added, ignoring the raised hands. "These are complex issues. I may not have every answer right at my fingertips, but I'm sure as heck determined to help you all."

His attempt to be folksy fell flat with most.

"We'll get this business straightened out," he went on. "Maybe not tonight, but soon. You can count on me."

Annie listened to more reassurances that sounded like casual lies, even to her inexperienced ears. She glanced at Marshall. His jaw was set and there was a hard gleam in his eyes. She considered asking him for his opinion on exactly what was going on. But he was watching Connally intently.

"He sounds like a con man," she whispered to Stone.

He only shrugged. "Prove it. He can say what he likes. It's a free country."

Stone's indifference irked her, but she kept it to herself.

"Say, it might be best if you all could write down your questions," the consultant added. He took out a handkerchief and mopped his forehead. "Then I could address each case individually, maybe do some research ahead of time in the town records. With permission, of course. Just keep in mind that I'd be happy to speak privately with any of you, if that is your preference."

Another red flag, as far as Annie was concerned. She made another note. *Private meaning no witnesses and no official record?*

She wasn't the only one with suspicions. The low murmurs in the room were threaded with concern, even though she couldn't make out every word. But a few homeowners seemed to be jotting down their thoughts. Connally glanced downward at the ones who were closest to him, smiling affably.

Offering private talks was a shrewd move, she thought angrily. The proceedings of the town meeting were supposed to be transparent, but not everyone wanted their business out in the open. Some of the older people on fixed incomes had financial troubles that they kept to themselves.

Annie had overheard her mother saying as much to her dad more than once, but Lou always glossed over the details.

Well, at least everything Connally said tonight would go on the public record. The trouble was, he hadn't said anything definite or with substance.

Even though the mayor hadn't attended, his secretary was dutifully taking notes on a steno pad. She sat next to the video camera taping the meeting for good measure.

The head of the town council wrapped up the meeting, and people milled around.

Marshall Stone stood first, his dark gaze on Annie. She couldn't read it or his neutral expression as she gathered her things and got up.

"Want to go outside and talk for a bit?" he asked.

Annie hesitated.

"I heard someone say it's snowing again," he continued. "Besides, it's stuffy in here."

"That would be from all the hot air being generated by that guy." She indicated Connally with a discreet nod.

There were people gathered around him, including several senior citizens—a married couple in their eighties and a widow Annie thought her mother might know, and a bachelor farmer who was so old and stooped his overalls looked hollow.

"You have a point," Marshall said in a low voice. He waited for her answer as Annie took off her tortoise-frame glasses and tucked them into her bag, which already held her notebook and printed information handed out before the meeting. "Just a sec."

Annie got her father's attention by waving at him. "I'll be outside," she called.

"Okay, honey." He turned to discuss something with her mother before he could see that Marshall Stone was going with her. Annie pushed open one of the double doors of the town hall's entrance.

A light snow was falling straight down, since there was no wind. She stopped for a minute to take in the lovely sight. He did too. Neither spoke.

She walked a few steps ahead of Marshall, knowing he had to shorten his long strides to follow her. But she wanted to be the one who decided where they'd end up. Annie stopped by the tiled entryway of a closed restaurant, moving right next to the narrow side wall so that he'd have room to stand a few feet away.

She had wanted to talk to him without half the town being able to listen in. And that was all. The entryway would do.

"Nice," he said, looking up at the sparkling snowflakes that twirled down from on high. The street lamps' illumination made each one stand out before it vanished forever. Annie held out a hand to catch a few, unable to resist, even though the crystalline snow melted almost instantly on her warm skin.

"You must be used to a lot of snow where you're from."

"That's so. Wyoming gets its share." His deep

voice echoed against the tiles of the entryway. His reply was to the point, but it held a thoughtfulness that she liked.

He was a man of few words, and each of them seemed to count for something. The warmth in his voice was genuine.

She hadn't picked up on that while the meeting was in progress, when he'd seemed so indifferent to what was going on in Velde.

She told herself to cut him some slack on that. It wasn't his hometown and he didn't have to have an opinion on local politics. The meeting could be the first time he'd seen a different side of his employer.

Annie now understood why her dad just didn't trust the man who owned the land adjacent to his. The conflict might never amount to more than the occasional spat over boundary lines, but the Bennetts could handle themselves. She was much more concerned about the elderly residents who had flocked to Shep Connally after Chuck Pfeffer introduced the man.

Call it a rude awakening for her and Marshall Stone.

Annie wasn't going to obsess over it.

Not when he was this close to her and they were as alone as they might ever be. She turned to look at him, realizing that he was keeping the same respectful distance. But when his eyes met hers, she felt a much stronger connection.

"Are you—going to be staying here in Colorado for a while?" The question hung in the air. She almost felt like someone else had asked it.

"Maybe," he replied.

With a flash of chagrin, Annie guessed from the amused gleam in his eyes and her own sentimental rush of emotion that she had to be looking up at him as wistfully as a lovelorn teenager. Which was so not like her. And she certainly didn't want to give him the impression that she'd dragged him into a doorway with the intention of kissing him. Still and all, it had been way too long since she'd kissed anyone. And there he was. Everything she wanted in a man and then some.

Stone closed the distance between them with one long step and took her in his arms. Then he angled his head over hers, supporting the nape of her neck with one large hand and pulling her body nearer to his with the other. Gently but insistently, he brushed his lips against her cheek and pressed a kiss to her closed lips.

She wanted him to. She sank her hands into his hair, loving the silky thickness of it.

With an almost inaudible moan, she parted her lips. He deepened the kiss and strengthened his hold on her, sliding his hand from her neck to slowly caress her back. Up and down. The pressure of his hand was sensual and easy, but it soon intensified. The hand around her waist went lower too, rounding over the back pockets of her jeans in full appreciation of the curves beneath the snug denim.

Soon both of his hands were well below her belt. Gently, he lifted her up by her behind so she could easily throw her arms around his neck and kiss him back just as hard, once her mouth was level with his.

Annie was literally floating in air, her boots off the ground. The sensation was strongly erotic. She used her thighs to get a grip on him, clasping his narrow hips with the same muscles she used to ride horses.

He might not be a cowboy, but he sure as hell kissed like one.

Murmuring some interesting ideas in her ear about taking this as far as she wanted to go, Marshall pressed her back against the narrow wall, swiftly freeing his hands and helping her support herself by pressing into her. She tried to concentrate on staying up, but it was far from easy when those big hands moved to her breasts, circling both at the same time.

He stopped and inserted an exploring finger between them, looking at her hopefully. "Front clasp?"

Annie shook her head. Stone seemed a little disappointed, but he went back to what he'd been doing.

A button on her shirt gave up and popped. He bent his head.

Annie breathed raggedly, her mouth open against his, her body quivering with excitement, not quite believing that this was still only a kiss.

The cool tile was a sharp contrast to the heat of the big, muscular body that had her pinned. They weren't in plain sight, because there was no one on the street, but if anyone walked by, they could be seen.

Annie almost didn't care. The way he handled her—with tender care and a dash of roughness that conveyed the ultimate in masculinity—had her dazed and craving much more.

Distantly, she heard the doors of the town hall creak. Men came out, talking loudly and joshing each other. She didn't recognize the voices. Not anyone she knew. She couldn't see them.

But Marshall swore under his breath and released his grip, letting her slide down and out of his embrace. "That's Chuck. Gotta stop. Sorry. I don't want to get caught."

"Excuse me?" She stared at him, wobbling a little when she touched down, off balance. She dragged a hand through her tangled hair. It hurt enough to snap her back to reality. *You're a grown man,* she wanted to say.

Too quickly, like an overgrown, shame-faced teenager, Marshall Stone straightened his shirt and smoothed the dark locks she'd tousled.

Annie was dumbfounded. But she couldn't stop him or scold him.

If that was his employer—and she had to assume that Stone had guessed right—she could understand, sort of, why Marshall wouldn't want to get caught necking in a doorway.

"Go," she said in a low voice. "Just go."

Marshall hesitated, reaching out to stroke her hair. She pushed his hand away and gave him a shove. "I mean it. I need a minute to myself."

He seemed to get what she wasn't saying. Her parents would come out sooner or later. She didn't want them to see her with a blurry mouth and high color in her cheeks and messed-up hair.

Since she'd moved home, they hadn't bugged her about any of her infrequent dates or what she'd done or even when she came home, except that time at four in the morning when she'd had a flat tire on a girls' night out. Which was reasonable.

She moved back into the shadows of the doorway, watching Marshall Stone walk away from her. There was nothing about the way he made her feel that could be described as reasonable.

What on earth had she just done? She usually insisted on getting to know a man fairly well before she kissed him. But she and Marshall had put the kissing first and the conversation second. Actually, no. They'd never exchanged enough words to add up to a whole conversation.

Something about the man from Wyoming shredded her common sense, to say nothing of her self-respect. She wanted him too much. For no good reason.

She saw him approach Chuck Pfeffer, who was standing with the councilman named Gitterson near a huge new truck, a dark color that looked iridescent under the street lamp despite its dusting of snow.

"There you are," Chuck called to him. "We were looking for you inside. Did you come out for a smoke or something? Can I bum a cigarette?"

"I just needed some fresh air. And no, I don't smoke."

"Aw, hell. Are you telling the truth? You look like

an ad for smokes, pal. But I guess they don't have those billboards anymore." Chuck paused, chuckling at his attempt at humor. "Sure you don't have some cigs in your truck?"

He thumped the hood of the huge new vehicle, making the snow dance. Marshall didn't tell him to quit. *Some cowboy,* Annie thought. *So not.*

From where she was, she took a longer look at the truck. It was not only new, it was expensive and loaded with custom features from what she could see. Did surveyors make that much money? She didn't get it.

Marshall Stone wasn't who she'd thought he was. It dawned on her that he might have earned enough to pay for a truck like that by doing something else. But what? His trade didn't lend itself to crooked dealings. Surveying was all about straight lines. Measurements had to be accurate.

"Just kidding." Pfeffer slapped Marshall on the back. "Listen, me and Joe wanted to talk to you about that old buzzard Tyrell Bennett. I don't know who he thinks he is—"

Annie froze. Marshall Stone said not one word in her father's defense, just let Pfeffer lead him away, when the loudmouth seemed to realize that someone might overhear.

She regretted what she'd just let him do to her in the doorway. Deeply regretted it.

Annie stepped out of the doorway, heading back to the town hall. She walked quickly past the alley that ran alongside it, stopped by a hooting voice she now recognized.

Pfeffer and Gitterson were standing by a row of

garbage cans. It would have been an ideal photo
opportunity if she'd had a camera. Marshall was
nowhere to be seen.

"Hey there. Annie, isn't that your name? Aren't
you a Bennett?"

"Yes." She kept walking.

"Just saying hi." Chuck seemed to be talking to
the man at his side, not to her. "I heard she used to
be a snow bunny up in Aspen. Bet she likes this
weather."

The stupid comment was too annoying to ig-
nore. She gave him a withering look instead of an
answer and ran up the stairs to the town hall entrance, going inside to find her parents.

Marshall rejoined the two other men, coming
back around the hidden side of his truck. Annie
had to have heard Pfeffer refer to her father as an
old buzzard. The hell of it was he couldn't have
said anything or argued with the man.

Not without tipping his hand about the ongoing
investigation of Pfeffer's new best friends, Joe Gitterson and Shep Connally. Chuck was only a side
note to the real-estate fraud Connally intended to
pull off in Velde, a scheme very similar to one in
Arizona that he'd gotten away with. Or had until
now. The FBI was still putting the pieces of the
puzzle together and tracking the money.

One wrong move and Stone would go in front
of a judge and request an arrest warrant for Connally. So far, Joe Gitterson hadn't officially made

the list of bad guys. Stone just hoped Annie would believe him when the time came.

He felt guilty for giving in to the temptation of her lush mouth and incredible body. But the way she'd looked up at him once she got him alone had shredded his self-control. That kiss had blown him away. It was a rash act that could get him taken off the case and fired in a heartbeat.

Chapter 4

"What are you worrying about? The snow is mostly melted. The road won't be icy."

Tyrell Bennett stood by the window, looking out over the fields. "I suppose you're right. The way it was coming down after we got home from the meeting, I was thinking we might need to get the snowplow onto the truck, and then I started thinking about how best to fix the roof again."

"Zach said it would hold through for the winter," his wife reminded him.

"Well, I hope so. At least we got the horses boarded out and the cattle to market," he mused. "But then I started thinking about—"

"Just stop thinking," Lou admonished him. "Everything will get done eventually, as soon as we can afford it."

She went into the pantry and came out with a long white receipt from the supermarket that Annie had tacked to a bulletin board, waving it at him.

"We've got a freezer full of beef, but everything else we have to pay for. You can add it up yourself."

"No, thanks. I sure wish the boys were coming home for Thanksgiving," he muttered. "Annie does what she can, but her leg ain't fully healed yet. I still see her limping when she's tired."

"I know." Lou was quiet for a moment. "She did last night when we were coming in from the truck."

"Well, that's why I need Zach and Sam for the heavy jobs. I'm not sending her up a ladder."

"They promised us a whole week at Christmas. I'm not going to complain. And speaking of the holidays, we need to buy flour and sugar and what-not in bulk for baking."

The discussion floated up to Annie's bedroom, where she lay under the comforter, her head cradled on a pillow. She watched the morning light move across the ceiling. Bright as it was, it did nothing to improve her mood.

She felt like she'd been had. The worst part was that she'd wanted so badly to *be* had by Marshall Stone, that snake. But wallowing in bed wasn't going to help her figure him out. It sounded like her mom could use her help anyway.

Annie sat up and let her feet rest on the smooth wood floor. Then she stood and stretched and did side bends, and threw in a couple of downward dogs and sun salutes for good measure. Yoga helped her flexibility—a lot of skiers did it. She quit when her leg began to twinge again.

The way she'd stormed into the house last night had done that.

Annie entered the kitchen still in pajamas. "What are we out of? Wish I'd known when I went to the supermarket."

"Lots of things. It's all right, honey. It'll be more fun if we shop together."

Annie nodded in agreement. "Let me brush my teeth and get dressed." She hadn't been able to brush away the sensation of Marshall Stone's amazing kisses last night. Maybe she'd have better luck this morning.

Her mother sat down to review the receipt. "They do have good prices."

Tyrell brought over a cup of coffee for his wife, fixed the way she liked it. "You making a list?"

"Yup." She slid over a piece of paper when he sat down next to her. "Add anything you like."

"Do they have those taco chips that I like? The extreme-cheese flavor?"

"Yes," Annie confirmed.

"Get two bags," her father said. He wrote it down. "There's a football game this weekend. Can't watch football without taco chips. Gotta keep my strength up."

She and her mother didn't talk much on the way to the supermarket, just drove along in companionable silence, until Lou got a call from Cilla.

Annie listened absently to the flustered female voice describing the joys of life with two kids under six in the house and her mother's soothing reassurances.

She definitely wasn't ready for that. But maybe

one of her brothers was. No telling which one, though, and of course her sisters-in-law had fifty percent of the vote on that subject.

But Annie wouldn't mind a little niece or nephew. Not at all.

Annie pulled a cart from the rack at the supermarket and handed it off to her mother, pulling out a second one for herself. When they shopped together, they tore the list in half and started at opposite ends of the supermarket, meeting in the middle.

Her mother held up the list. "Ready?"

"This is like a wishbone," Annie said.

"I folded it exactly through the middle. No one gets the short end."

Annie got the produce and dairy half. Her mother headed off to buy the dry staples that she needed.

She dawdled over the stacks of colorful fruits and vegetables, patting a large, light orange pumpkin pie and hoisting it to see how heavy it was before putting it back. Seven or eight pounds, by her guess.

She'd always wanted to make pumpkin pies from scratch. There were recipes in a wire rack above the heaped pumpkins. Annie took one and perused it, then replaced it in the rack. Five cans of puree would take care of all their pumpkin needs and be a lot less trouble.

Someone bumped her cart. She glanced up, assuming it was a mistake. It was a mistake. A tall, ruggedly handsome mistake in jeans and a flannel shirt, with a sad look in his dark eyes.

Marshall Stone's cart had bumped hers. He looked like he hadn't slept a wink either. She felt not one iota of sympathy for him.

"Did you do that on purpose?" she asked him.

"No. Sorry."

She angled her cart away. He blocked it with his. "Stop it," she ordered. "Go away."

"In a minute. Want to tell me why you're mad at me?"

"You know exactly why." Annie was ready to walk away and stepped out from behind the cart. It wasn't like she owned the damn thing or was somehow responsible for the few items she'd put into it.

Marshall caught her arm. "Let go of me." He didn't, but his grip relaxed slightly. Something about his touch made her irrational, because she didn't pull away. "Listen," she began. "You can't be on both sides of the same fence. I would think a surveyor would know that."

He looked at her like he wanted to say he was something else and not just a surveyor, that he was really a misunderstood knight in slightly tarnished armor.

"I'm sorry. I didn't know Chuck was going to say something like that about your dad. I should've told him to shut up, but . . . he wouldn't let me get a word in edgewise. He's a jerk."

"And your boss."

"True."

He let go of her. Annie couldn't think of anything else to say. She looked down, noticing what he had in his cart. Hamburger meat and buns. A tub of dip. The same brand of extreme-cheese taco chips her father liked.

Annie felt herself relenting ever so slightly. Inwardly. Not outwardly.

"Just the usual," he said. "Big game this weekend."

"I know." She realized he might watch the football broadcast with Chuck, mostly because he didn't know anyone else around Velde besides her. Tough luck. He was not forgiven for letting the rude comment about her father go past him, and she still didn't know the whole story behind what he was doing and how he could earn enough doing it to afford a tricked-out truck like that.

Although he wasn't eating filet mignon and drinking champagne. She looked down into his cart again and frowned.

"What? You don't approve?" he asked. "Those are the basic four man-food groups."

"Don't forget crow." She gave him an icy smile. "And a big, juicy slice of humble pie. Made from scratch."

Annie pushed past him without a backward look, abandoning the cart. He didn't even try to stop her.

There were youngsters decorating storefront windows all over Velde the next time Annie went in. The pre-Thanksgiving event was a yearly tradition sponsored by the scouts and local businesses. The kids wore bright new jackets against the cold snap, and their exuberant artwork made for a colorful scene.

Closely set together, the turn-of-the-century buildings along the main street each sported a different theme. The masterpieces on glass showed a lot of imagination. Annie spotted four-legged turkeys and Pilgrims on skateboards. A few would have to be defined as works in progress. She really wasn't sure what they were.

She stopped to admire an abstract painting in glorious shades of amber with splotches of white, thinking that it reminded her of something. Maybe it wasn't an abstract.

The artist, a towheaded boy of around eight, stood to the side of his creation while his scout leader took a quick photo with a smartphone.

"Great job," Annie said to the boy. "I love the colors. But what is it?"

"Candied sweet potatoes with marshmallows," he said proudly.

"Aha. Of course." She just hadn't recognized the side dish at nearly billboard size. "Well, keep up the good work."

She strolled on, seeing Cilla Rivers on the next block with the two little girls her mother was always talking about. Brushes in hand, they were busily dabbing color onto a storefront window that was low enough for them to paint.

"Hi, Cilla. Nice day."

The older woman nodded, even though she was shivering a little inside a lightweight fleece top. "Jenny and Zoe are having a great time."

With their tumbling brown curls and wide green

eyes, it was easy to see the resemblance between the sisters, who were working on the window at different heights.

Jenny, the older one, was adding a rainbow to a snow scene, arching stripes of color over something that looked like an upside-down broom stuck in a snowdrift.

No. Brooms didn't have red wattles and beady black eyes.

Jenny stepped back, casting a critical eye on her artwork. "I didn't do the turkey so good."

"Looks fine to me," Annie said, and laughed. "We used to have one just like that running around the ranch."

A thick brown brushstroke at the bottom marked the line between Jenny's painting and her sister's. Zoe squashed her brush into a blob of red and yellow paint and dabbed at a green background that was already dry.

Annie squatted down to talk to the little girl on her level. "And what are you painting?"

"Flowers. Under the ground. That's because it's winter," the child replied, a serious expression on her face. "My mommy says snow helps them grow in the spring."

"She's right," Annie said. "Which do you like better, winter or spring?"

"I like them both better."

Cilla exchanged smiles with Annie, who got up again, stepping back to admire the whole painting one more time. Cilla dug in a pocket and took out a smartphone.

"Annie, would you take our picture?"

"Of course."

"Here comes Ed. You can get all of us together."

"Can we send it to Mommy?" Jenny asked.

"That's the idea," Cilla said. The girls put down their brushes and she moved them in front of her, smiling at her husband as he walked up and put an arm around his wife's shoulders.

"Say cheese, ladies," Ed told the others.

Annie held up the smartphone and clicked it.

"Take another one," Zoe piped up. "So Mommy has just me and Jenny."

Annie laughed and obliged.

The ranch kitchen was warm, what with the oven going all morning. Tyrell Bennett didn't seem to mind. He was reading the paper, enjoying the mingled scents of cinnamon and brown sugar that wafted through the air as his wife bustled around, talking to him as she worked.

"They have their own lives now, Tyrell. I consider myself blessed to have two wonderful daughters-in-law."

"I just wish they were able to come home more often." Her husband nodded in agreement. "You're right about Nicole and Paula. I'm always telling Sam and Zach how lucky they are."

He fell silent for a little while, studying the column on school sports in the local newspaper. "Says here in the *Voice* that the high school has a stellar lineup for the football team. Remember when the boys were on it?"

"Do I ever." Lou laughed. "I was the one who

had to wash all those muddy jerseys and britches and knee guards."

"Until I made them see to it themselves," Tyrell pointed out. "What'd you do with that stuff, anyway?"

"Donated it all," she said briskly. "Ages ago. No sense keeping things some other kid could use."

He nodded, his gaze moving to the social column. Absently, he read aloud. "Albert and Gloria Sanchez have announced the engagement of their daughter Teresa to Ned Dawley of Denver. Who's he?"

"I'll ask Gloria next time I see her. But when did you get interested in stuff like that?"

"I read the whole paper. I like to be well informed," Tyrell said with lofty dignity. He kept on reading. "Think Annie's ever going to get herself married?"

"Of course. She just needs to find the right man."

Tyrell leaned back in his chair until the front legs lifted a few inches off the floor, and folded his arms behind his head. "That could take a while."

Lou flicked a dish towel at him. "Let her figure it out. And don't you try to do any matchmaking."

"I wouldn't dare," Tyrell said mockingly. "I believe that's still a woman's job."

"Don't look at me."

He waggled his eyebrows and did just that. The chair legs came down on the floor as Tyrell reached out and pulled his wife onto his lap. "How long do you think Annie's going to be in town?"

Lou giggled. "I don't quite know. But she's only

been gone a half hour and she said she was going to the mall with Nell."

Tyrell put his arms around her. "That's a forty-five-minute drive one way. Add in at least an hour of shopping and we have the whole afternoon."

"To do what?"

"As if you didn't know." He gave her a good squeeze that made Lou giggle again.

Chapter 5

Nell dropped Annie off by her truck, which she'd left in the town's parking lot, and rolled down the window to say good-bye.

Annie poked her head in. "Wait. That bag's mine." She'd bought silver nonpareils and multi-colored jimmies in advance for Lou's upcoming Christmas-cookie-baking marathon. Her mother liked to go all out, though she had given up on making the much less popular fruitcakes.

"Only one?" Nell asked. The saloon owner had at least ten bags of her own to wrangle.

"Yup. Sure you don't want help with yours?"

Nell shook her head. "I didn't buy anything heavy. Do you have everything?"

Annie took a second look. The other bags were too full to close. Bristling foil garlands bulged out of a few, and boxes of glass ornaments were stacked in others. "Yes. That was fun. Thanks again."

"You bet. Take care now." Nell drove away when Annie stepped back.

As she walked toward her red pickup she remembered her next errand: stamps. Her mother had asked her to get two sheets with holiday themes.

Annie did an about-face, heading for the Velde post office instead. Looked like she wouldn't have to wait long. There were only two people ahead of her.

She stood, her hands crossed in front of her, looking around idly. Her gaze lifted to the mural above the counter, painted decades ago and still in remarkably good condition. She remembered studying it as a kid, feeling uplifted by its sunny depiction of mail delivery in the West. A Pony Express rider at full gallop rode toward modern times, represented by a small white truck on a rural road, an apple-cheeked mailman at the wheel.

Annie turned her head when someone bumped into her.

"Sorry, dear. I didn't see you."

"That's all right."

The speaker was an elderly woman whom she didn't know by name. But Annie had seen her at the town hall. She and her husband had been among the group who'd approached Shep Connally after the meeting.

The woman held a certified letter she'd just received in one thin hand. Annie couldn't help noticing the bold black lettering on the envelope: *Department of Taxation. Official Business. To Be Opened By Addressee Only.*

"I'm just distracted, I guess." Her hand shook and she dropped the envelope. "Oh, goodness. What is the matter with me?"

"Not to worry. We all have days like that." Annie bent down to retrieve it and read the names, *Jack and Elsie Pearson.*

"Here you go." She handed it over.

"Thank you. I appreciate it."

"Yes. My name's Annie Bennett, by the way."

"Oh," the woman said a little vaguely. "Well, I'm Elsie Pearson."

"I'll remember that." Annie smiled reassuringly and stepped toward the exterior door to hold it open for Mrs. Pearson. "I hope you don't have far to go. I could give you a ride if you like."

She could get the stamps some other time. Her mother would understand.

The old lady opened her purse and slipped the certified letter next to a plain envelope with no stamp on it and a printed company name in the upper left corner, *Connally Associates.* There was no street or number. Just a town she'd never heard of. Dehia, Arizona.

Annie bit her tongue. The old lady closed her purse and buttoned up her coat before she answered.

"No, that's all right. I live just around the corner. But thanks."

She walked somewhat uncertainly away, her shoulders bent. Annie looked after her through the glass of the closed door. The two envelopes she'd glimpsed proved exactly nothing. But there was a story behind them. And she knew someone who might be able to help her find out more.

*   *   *

Annie paused in front of a limestone building crowned with a carved pediment, then went up the steps through the columned facade. Her boot heels clicked against the inlaid marble floor of the half-size rotunda. The founders of Velde had spared no expense. There were paintings of them on the walls, in high collars and whiskers, and a smiling portrait of the current mayor. It was a safe bet that he wasn't around this afternoon.

She barely spared them a glance, intent on her errand. "Harriet? You in?"

The town clerk appeared at the doors to a corridor next to the mayor's chambers. "Yes. Hello, Annie. What's up?"

They'd met last quarter, when she'd accompanied her parents into town. They liked to pay taxes in person.

"Hey, do you have a minute or two? I just wanted to ask you a few questions about town records—the ones that are open to the public."

"Sure. Come with me." Harriet Sargent led the way into her work space. "Have a seat." She lifted a stack of manila files off the chair beside her desk.

"Still using hard copies?" Annie teased her.

"Of course. The town files aren't going to be digitized in my lifetime. Besides, paper lasts longer than some computerized records. Remember floppy disks?" She held one up. "I use this for a coaster. Haven't been able to access the data on it for years."

The flat screen monitor and CPU on Harriet's

desk was the latest model. Annie's laptop was older.

"So what can I do for you?"

"I need an answer to a general question."

"Let's hear it."

Annie collected her thoughts, which had gone in a lot of directions after the encounter with Elsie Pearson.

"If someone wanted financial information on someone, like tax assessments, could they just walk in here and get it?"

"Property assessments are available to the public online. And yes, here too, if folks fill out a form and request one. Why do you ask?"

"Well, if you were a senior citizen on a fixed income and you had a big tax payment coming up and someone was able to find out about it and pressure you into deeding over your house in the future in exchange for cash now, or something like that—"

Annie stopped and looked at Harriet. Maybe she was letting her imagination run away with her.

"That does happen. Unfortunately, it's kind of a gray area. If a bank does it—and they're not allowed to use high-pressure sales tactics, by the way—it's called a reverse mortgage. Are you concerned about an elderly individual you know personally?"

"No." It wasn't exactly a lie. Annie hadn't even known Elsie Pearson's name until today. "I was just wondering."

"Oh."

Annie glanced down at the newspaper on Harriet's desk, frowning at the front-page photo of Shep Connally shaking hands with a member of the town council as the others looked on. Speak of the devil.

"My folks dragged me to that meeting, but I was sort of glad I went. I didn't like the consultant guy, though."

Harriet fiddled with a pencil. "I didn't either. But as far as I know, he hasn't done anything wrong," the clerk added.

"It bothered me how some of the older folks seemed to trust him right away. Why would they? He really didn't say anything that made sense to me."

"I would agree. And let's all hope he's not setting them up. But it's a free country. You can say anything you want. It's what you do that counts more."

Annie blew out a breath. Marshall Stone had said essentially the same thing. And both he and Harriet were right. But that didn't do much to ease her mind at the moment.

"If it's any reassurance, Annie, no one has come in here asking to see tax assessments. I suppose people will, since quarterly payments are due at the end of the year. But it's been quiet."

"Okay. Well, I guess that's all. I appreciate you letting me pester you."

"Anytime. And you're not a pest."

Annie thought once more of Elsie Pearson and how troubled the old lady had seemed. "I just wanted to make sure on that one point." She knew she was going to think of more questions as soon as she was out of here. "All right. Thanks again. I know you have work to do."

"Yes. Filing. It never ends." Harriet shifted an uneven stack of papers to an open spot. "If Velde keeps growing, I'm going to have to beg the mayor for an assistant. Maybe two. Know anyone who'd be interested?"

"Ah—" Annie didn't want to put herself forward as a candidate. But she could learn a lot more if she was inside this office. It was something to think about.

"It's just not possible to get everything done on a computer," Harriet was saying. "And between you and me, I don't quite trust the darn things. One wrong keystroke and the hard drive eats a whole day's work. Or if there's a power failure, it can take hours to get online again."

Annie gave a sympathetic nod.

Harriet patted the heap waiting to be filed. It contained so many different sizes and types of paper that it would have been impossible to stack neatly. "You're looking at the original database. I'm glad we still have to keep them."

Annie wished she could look through it all. From where she was sitting, the papers didn't seem to be just documents. Drawings, old ones in faded ink, of property boundaries, and brown-spotted maps were mixed in.

"How do you keep track of it all?"

"You caught me on a bad day, Annie. Usually I'm more caught up than this. Although I couldn't say my desk is ever completely clear."

Annie had never worked at a desk. She didn't have anything to say on the subject.

"For the most part, I do know where everything is," Harriet said. "It helps, let me tell you." She indicated a piece of paper sticking halfway out, near the top of the stack. "That right there is a map of your family's ranch."

"Really?" Annie peered at what she could see of it. "Mind if I take a look?"

"Not at all." Harriet pulled it out carefully and handed it to her. "A surveyor requested it a day or so ago. He wanted to compare the old boundaries on file with his new measurements. I think he said he was surveying for the rancher whose land adjoins yours."

Annie's eyebrows went up. "Do you mean Marshall Stone?"

"That was the name, yes."

"He was on our property several days ago. He didn't say anything to me about coming in here."

"Standard procedure." Harriet seemed unconcerned. "Showed ID, filled out the form. I have it on file."

"Hmm." Annie thought about asking to see it, thinking it might be possible to find out a little bit more about Stone without having to ask him personally. But she didn't want to bug the clerk any more than she already had. "Well, thanks for showing me this." Annie gave her back the old map. "I know my father would be interested."

"I could make you a photocopy. I can't let you take the original out of the office, though."

"That's okay. He could come in and see it for

himself, right?" The clerk nodded. "I'll tell him about it. And now I really should get going."

"All right. I'll be sure to file that map first," Harriet promised. "It won't go astray. And if it does, don't worry. I've never lost anything for longer than a day."

Chapter 6

That conversation had taken up the rest of the short afternoon. Annie didn't know much more than when she'd started, but she was determined to have it out with Marshall Stone. Maybe it was standard procedure and maybe it wasn't, but she didn't like the idea that he had researched their property without ever telling her. As if her father didn't respect other people's boundaries. That would be Chuck Pfeffer's game. She felt more than a little ticked off.

She kicked a pebble down the stairs and headed for her red pickup.

What next? If she wanted to talk to him, she'd have to find him first. That fancy truck of his ought to stand out even more during the day—although sunset wasn't far off. Still, it would take less than half an hour to drive through every street in Velde.

She had several good reasons to stick to conversation this time around. Annie vowed not to let herself get distracted by his long, lean good looks and potent attractiveness.

He might have worked both to his advantage the night of the town meeting, but he hadn't apologized at the supermarket and he wasn't likely to now either.

His conduct raised questions. The way Annie saw it, Marshall Stone owed her some answers.

She got into her truck and drove away.

About ten miles out on the road into Velde, Marshall Stone was cleaning out the cab of his truck. Strictly speaking, it wasn't his.

Where he was from in Wyoming, no one would ever drive something so showy. On principle, they'd be likely to bang it up a little, just so the truck knew who was boss.

He had thought when it was assigned to him that the gleaming new vehicle would stand out too much in a town like Velde. Maybe not in Aspen or Vail, but in cowboy country it just looked too damn new. Still, he couldn't complain. There was no way the IT team could retrofit a vintage one with the wireless gear and encrypted satellite connection he needed to stay in touch with his colleagues on the fraud case.

Which was going slower than he liked. If he could wrap up this investigation before Christmas and get out of Velde, that would be fine with him. Hell, if he could wrap it up before Thanksgiving, that would be even better.

He didn't think for one second that a certain

beautiful brunette would miss him. Marshall crumpled up a handful of fast-food wrappers and stuffed them into a plastic bag. He'd had about all he could stand of steamed burgers and stale fries.

However, it seemed best to stay out of restaurants, especially restaurant doorways, for the time being. Then again, lightning wasn't supposed to strike twice. The kiss he had shared with Annie had been the kiss of a lifetime.

Yesterday he'd done himself a favor, and swung off the road when he'd spotted a lunch truck out by the sawmill, figuring that hungry loggers knew how to chow down.

The roast beef sandwich he'd selected had been about as big as his head and truly tasty. But he hadn't been able to eat the whole thing and he'd forgotten about the remains, which he tossed into the plastic bag too.

Holding it closed, he walked toward a Dumpster in the parking lot that several small businesses shared. All of them were closed. About to toss in the bag of trash, he heard an echoing bark. Then the scrabble of claws.

Marshall was just tall enough to peer in over the side. The Dumpster was empty . . . except for a black-and-white dog that was staring up at him, wagging its fluffy tail. Didn't have a collar. Looked dusty, but not too bad otherwise.

"How'd you get in there?"

It jumped up toward him and fell back again on all fours.

Marshall looked around. There was no one else in the parking lot. It was possible that the dog had jumped in somehow, unless some son-of-a-bitch had put it in there.

He sighed and went to get a heavy-duty plastic crate stashed behind one of the businesses. He fished out what was left of the roast beef sandwich and tossed the bag of trash into a tall can by the locked back door.

Then he brought over the crate and stood on it to peer over the Dumpster's side again. The dog came right to him, stretching up to sniff at the remains of the sandwich he held out.

There were only a few shreds of roast beef and a glob of mayonnaise on the roll, but the dog seemed interested. More than interested. When it got a whiff of what he held in his hand, the tail really got going.

"Come and get it," Marshall coaxed.

The dog made a jump and fell back. Its eyes fixed on the prize, it backed up a few steps and crouched, then sprang high enough for Marshall to catch it by the furry scruff of its neck.

He wrangled it over the side of the Dumpster and let it jump down the rest of the way. Wonder of wonders, it sat right down without him saying a word. Maybe without knowing it, he'd given the animal some kind of signal it recognized. Someone had trained it. Maybe the dog hadn't been abandoned. Some practical joker could have put it into the empty Dumpster.

"Who taught you to do that?"

The dog grinned, letting its tongue loll out. Marshall was about to reward it with the sandwich when he realized his hand was empty.

"Hey. That wasn't polite." The dog didn't even bother to look guilty. If he got close, he would probably smell the mayo on its breath.

"You're pretty slick." Its tail thumped on the ground; the dog seemed to agree. "So. Now that you're out, what am I going to do with you?"

He patted his pockets, looking for his phone, and remembered that he'd left it in the truck. Marshall walked back to it and the dog accompanied him, heeling like a champion. "Good dog," he said.

It wasn't that obedient. Before he gave it a command, it jumped past him through the door he'd left open and landed on the front seat. "Hold on. I didn't say you could do that. Now get down."

The dog eased down into the foot well and popped up its head, grinning again.

"Not quite what I meant."

It stayed there for a few more seconds, then clambered back up onto the seat and stared out the passenger window like it had important work to do.

Marshall looked it over. It was clearly some kind of stock dog mix, male, probably smart as hell and too adventurous for its own good. He ran his hands along its sides, feeling definite ribs, but it wasn't starved. Just hungry. He picked up a back paw, noting the worn pads and a split nail. It had to have covered a lot of miles lately. No identifying tattoo that he could find. He doubted it was microchipped, but a vet would be able to tell him that.

"Do you have a name? Are you someone's dog?"

The dog turned intelligent amber eyes on him, as if the answer was obvious. *Yours, pal.*

"All right." He sighed. "You need a bath and a collar, for starters. It's late in the day, so you get a reprieve on the vet visit." Marshall got into the truck and slammed the door.

Chapter 7

Annie had no luck finding Stone and didn't particularly want to ask around. The gleaming black truck was nowhere to be found in Velde and she felt like a dope trying to play detective when she couldn't find a man who was taller than anyone else in town and owner of a great big shiny new vehicle that had to have caused comment.

By the next day, she sucked it up and contacted Nell.

Not face to face. Annie could do without the tactfully phrased questions the saloon keeper was sure to ask. E-mail was preferable. She reached into her jacket pocket for her smartphone and scrolled through for Nell's contact information, then typed a message that was too long to text.

Hey. Do you happen to know where that guy is who came in the night we tested the Christmas lights? He left some surveying gear out at our place.

Technically, that was true. There were neon pink ribbons fluttering in a few places along the fence lines where he'd set a marker in the ground below. Her sharp-eyed dad had spotted them, pitched a minor fit, and vowed to remove them all.

Her phone chimed. Nell's answer came surprisingly quickly. I sure do. Marshall Stone is renting the cabin on that land I own outside town. Nice to have such a responsible tenant. And so easy on the eyes. You should stop by and say hi, Annie.

Did that qualify as a hint? It was more like a blunt instrument. Nell obviously thought Annie should be actively looking for l-o-v-e, not that it was any of her business.

So he was at the cabin that Nell had recently restored with an eye to renting it during ski season. Annie hadn't been out that way, hadn't even thought of it because she hadn't imagined Marshall Stone was in town for very long.

Annie guessed there hadn't been enough snow for Nell to find other takers. But she knew Nell wouldn't have rented it without doing some kind of background check.

Asking Nell about that wasn't likely to get her much information. The saloon owner kept up with all the town doings and occasionally indulged in gossip like everyone else, but that didn't mean she would reveal private information about a paying customer. Safe to assume that Stone had passed inspection with Nell, which was a good sign.

For now, Annie just wanted to talk to him. That was all.

She didn't have his phone number or his e-mail.

Nell hadn't offered either. Another hint. All right. Annie would play friendly and stop by the cabin.

Marshall opened the door about a minute after she knocked. Right away she saw why it took him so long. He had a black-and-white dog by the collar, some kind of herding breed by the looks of it and the level of energy. It seemed awfully interested in getting outside.

"You have a dog?" she asked, surprised. "Down, boy." She reached out a hand to pat the wriggling animal, who licked it eagerly.

"Stop that, Rowdy. I found him in a Dumpster, got him out and got him shots and a checkup straightaway. Healthy and full of beans. The vet said he wasn't microchipped. So the answer is yes, I now have a dog."

He'd rescued a stray. Uh-oh. Annie could feel the beginnings of a dangerous thaw in her mixed feelings about Marshall Stone. But until she knew more about who he was and what he was doing in Velde, it might be wiser to keep this supposedly social call on the short side.

She stayed where she was until Marshall motioned her inside, still hanging on to the dog's collar. "Come on in. He's not completely nuts. But I'm getting there."

"He's cute. Rowdy is a good name for him."

"He lives up to it, believe me."

Annie looked around the snug cabin, which was one big room, the old log walls sanded and varnished to a honey color and the restored chinking between them thick as sugar icing. The floor was made of split hackberry logs, worn smooth long ago and recently refinished. A crackling fire was visible through the isinglass panes of an antique woodstove in the corner. Super cozy.

She checked out the rest of the décor, never having been inside, although she'd seen pictures. There were knickknacks on a whatnot shelf dripping with doilies and vintage books for après-ski entertainment. No television. Annie wondered if there was Internet access.

Then she saw the router, also on a doily. All the modern conveniences with a touch of yesterday.

Obviously Nell had intended the cabin to be a romantic retreat for vacationing couples. Unfortunately for Annie's peace of mind, there was only one piece of furniture big enough for two people to sit on.

A love seat faced the bed, which was a king-size affair of poufy, down-stuffed white supported by four tall posters carved from dark, heavy wood. It was the kind of bed you could run at and fling yourself into and not come up for days.

Or, she thought uneasily, be flung into. By a man who had just swept you up in his arms and whispered all the things he was going to do to you over the course of a passionate weekend.

Sign her up. As far as she could tell, Marshall Stone was single.

Annie'd had a fair amount of experience with figuring out who was and who wasn't. Some of the corporate types who took ski weekends liked to remove their wedding rings before they picked her for an instructor. "Didn't fit into the ski gloves" was only one of the ridiculous reasons she'd heard. But she could tell. Married men tended to look guilty in advance, even if they never made a move.

"Would you like some coffee?"

Startled by the mundane question, Annie looked around at Marshall. "What? Oh—no, thanks."

He shrugged and bent down. The rattling sound of kibble told her he was filling the dog's bowl.

She wasn't quick enough to move toward one of the high stools by the counter that served as a dining space. Marshall came out of the kitchenette and headed straight for the love seat.

His eyes caught hers. He must have read her mind, because he went to the love seat and quickly rotated it to face the woodstove in the corner instead of the poufy bed.

Annie breathed an inward sigh of relief. She took one side of the love seat. He took the other. Still and all, she couldn't fight the feeling that she'd been put in the corner for having such wayward thoughts. But Marshall's demeanor was matter-of-fact. He didn't seem inclined to quiz her about why she'd stopped by or even how she'd found out where he was staying.

"So where are you from exactly?" Annie began, trying not to sound too curious. "I never did ask."

"Garrick. Bet you never heard of it." He smiled when she shook her head. "It's a small town," he said. "Smaller than Velde."

That wasn't a whole lot of information, but it was a start. She found herself wishing he were a little more communicative. But Marshall Stone fit the profile of the strong, silent type. Annie searched her mind for other topics to discuss.

"That's quite a truck," she said encouragingly. Men always liked to talk about their wheels.

"Gets me where I'm going." That was all he had to say.

Another subtle inquiry shot down. But she wasn't giving up.

"Surveying must pay well," she said.

"I do all right."

She was stymied until she spotted a throw toy for Rowdy and played with him for a while. The dog's antics filled the lull in the conversation. Marshall Stone just didn't much like to talk about himself.

But she hit another invisible wall when she brought up the town meeting.

"So whose side are you on?" she asked, not really making light of it.

"I'm not on anyone's side. Why do you ask?"

"You work for Pfeffer, and Shep Connally is his pal. Do you know anything about him?"

There was the barest fraction of a pause.

"I saw what you saw that night, Annie. I've never been personally introduced to the man, if that's what you mean."

He'd sidestepped the question. She decided to let it go.

"I know I should have told Chuck Pfeffer to shut up when he made that obnoxious comment about your father," he said finally.

"Well, yes. But I'm not going to be a sorehead about it indefinitely. Besides," she added honestly,

"I couldn't say my dad is ever going to be your biggest fan."

"I suppose not." Marshall had to smile. "He's entitled to his opinion."

"Those surveyor flags on the fence line got him riled again."

"I have to leave them there until the job's done, but I'll be sure to take them down when I go," Stone said agreeably.

Like, she thought with a pang, *he can't wait to do that.*

"Chuck Pfeffer wants me to double-check my work, by the way."

"He's your boss." She found it in her heart to forgive him for that, sort of, without actually saying those exact words.

"Only for this one job. And I'm pretty much finished."

"Which reminds me. I stopped by the town clerk's office. She said you'd been in."

"Yup. Strictly routine. I have to check my measurements against the old ones. They're almost always different."

The town clerk had said as much. Annie wasn't sure how exactly to keep up her end of the conversation if they were going to talk about surveying.

"I wouldn't know. So how long have you been a surveyor?"

"Years. All over the western states. I come and go. Never in one place for long."

Annie got the unspoken message. He wasn't the kind of man who stuck around, even if he was single. The guardedness in his tone put her ever so slightly on edge.

No holiday flings, she warned herself silently. She'd had exactly two in her life. The first, she'd chalked up to being only twenty and too naive to know better. The second, a few years later, she'd just been too lonely to say no. January could be cold in more ways than one.

"How'd you get started with that? Do you work for a company?"

He only nodded at first. Then, as if he'd read her mind, he filled her in.

"I answered an ad right out of college. *Assistant wanted, will train.* I was the guy who held the pole. I learned on the job."

"How come you don't have an assistant?"

"I don't really need one, not with electronic instruments. I use a remote to confirm the mark on the opposite side."

"Oh."

He didn't seem to mind answering her questions. It took both their minds off what would have been too weird to talk about: that incredible kiss in the darkened doorway.

For a long moment, she forgot the rest of the pointed questions she'd intended to ask him. To make matters worse, the dog jumped up and wedged himself between them on the love seat, looking from Marshall's face to hers as if he was watching a tennis match.

"Rowdy. Get down," Marshall said after a while.

"It's all right." Annie patted the dog's silky fur.

"I don't mind him." Truth be told, she was grateful for Rowdy's presence. A staring dog made a pretty good chaperone.

"Well, I do. Down." The dog picked up on his stern tone of voice and jumped down, heading for a brand-new dog bed that she hadn't noticed.

Aww. Marshall had gone all out for the stray. "I hope Rowdy knows how lucky he is," Annie said.

"The word is *spoiled*. My guess would be he's never slept on anything but a pile of feed sacks in a barn." He shook his head and shot a look toward the dog that was a lot more affectionate than annoyed.

Annie was definitely melting. Marshall turned and looked in her eyes. Maybe he really could read her mind, because he leaned over and kissed her. It was better than the first time. In fact, it was sublime.

It just didn't last long enough. His lips brushed her cheek, raising a scorching heat in her sensitive skin that had nothing to do with the fire. Then he claimed her mouth with his, teasing her sensually with his tongue as his strong hand slipped into her hair, stroking through her dark locks and finally coming to rest on the nape of her neck. Dreamily, Annie surrendered to the sensation, desiring nothing more than the feeling of his hand cradling her head while she kissed him back.

She was expecting him to go further, to take her in his arms, but Marshall drew back. There was a hot gleam in his half-lidded eyes as he looked down at her. Curled on the love seat beside him, thinking about jumping into his lap, Annie only gazed back at him. Thinking hard. And trying not to think at all.

She'd gone too far with him once already. Allowed him to hold her so close it had been difficult to breathe, let him caress her as gently and as roughly as the impulse demanded. Stayed in his arms in the restaurant doorway, kissing him like she'd never kissed any man. What should have been a deeply private encounter had essentially taken place in public, considering that anyone in town might have seen them.

It wasn't like she had anywhere private to go in Velde besides back to her parents' ranch. Of course, she hadn't known about the cabin he was renting at that point. Even though she loved being back on the home place, it was tough not being able to come and go without comment. But her shared condo in Aspen hadn't really been all hers either, and she'd managed.

Public or private, what had happened between her and Marshall Stone had been a first for Annie. He'd demonstrated the ultimate in skilled masculine passion, in fact, but he'd also been intensely focused on her pleasure.

She'd found him powerfully attractive, but maybe that was because she'd been single herself for longer than she'd ever thought possible.

The romantic setting had weakened her resistance.

What with the soft snow coming down outside the sheltered space and the way he looked at her just before he took her in his arms—damn. It didn't really need to be analyzed. The heat of his sensual embrace and the bold way he kissed had made her forget about everything but him.

"We probably shouldn't do that too often," he said in a low voice.

"Maybe not." She wriggled into a more upright position. "What were we talking about?"

"Surveying."

"Right. You're almost done but you're not done. So why does it take so long to survey a piece of land?"

"Many reasons. For one, you have to try to reconcile the past and the present, and that's never easy."

Annie thought that could apply to a lot of things in life. She nodded.

"Used to be stones and streams served to mark boundaries and corners. And trees," he added. "But stones get buried and streams dry up and trees die or get hit by lightning or chopped down. Did your dad ever walk the lines with you, show you the landmarks of your ranch?"

The ritual of walking the property lines was a long-standing custom in the country and generally something that men did. She didn't ever recollect her mother going along.

"He walked the lines with my brothers," she replied. "Not me."

"Sounds about right. It was always a man's job. Father and son, grandfather and grandsons. Just try talking to some of these old birds about what a satellite can see or how accurate measurements are now."

Annie bristled. "Excuse me?"

"Whoa. I didn't mean your dad. He was just concerned that I was on his property. He actually seemed to have a very good idea of where the lines were, considering your land hasn't been surveyed since his grandfather's day."

"Did he tell you that?"

Marshall nodded. "Before you showed up, yes."

"Just out of curiosity, do your measurements favor us Bennetts or Chuck Pfeffer?"

"The data could go either way. I really need to make sure," Marshall replied.

Annie narrowed her eyes. His answer could be interpreted as evasive.

"By the way," he added in a bland tone, "I don't automatically favor the side that pays me. Measurements are measurements, and numbers don't lie. Pfeffer could end up with what we call a dirty title. Meaning his claim to the land can be contested. And if he wants to sell, he won't be able to."

"Is that why he's having his ranch surveyed?"

"To be honest, he never said."

"I wonder if he tried to do it himself. My dad would have complained if he'd seen Chuck out there too often."

"I don't doubt it."

"This is the time," she said, "I remember my dad and my brothers doing it, around Thanksgiving, before we got really snowed in but after the hay was cut."

"How many brothers do you have?"

"Two. Sam and Zach. They're almost as overprotective as my dad."

Stone raised an eyebrow, but seemed otherwise indifferent to the information.

"They're both married now. They'll be back for Christmas with their wives."

"Well, maybe your dad will walk the lines with you this year. Thanksgiving's right around the corner. He could follow the surveyor's flags," Stone added with a wink.

"If he wanted to take me along, he would have asked. He's never mentioned it." She looked his way. "You could go with me."

"Nothing doing," Stone said seriously. "I don't want your daddy to see us traipsing over the fields with no warning. He might come after me with a shotgun."

"Oh, please. He's not that old-fashioned."

"He never saw me kiss you," Marshall muttered. He got up and walked into the kitchenette without giving a reason. She heard things being shifted around in a random way.

Good move. She breathed a little easier.

"And he never will," Annie confirmed. "But we're getting off the subject. I really wouldn't mind learning a little about surveying. You could teach me."

"It's all about straight lines," he began.

She watched him walk out of the kitchenette and stand there. The phrase described him to a T, except for his biceps, rounded with muscle under his checked flannel shirt.

"No curves? Not ever?" she asked flippantly.

"Depends on what I run into," he replied. "Or who."

"I see."

He didn't seem to realize that he'd put her into a box marked *Random Encounter*. So it really didn't matter to him who he kissed. Or why.

Okay. She could live with that. After all, she hardly knew him and he was just passing through.

Two steps more and he kneeled down to drag out a long, hard-shelled case from under the bed. "I'll show you the gear." He thumbed open the clasps and revealed the equipment he'd been using when they'd first met. "That yellow box is called a total station. It's a theodolite combined with a laser that measures distance electronically. There's the remote I mentioned."

"Oh."

"But old-style equipment works better if something blocks the laser."

"Like what?"

"Trees. Houses. Big boulders."

Her reply was meant in jest, but it fell flat. "Well, I can see where other people's houses might get in the way of what you're doing."

That got Stone's attention. "What's that supposed to mean?"

"Sorry. That kinda slipped out. But—" She hesitated. "Not everyone thinks you're just a surveyor."

Marshall closed the clasps. "Who exactly are you talking about?"

"No one in particular," she said hastily.

It was fairly obvious from the searching look he gave her that he guessed she was talking about herself.

"Okay, a few people. It's just that no one around here knows you."

He shoved the case back under the bed with a sigh. "Wouldn't be the first time I came in somewhere and got tagged as a suspicious character. Folks get scared their taxes will go up if their land is larger than they claim."

"That's not up to you, right?"

"No. Of course not." He dusted off his knees as he straightened up to his full height. "Maybe I do need an assistant. Someone to hold up a sign, not a pole. *He's Just Doing His Job. Please Don't Shoot.*"

"How about me?" The words were out of her mouth before she thought twice. Another out-of-nowhere suggestion. But it wasn't that crazy. She forced her mind back to the reason she'd come to the cabin in the first place: to find out more about him. So far she'd struck out.

She thought of Chuck Pfeffer and his pal Shep Connally, who'd showed up at the town meeting with an obviously hidden agenda. Most of all, there was Mrs. Pearson, a vulnerable old lady in some kind of financial difficulty, and probably a few others like her that Annie had no way of knowing about. Something was up. Whose side was Marshall Stone on?

If he said yes to her suggestion, then he had to be a good guy. He wouldn't let her follow him around if he wasn't.

"I mean—you could take me out into the field, show me the basics. Could be the start of a new career," she joked.

He eyed her speculatively. "What is it you're doing now?"

"I'm a ski instructor. But I broke my leg pretty badly last spring and it's still healing."

"Sorry to hear that. Risky sport."

Annie studied him for a long moment. "I take it you don't ski."

"Good guess. But what made you think so?"

"You seem like the cautious type."

"Do I?"

She just couldn't read the expression on his face. She got the feeling there was something she ought to be able to figure out about him, but Stone was living up to his name.

"Well, I love it," she forged on. "And I'm waiting for a go-ahead from my doctor to get back on the slopes. My mom and dad took care of me during the worst part—I moved back here from Aspen—and now I'm returning the favor."

He nodded with approval, but he didn't say yes.

"So do you want to give me a try?"

Stone gave a shrug. "I don't think it's a great idea. Surveying involves a lot of walking."

"I can walk just fine." Not entirely true. Her leg still ached when she overdid it. "I just can't ski."

Marshall looked dubious. "Some days I end up walking for miles."

"I'm game," she said with bravado.

"Ask your doctor first. As for the actual surveying, you could probably pick it up fairly quickly."

"How complicated can it be?"

She knew damn well that the answer to that rhetorical question was *very*. But she wasn't going to chicken out.

"Depends," he said. "Of course, you don't have

to do the triangulating. There's software for that and it also factors in all the variables you enter. You really don't have to know much math."

"Good. It never was my best subject," she said honestly. "But I'm interested," she insisted.

"Okay," he said, a faintly mocking tone in his voice despite his acquiescence.

Tough luck, Annie thought. She wasn't going to leave with nothing but a memory of a second kiss.

"Lesson One," he began. "Surveying is pretty much about finding the distance between two points however you can. So the first thing you do is make sure the sight's level before you look through it and fix on an immovable object. Then you—"

"How big does the immovable object have to be? Just give me an example." She raised herself halfway and peered over the back of the love seat, trying not to look too hopeful about him coming back.

He was grinning at her. "How about a lady on a love seat who won't budge?"

"What?"

For some reason, he had his jacket on. Then he took a dark brown winter Stetson from a hook and set it on his head just so. The angle of the light meant his face was partly hidden. But not his mouth. Which kicked up.

She wasn't sure if he was laughing at her. "I'm—just very comfortable. I wasn't aware I'd overstayed my welcome."

"You haven't. Rowdy needs to get out, that's all." He held up the leash and the dog ran to him. Stone bent down to clip it to his collar.

"Maybe we could go over some more concepts tomorrow." Annie got to her feet. "I really think we would need to be out in the field for me to understand completely."

"That's not possible. Not tomorrow. I'm starting a new assignment just outside town. Chuck referred me."

Him again. Their obnoxious neighbor was a little too connected to Marshall Stone for her liking. She sensed even more strongly that he was concealing something from her—and that he was good at it.

"Want to go with us?" Stone asked. "Rowdy, sit."

She couldn't help noticing how well the dog behaved. Either Marshall had the gift of teaching instant obedience or the dog had been carefully trained by someone else. "Why not?"

She found her jacket and turned up the collar. It couldn't have gotten any warmer since she'd arrived at the cabin.

Stone opened the door and he and his dog stepped aside. "After you."

Annie let him lead the way once they were outside. She found it hard to keep up with his long strides over the rutted dirt road that wound through the undeveloped land in back of the cabin. She wondered idly how much of it Nell owned.

"The moon will be up soon." Stone's words echoed in the crystalline mountain air. Night had fallen an hour ago.

"Too bad," Annie said. "Look at those stars." Thousands upon thousands of glittering points of light decorated the dark sky.

He was bending down to unclip Rowdy's leash. "Go," he told the dog, which bounded away, barking for joy.

"Is that a good idea?"

"He comes back. I don't think he likes the leash much. I guess I could say he tolerates it to make me happy."

They walked on. Stone seemed to be matching his pace to hers so that she wouldn't stumble. An otherworldly glow along the horizon hinted at the imminent arrival of the moon.

They stood together in silence as he gave a low, piercing whistle. In the distance, the lights of a little ranch house came on, warm squares of yellow in the overall deep blue.

In another minute, Rowdy appeared, racing toward them. The dog circled his master's legs, panting. Eventually he sat.

Then the moon appeared over the ridge, huge and brilliant. Annie couldn't help but look at Stone's face as he took in the sight of it. The chiseled lines and strong jaw seemed to be sculpted in silver.

He lifted his head and his dark eyes shone as he turned to look at her. There was the hint of a sensual smile on his firm mouth as he closed the distance between them.

Annie had the feeling he was going for Kiss Number Three.

She wanted it as much as he did. He tipped the Stetson back. Somewhere in the mix that was Marshall Stone there had to be a rancher or a cowboy. Only they knew how to kiss with a hat on.

He drew her into his arms, holding her close and warming her instantly with the heat of his powerful body. His mouth claimed hers with assertive skill that felt too good to resist. She gave in and gave the kiss all she had.

Annie pressed herself against him, rubbing like a cat seeking a haven from the cold, slipping her hands inside his jacket and running them over the hard muscles of his chest. His warmth and his strength were irresistible. The hard contours of his thighs supported her as she stood on tiptoe to kiss him again and again. The rising moon drenched them in silver light. The little ranch house was far away. There was no one to see.

They were both quiet as they walked hand in hand back to the cabin over the same rutted road. He led her around to the front and stopped when Annie gasped.

"What's the matter?"

She pointed. A shadowy figure ran away from Marshall's truck.

Stone swore almost inaudibly under his breath. "I'm not going to leave you to chase him," he muttered.

The warmth of the kiss still lingered in her body, but the fear she felt quickly dissolved it. "Do you know who that was?"

"No."

Keeping her close to him, he walked around the truck, looking for damage and checking the locks.

"Looks like we got back just in time," he said. "But I wonder if he watched us leave."

Annie's reply was troubled. "No one from around here would do that. Break in, I mean."

"Maybe that's so. Could have been someone from out of town, of course."

"What are you saying?"

He sidestepped her question again. "There's no telling who it was. I don't see any damage and the doors are still locked. I do keep some gear in the cab."

"Is it something worth stealing?"

His answer was slow in coming. "That would depend on the thief."

Annie looked down. Rowdy was sniffing the ground around the truck. The dog stretched up and rested on its front paws to give the passenger-side handle a good going-over.

"He smells something," she said uneasily.

Marshall nodded, his jaw set in an angry line. "Let's check inside, see if anything was taken. Then I'll follow your truck back to the ranch. I want to make sure you get home okay."

"You don't have to do that."

"It's not your decision," he snapped. "And I think it'd be best if you stayed away from here—and from me—for a little while."

"Are you kidding?"

"No. And don't argue."

Annie stared at him. Marshall Stone seemed to be genuinely angry. Whether it was at her or at the prowler they'd scared off, she couldn't tell.

His dark gaze met hers. If he wasn't going to explain himself, she would just have to live with that. She didn't have to know everything about him.

What she felt in his embrace was reason enough to trust him for now. He cared about her.

She knew it.

Chapter 8

"**M**om. Step away from the baking aisle. Keep your hands on the shopping cart." Annie did her best to sound like a cop and not laugh.

Her mother shooed her off by waving the list in her hand. "Oh, stop it."

Lou Bennett looked yearningly at the displays of sugar, spices, flour, and holiday bakeware. "I still need a few things for Christmas. Those elf cookie cutters are very cute. What if they sell out?"

Annie looped her arm through her mother's and steered the cart on. "You can order things like that online."

"But the store's so crowded and the good stuff's going to get snapped up. I know lots of people who'd love those cookie cutters. It's not just me."

"You're obsessed."

"Okay, so I like to make cookies. And not just for you. Do you know how many of my friends have grown kids coming for the holidays? They always ask what I'm baking this year. By the way, I ran into that girl you used to know in high school, Darla Something, and she said you should call her."

Darla Ulrich was nice enough, but she loved to gossip. Annie would have to set aside an afternoon just to listen without getting a word in edgewise. All her other former friends in Velde had either moved away or married or both. Annie had lost count of the number of baby photos on everyone's Facebook page. Still, she was glad that they could all sort of keep in touch online. Her pals in Aspen and Vail were way too busy during the holiday season to do more than post a few words now and then.

"Darla. Yes. I'll call her soon," Annie promised, humoring her mother. "But right now we have to finish shopping for Thanksgiving and there's no room in the cart."

Somewhere under bags of sweet potatoes and onions and fresh cranberries and a hundred other things was a twenty-five-pound turkey.

"I really don't think we need such a big one. It's going to be just us three," Lou murmured.

"Dad insisted. He said a puny bird won't look right on our big platter. And he loves turkey sandwiches with your homemade gravy the next day."

"Don't I know it," Lou said with fond irritation. "Ty plows through the leftovers before I can make a potpie. I don't know where he puts it. It's not fair the way men can eat anything and not gain weight."

Annie let go of the cart to stand back and assess her mother's slim figure. "You have absolutely nothing to worry about."

"Thanks, honey. So. Are we done?"

Annie consulted the list. "Yes. Except for the marsh-mallows."

"Those are in the baking aisle."

"I don't trust you," Annie teased her mother.

They both looked ahead when they heard beeps and giggles. Cilla Rivers had the two little girls in the toy car attached to her shopping cart.

"Jenny, Zoe, say hello," Cilla reminded them. "This is Annie's mother, Mrs. Bennett."

"Hello, Mrs. Bennett," they chorused. "Hi, Annie." They spun the wheels they clutched to the right and to the left. An unknown genius had thought to put two steering wheels into the toy car as an anti-squabbling measure.

"You two look like you're having a great time," Lou said.

"I want to get a driver's license," Jenny, the six-year-old, said.

"Well, I want to get a ticket," her younger sister replied.

"What for, silly?"

"Then I could go to a movie. You need a ticket to go to a movie."

Laughing, Annie squatted down so she and the two little drivers were eye to eye. "Tell you what. My mom and Cilla want to get a head start on all the cooking, so I'll take you to a movie tomorrow afternoon if it's all right with Cilla."

The children let go of the wheels long enough to applaud. "Can we go, Aunt Cilla? Please?"

"Sure." Cilla beamed at Annie. "Thanks so much. I really have my hands full. There's an animated movie out at the multiplex they'd enjoy."

The women planned the excursion on Annie's smartphone as they headed for the checkout register, the little girls beeping all the way.

A day later, Annie found herself shepherding Jenny and Zoe through the lobby of the theater as they discussed the plot of the movie they'd just seen.

There wasn't much to it. A dastardly villain planned to steal all the lollipops in the world, but a gang of plucky kids stopped him in time, for a happy ending with candy for all. But they'd enjoyed it.

Jenny turned to her. "Did you go to the movies when you were little, Annie?"

"Sure. Lots of times. I used to wish I had a sister to go with because I had to sit next to my brothers. They didn't behave very well. You two were great."

"Thanks for taking us," Jenny said politely.

"My pleasure."

The girls stopped to peer at the candy under the glass counter, but Annie steered them away.

"What's next for you two?" she asked as a distraction. "Are you ready for the holidays?"

She was surprised that they didn't launch into a breathless discussion of their Christmas lists or talk about how they couldn't wait for Santa. Jenny didn't even answer. Her baby sister took the lead.

"We want to see our mommy," Zoe mumbled.

"She's coming back," Annie reassured her.

"Sometimes we talk to her on Aunt Cilla's computer," Jenny said. "It's nice to see her face, but it's not the same."

Annie reached down and took their hands. "I know what you mean. We're doing that with my brothers this year. They can't be with us for Thanksgiving, so a computer is the next best thing."

"Is Mommy really coming back, Annie?" The younger girl looked up anxiously.

"Of course she is." Annie smiled. "Don't you worry."

"It's going to be just you and me, pal." Marshall spoke to Rowdy, who jumped out of the dog bed at the sound of a grocery bag being unpacked and came over to the cabin's kitchenette.

The dog's bright eyes tracked the items as they were removed. There was half of a precooked turkey breast encased in clear plastic. A can of cranberry sauce. A box of seasoned dry stuffing. A jar of gravy. A frozen pie. Marshall put that and the turkey into the small refrigerator. With the basics, there was something green in the crisper to microwave and throw on the plate.

"Don't look so eager. What if I screw this up?"

The dog barked once and grinned, as if it knew for sure that such a brilliant, warm-hearted guy couldn't possibly screw anything up.

Marshall went into his gear bag and pulled out a laptop. "There's gotta be a football game on somewhere." Rowdy wagged his tail.

Up here in the high country, he couldn't download the movie of his choice—he was thinking fist-fights with robot combatants up against a heroine in a slinky outfit. Everything else on offer around Thanksgiving seemed to be mostly heartwarming fare. Bad enough he had to celebrate by himself.

It'd been a long time since he'd celebrated the holiday with anyone. Since his parents had passed away years ago, he'd gotten in the habit of saying no to kind offers to join friends and distant relatives at their festive tables, and just got through the day as best he could.

He wondered what Annie was doing. Besides celebrating with her family, of course. What he wanted to know was if she was thinking about him. The downside to telling her not to argue with him was that she hadn't—and she'd stayed away. He hadn't found out anything about the potential prowler. His contact at the police department said there'd been no break-ins or any other criminal activity anywhere in Velde. According to the officer, the little town was the same as always—peaceful and prosperous—and the inhabitants were going about their business just as usual and preparing for the Christmas season.

So maybe he should take on Annie as his assistant. Except that would involve telling her who he actually was and what the investigation was all about. Forget it. She would drive him crazy in minutes and it had taken him months to get this far.

Marshall scrolled through the sports networks that were available and found something worth watching.

Rowdy looked longingly at the packaged foods

on the counter, then settled down beside his new master on the floor.

The Bennetts' table was swathed in deep red damask and sparkling with the good china and crystal. Then there was the food.

"I made too much," Lou fretted, finding room for a bowl of cranberry-orange relish between a platter heaped with stuffing and the gravy boat.

"Don't say that, darling." Tyrell was beaming with anticipation. "I bet I can eat about half of everything here. You and Annie outdid yourselves. Now sit down and let's say grace."

They bowed their heads. Their three voices were joined by four others as they all murmured the familiar words of blessing. Smiling, the Bennetts paused for a few moments before serving up the feast.

Tyrell turned to the open laptop at his side, offering a slice of turkey to the man on the screen. "White meat or dark, Sam?"

His oldest son held up a well-browned drumstick in answer. "I'm good. Working on this."

"Looks good."

Lou peered at the screen. "Are you all there? Can you hear me?"

There was a chorus of yeses from Sam and Nicole in Chicago, and Zach and Paula, patched in from somewhere in Oregon.

"Well then," the patriarch said. "Let's eat."

* * *

"So how was your Thanksgiving?" Dr. Bert Lyon slipped Annie's latest X-ray into the viewer. The overhead light of the examining room made his gray hair look almost as white as his office coat. He pushed up the glasses that rested on his beaky nose and studied the ghostly image.

"It was really nice. We didn't do anything special, though."

"Sometimes those are the best holidays." He tapped the X-ray. "You're making progress."

She would have cheered, if not for the expression on the orthopedist's face when he turned to her. She didn't see the usual twinkle in his eye, which was familiar to every Velde kid who'd ever fallen out of a tree or slipped on the ice.

"But I wouldn't say the bone is one hundred percent healed," he added.

Annie groaned theatrically. "Aarrgh. Will it ever be?"

"Yes. You've got to give it a little more time, that's all."

"I suppose I don't really have a choice."

"Be patient. Now let's have a look at that leg."

She rolled up one leg of her sweatpants and pushed down her sock when he settled himself on a wheeled stool and rolled over to the examining table.

Dr. Lyon asked her to flex her foot as he ran his hand over her calf. "You haven't lost much muscle. That's a plus. Do you think you can stay off the slopes until January?"

Annie made a face. "If you say I have to, then I can."

The orthopedist pushed away from the table and rolled toward the low counter where her file was. She covered up her leg and pulled up her sock. Dr. Lyon flipped open the manila file and leafed through it.

"Don't take chances," he advised. "Agreed?"

"I won't. But it's going to be a long December."

He chuckled as he took a pen out of the pocket of his white coat and jotted down a few notes. "You'll get through it."

Annie brightened as she thought of a halfway measure. "I can ride the ski lift, can't I?"

The town boasted a decent slope that petered out where the main street began. It wasn't a black diamond run and no hotdogger would give it a second look, but it was popular all the same, especially with the locals. The creaky but serviceable ski lift started up when the snow did, around the end of September, and kept going until March and sometimes into April.

Dr. Lyon peered at her over his half-glasses. "Sure. In bedroom slippers. No skis. I mean it, Annie. Your mom and dad would skin me alive if they thought I encouraged you before it was time."

"I won't ski, I promise. I was only thinking of taking a friend with me. The view from the top is great."

"Can't remember the last time I saw it. Guess it hasn't changed much." The orthopedist took a last look at her file as he capped his pen. "You going with someone from here?" he asked absentmindedly.

"No. He's from Wyoming."

The nurse poked her head in through the door. "Dr. Lyon, your next patient is in room three."

That spared her any more explaining. But the doctor's question had been routine.

"Thanks, Gina. We're all done here."

Annie slid off the table and found her boots as the doctor exited. She walked through the narrow corridor to the front reception area to make an appointment for early January.

The first month of the new year to come seemed like a long way off, but it was only a few weeks away. Marshall Stone would be long gone by then.

She waited until she'd left the office and was warming up her car to try and reach him. The call went straight to voice mail.

Disappointed, Annie didn't leave a message, deciding to send a text instead. Meet me on the mountain? She suggested a date and time and a few other details just in case he needed them.

He texted back immediately. Can't make it then. Some other time, okay? Thanks.

She bit her lip. His terse reply could be interpreted in a lot of ways. Maybe he really was busy, because he'd replied to the text just a few seconds after he'd let her call go to voice mail.

But why had he refused so quickly when she'd used the words *how about* so he wouldn't have to commit to a specific date and time?

And to think she had once been so inundated with male attention that she never analyzed phone calls or texts on a molecular level, she thought ruefully.

The more she thought about it, the more his

reply seemed like a brush-off, one she had never expected.

And she'd been so sure, briefly, that she'd known how he felt about her. Maybe it was all in her imagination.

Annie tapped the screen to make the text go away, silently chiding herself for trying to read between the lines of such a short message.

She had arrived at the ranch and was parked in the driveway before she texted someone else. Darla would do.

She could ski and Annie could—well, she could bird-watch from the top of the mountain. That was about it. She wasn't much of a bird-watcher, but she did have binoculars somewhere. Then they could talk over coffee in the small lodge. Annie knew for sure that Lou wouldn't be there. Her mother hated heights.

Chapter 9

Bundled up against the cold, Annie settled herself on the attached bench of an outdoor picnic table and took in the glorious view. The day was incredibly clear and the mountains seemed much closer at this elevation. The dark pines dominated now that the aspens were leafless, dusted with snow that also lay in deep drifts within ravines no longer hidden.

She'd somehow forgotten that most birds went elsewhere in winter. The binoculars went back into her pocket once she'd watched Darla hurtle downhill a few times and wave from the ski lift on the way up again. Annie pulled the drawstring of her hood to tighten it around her chilly cheeks and lifted her sunglasses to see what the white world looked like without them.

The intense sunlight made her squint. Annie put the sunglasses back in place and turned to look in a different direction.

Velde had gotten at least two inches of snow overnight. Still, it wasn't much for early December. Snow machines were providing an acceptable depth on the trail. But the town at the foot of the mountain sparkled.

Annie played the game of identifying local landmarks for a while. There was Jelly Jam Café, her mother's favorite hangout. And there was Albert's Mercantile, where you could still buy everything from overalls to canned ravioli. And there was Nell's saloon at the center of town.

She took out the binoculars again to check out the decorations affixed to the old-fashioned lamp posts. There were tall candy canes tied with giant red bows on every one. She could just make out garlands of lights hanging high over the streets that would add a delicate touch of sparkle at night. Nice. It was beginning to look like Christmas. She just wished she were more in the mood for the holiday.

With nothing to do, she peered through the binoculars. They weren't that powerful and she was too high up to recognize any individual on the streets. But it was fun to watch everyone bustling about below.

Her gaze moved to the outskirts of town, stopping on the new development she'd noticed before. The raw lots were visible under the light snow, rectangles of flat dirt and nothing more. No structures of any kind were in evidence, not even a construction-site trailer. Just the same winding street lined with lamp posts, which were, oddly, also adorned with candy canes and red bows, even though there wasn't a stick of lumber in sight, let alone finished houses.

But there was a truck parked out there. She adjusted the focus knob.

It was a big black truck, so new that the bright light hit it like a diamond. She knew whom it belonged to.

Marshall Stone must be inside it. Unless he'd just parked it and was walking around somewhere out of sight. She swept the field of vision with the binoculars, seeing no one. Maybe he was finishing up a survey with the gear he stashed in the cab.

Was it a point in his favor or not that he was actually working at the time he'd told her he couldn't make it? Yes, she decided. If he *was* working.

But what could he be doing out there? The subdivision had to have been professionally surveyed before ground was broken or permits wouldn't have been issued. The site had been parceled out with mathematical precision. The development company didn't need a freelancer to second-guess their measurements.

Although he didn't freelance. Stone worked for a company he hadn't named. Hmm.

She peered at the truck from several angles without seeing him, but noting that his tire tracks were the only marks in the snow. After a while, she stuffed the binoculars back into her pocket. It felt weird to be spying on Stone and she didn't want to do it.

A muffled clomping made her turn around. Darla was approaching, wearing abominable-snowman boots that looked awful, but comfortable.

"Hey, Annie. Whatcha doing?" she called. Her face was flushed with the exhilaration of her swift downhill runs.

Annie fought back a pang of envy. "Soaking up the sun."

"You must be freezing, sitting there like a lump," Darla said cheerfully. Darla had never been particularly tactful, but she meant well.

"I'm a little cold," Annie said.

"I say we treat ourselves to hot cocoa and to hell with the calories." Darla turned, stumbling in the huge boots but quickly righting herself with a skier's honed sense of balance. She pushed open the sliding glass door to the lodge interior.

Annie allowed herself one last look below. The truck was in the same place.

They had to shed a few layers of outerwear shortly after they got inside the lodge. Darla tossed her jacket over a sofa positioned in front of a stone fireplace, and Annie did the same. Blazing birch logs were piled high and would burn for hours, radiating heat throughout the great room.

Darla led the way when they returned with two cups of marshmallow cocoa, which Annie carried. She set hers down on the low table in front of the fireplace and gave the other to her friend.

"Ahh." Darla's hands curled around her cup as she sipped it slowly. "Bliss."

There weren't very many people in the lodge on a weekday and Annie was fine with that. She listened absentmindedly to Darla, getting in a soft-voiced question or comment now and then.

Darla was as talkative as ever, but not as nosy as

Annie remembered. Still, she seemed to think it was her obligation to get Annie caught up on everything and everyone in Velde.

"So what was it like being the queen of Aspen and Vail?"

Annie gave a low laugh. "Some queen. I worked really hard. But I had a great time."

"We were wondering about you coming back home to this little town."

Those would be the friends Annie still kept up with online, who had scattered all over the West. Only a few had stayed on in Velde. Facebook was better than nothing, but she didn't check her page too often. After the initial flurry of get-well wishes and concern, the news tended to be about the same and she wasn't into posting her every thought and what she had for lunch.

"Are you going to keep on being a ski instructor?"

The direct question rattled her a little. "That's what I do," Annie answered vaguely.

"Aspen and Vail are so pricey. I've been to both, but I had to stay in some funky places. Still and all, I pretty much had a blast."

"It's not any less expensive when you work there."

"Do you think you'll go back?"

Annie gave herself a few seconds to respond. Even though Darla had mellowed some, she was still a talker. Annie didn't want her plan for the future broadcast all over town. Mostly because she didn't have one.

More and more, she felt like one part of her life

had ended and the next part had yet to begin. She didn't know what she would do next or where she would go.

"I haven't decided," she replied. That was true enough and Darla seemed content with the simple answer. She returned to her favorite subject: herself.

Warmed by the fire and the hot drink, Annie paid minimal attention—until she heard Darla mention Marshall Stone.

"You should check him out. What a hot guy. He's, like, a surveyor or something."

"I know who you mean." Annie's answer was nonchalant. "He was at the town meeting. I went with my parents."

"Oh. I didn't go. Too boring. But I would have showed up with bells on if I'd known he was going to be there."

Annie breathed an inward sigh of relief. Now she knew with absolute certainty that no one had seen her and Marshall kissing in the doorway. That was something Darla would have brought up right away.

"He showed up just in time," Darla added.

"Huh?"

"There's a man shortage in Velde. All the good ones are taken."

Annie smiled politely. "I don't think he's moving here."

"So you talked to him?"

"Yes. He was out by our ranch, surveying Chuck Pfeffer's land."

"Lucky you."

Annie braced herself for a barrage of curious questions. But Darla had more to confide on the subject of the handsome stranger, who apparently wasn't as reserved as Annie had first thought.

"Some friends of mine decided to go to Nell's saloon for beers and sandwiches and there he was, long legs and all. One or two of us made eye contact. From a distance. Nothing happened, but something could have, put it that way."

"So he was there alone."

The thought just came out. Annie bit her lip.

"No. He was with a woman. She was gorgeous," Darla emphasized. "I have no idea who she was, but they sure seemed to know each other."

Annie was quiet as she gazed into the fire, tuning out Darla's speculations on the subject. Apparently her own talent for fooling herself had led her to believe that she might have an exclusive on a man who'd made it clear that he was just passing through. But it didn't really matter. It wasn't like she and Marshall had done anything more than kiss a few times.

Darla stopped and poked her. "Hey. Are you listening?"

Annie only shrugged. "Sure. But he really can't be the only available guy in town."

"Please. He is," Darla insisted. "And right now he's at the top of everyone's wish list. I can't believe you don't want to get to know him better."

A small smile curved Annie's mouth. She wasn't going to fill Darla in on her efforts to do that so far. "Go for it," was all she said.

"How? Follow his truck around?"

"Whatever works."

A college-age waitress with a tray stopped by the sofa. "Can I get you ladies anything else?" she chirped.

"Nothing for me, thanks." Annie wasn't sure she liked being referred to as a lady. It made her feel— not old, but older than she was.

Darla handed over the cups. "Me neither. Here you go. Appreciate it."

"No problem." The waitress walked away, balancing the tray with the cups as if she was practicing.

Annie had started the same way, covering weekend shifts at ski resort restaurants and bars just to be close to the action and able to ski during the weekdays, when the slopes were less crowded. It seemed like a long time ago.

"You ready?" Darla asked. She pulled up the socks inside her huge boots.

"Yes." Annie stretched a bit, then put on her jacket, glancing up at the clock framed by antlers. They had been talking longer than she'd thought.

Darla went out first, lift ticket in her hand. Annie stopped briefly at the deck railing and looked for Marshall's truck.

It was still there. A flash of black and white circled it and stopped at the passenger side door. Someone opened it from the inside and Rowdy jumped in.

Annie was pretty damn sure that Marshall hadn't done the opening. The person had been wearing pink.

She blew out the breath she'd been holding.

Better to know than not to know, even though what Marshall Stone did was none of her business. It was no big deal. Life went on no matter what she might want. Annie was an expert at getting up and moving on. The trick was to stay busy and not brood. Maybe Nell needed her help with something.

Darla dropped her off in front of the saloon, but not before Annie looked up and down the main street for Stone's truck.

"Right here is fine," Annie said. "I parked around the corner."

"Okay. Nice talking with you, Annie. Let me know when you can ski again. I felt kinda guilty having so much fun."

"You shouldn't. I like doing nothing sometimes. It's probably good for me."

"Stay in touch."

"I will. Thanks for the ride."

She got out and waved to Darla as she sped away in her zippy little car.

Annie turned and looked through the windows of Nell's saloon. The sign said OPEN, but she didn't see her friend. Or anyone else.

She went through the swinging half doors to the winterized entry and took a final peek through the glass of the inside door, looking for a pink sweater or jacket. The booths were empty.

Annie heaved a sigh. She couldn't fault Marshall Stone for just being a man like all the others. She went in. "Nell? You here?"

"Coming."

The older woman appeared, maneuvering a hand truck stacked with liquor cartons. "Hi, Annie. Want to help me restock?"

"Sure."

The two of them filled in the empty spots in the display of bottles in front of the mirror and got set up for happy hour. There were no customers, which made the various tasks go quickly.

Nell stepped back and cast a critical eye on the display. "I think that'll do it," she said with satisfaction. "Thanks for your help."

"You're welcome."

"Lucky for me you were in town," Nell added.

"I was meeting a friend up at the ski lodge."

"Such a clear day," Nell enthused. "The view must have been amazing."

"Yes."

"So are you heading home now?"

"Might as well."

"I'll walk you to your car. I could use a breath of fresh air."

Annie slipped on her jacket again and waited for Nell to put on her coat and gloves. The older woman turned the OPEN sign to the side that said BACK IN FIVE.

They stopped to admire a few shop windows along the way, decked out with tinsel and gift-wrapped boxes to attract holiday shoppers. The Thanksgiving themes painted by the schoolchildren had been washed off, replaced by spray snow and glitter applied from the inside to frame the merchandise.

"Hmm. I'm trying to remember if I need something," Nell said thoughtfully. "Still haven't put up those Christmas decorations."

"I'll help you."

"You don't have to, Annie."

"Why not? It's fun. Something to do."

"You should be going on dates, not dusting off those old things."

Nell gave her a sympathetic look that Annie missed, because she was peering through the window at a scale model of a covered wagon.

"Now that is wonderful," Annie said in awe, reading the title on the placard by the display. CHRISTMAS CROSSING. 1880. "Bet that's exactly how it was back then."

"Yes indeed. I guess we don't have anything to complain about."

A small figure of an old cowboy dressed in worn denim and a sheepskin coat held the reins of a team of straining oxen, his slouch hat pulled down low and his shoulders hunched, as if he were bracing himself against a fierce, invisible wind. A tear in the covered wagon's taut canvas offered a peek at wrapped gifts amid barrels and boxes of foodstuffs and necessities.

Annie kneeled down to see the cowboy's face. "Look at his wrinkles. Can you see, Nell? The face is made of dried apple."

"It sure is. Can't you just feel the snow he's fighting against?" Nell leaned in, her breath frosty on the glass. "I wonder who made it."

Annie looked more closely at the placard. "An

original work created by Chester Byron Hamilton."

"What a romantic name. But I don't think I know him."

"Not everyone is from Velde," Annie teased her.

"Just you hush up." Nell straightened and bumped into someone behind her, apologizing automatically. "Oh dear. I'm so sorry. I didn't see you." With a look of surprise on her face, Nell reached out to steady a wobbly old lady. "Elsie?"

Annie recognized Mrs. Pearson from the post office. She had a crocheted hat over her wispy white hair and wore a heavy coat that looked as if she'd had it a long time.

"Hello, Nell." Her voice quavered just a little, but she smiled. "How have you been?"

"Just fine. And you?" Without waiting for an answer, Nell made the introductions. "Annie, I'd like you to meet Elsie Pearson. She was the school principal back when I first started teaching. Elsie, this is Annie Bennett."

"A pleasure." Mrs. Pearson nodded courteously and extended a thin, gloved hand.

Annie shook it carefully.

Nell looked as if she was just about to hug the frail figure, but she hesitated. The authority that Mrs. Pearson had once had wasn't entirely gone. The old lady still held herself with dignity.

"I haven't seen you for so long," Nell went on. "Would you mind if I came over some afternoon?"

Mrs. Pearson seemed to be trying to come up with a polite refusal. "That would be lovely," she said after a few moments. "But please call first.

Jack's health isn't what it used to be and he doesn't like unexpected company. He's been undergoing tests, but the doctor has no definite diagnosis."

"I'm sorry to hear that." Nell chose not to dwell on what was obviously a sensitive topic. "And of course I'll call in advance. If I stop by, you won't have to do a thing. I'll bring cake and coffee from Jelly Jam. Would that do?"

"Yes." Mrs. Pearson looked relieved. "Very nicely. That's thoughtful of you, Nell." She drew herself up to her full height of five foot nothing and fixed her clear gaze on Annie's for a few seconds. "Nice to have met you, my dear. Now I must be going."

They said their good-byes. Both Nell and Annie turned to watch the old lady's progress along the street. She walked without a cane, but not quickly, avoiding the icy spots.

"Goodness. Mrs. Pearson must be close to ninety by now," Nell said in a low voice. "There doesn't seem to be anything wrong with her vision. But I wonder what's going on with her husband. Jack was always such a stalwart man—he was a rancher. They sold the place shortly after she retired. It's a shame, really. I know how much she loved it. But moving to town probably made sense by then."

"Maybe we could help her somehow," Annie said. Her take-charge, get-it-done side was kicking in. Having something to think about besides a problem by the name of Marshall Stone would be a boon.

Nell's expression was pensive. "I had the same thought. But do you know something I don't?"

"Before you introduced us, I noticed Mrs. Pearson at the post office. She had a tax bill in one hand and an envelope from that speaker at the town meeting in the other. Connally."

"Really." Nell's penciled eyebrows rose. "I've been hearing that name. Of course, I don't try to eavesdrop on customers, but sometimes it's unavoidable. Some older folks have been discussing the man. He's looking for investors."

"I wouldn't give him a dime."

Nell gave a neutral shrug. "I gathered that he's selling shares in a high-yield private fund of some sort."

"Is that all?"

Nell studied her for a long moment. "What's gotten into you?"

Annie didn't quite know. Maybe she just needed to think about someone besides herself and do a good deed while she was at it. She'd gotten over the idea long ago that obsessing over some guy for weeks was worthwhile.

"Seeing Mrs. Pearson again, I guess," she said quickly. "I did worry when I spotted the envelopes, because I didn't like Connally, but she didn't know me from Adam and I didn't expect to run into her again."

"It's a sign. Is that what you're saying?"

"No. I don't believe in signs. But you just filled in a few blanks and got me thinking."

"I see." Nell didn't quibble. "Well, the Pearsons may need help of some kind. God knows they were thrifty, but they never had much money to spare.

Still, I doubt they would give someone like Connally the time of day."

"We could find out."

"Annie, the Pearsons were proud people and I'm sure they still are. Is their situation, whatever it might be, any of our business?"

Annie planted herself on the sidewalk. "You and I both know that quarterly property taxes are due by the end of the year. Maybe Mr. Pearson's health isn't the only thing she's worried about."

"I wish I had followed up when she stopped coming to church last spring," Nell fretted. "But I never seemed to have the time."

"Let's talk about what we can do right now. Something's going on in Velde and it has to do with real estate."

Annie left Marshall Stone out of it. Her initial sense that he was somehow involved in a secret land grab had been replaced with other suspicions that she was damned if she'd discuss with Nell or anyone else. She wasn't really able to believe that he would cheat anyone out of money or land. And she couldn't quite say that he had cheated on her when she had known him for only a few weeks.

But it still felt like it.

Nell snapped her out of it with a quick question. "Are you serious, Annie?"

"Yes. I even spoke to the town clerk. She wouldn't say anything specific, but she had her doubts about Connally too."

"Oh my. Harriet Sargent is such a levelheaded gal. What exactly did she say?"

"Not much. But I'd like to get your take on what I've figured out so far."

Annie steered Nell down the street toward the café just ahead. She opened the door, inhaling the mixed fragrance of cinnamon and caramel. Fresh-brewed coffee provided the top note.

Nell swept past her to a table by the window. She put her purse over the back of a chair and got comfortable before the waitress arrived to take their order.

"Tell me everything," she said to Annie. "Begin at the beginning."

Chapter 10

Nell was as good as her word. She called Mrs. Pearson and then Annie, to let her know that they were invited to the Pearsons' the day after next.

"Don't dress up," she told Annie. "Sometimes the housekeeping is the first thing to go for old folks. I don't want to make her feel awkward."

The Pearson house turned out to be neat as a pin, once Elsie had opened the door and quickly motioned them inside. "Hello, you two. So nice of you to come. Don't let the hat out."

She smiled, but Annie knew she wasn't joking. It was a charming old house—a cottage, really—with tall windows that let in abundant sunlight and bone-chilling drafts as well. Mrs. Pearson wore a thick, hand-knit sweater with a cowl collar that she had pulled up over her white hair. Annie didn't want to be rude, but she kept her jacket on.

Nell was braver and also better upholstered. She took off her swing coat and hung it on a foyer hook, over the handle of a cane that was much too long for Mrs. Pearson. Annie assumed it belonged to her husband.

"Everything is just the same, Elsie. Thanks so much for inviting us." Nell paused, looking around discreetly. "Where's Jack?"

"Taking a nap." Elsie glanced toward a room with a closed door.

"Oh. Well, we can save some cake for him." She held up the bag with take-out coffees and a small bakery box.

"Thank you, Nell. I'll be sure to tell him you were here. Please sit down, Annie." Mrs. Pearson led the way to a sunroom filled with plants and wicker chairs. It was warm enough for Annie to shed her jacket and relax a little.

Nell pretty much took over the conversation as the coffees were set out and the cake sliced and served up on small porcelain plates. Annie simply listened as the older women talked and talked. Mrs. Pearson sat up straight when Nell finally ventured onto the subject of money.

"Elsie, I want you to know something. Now, please don't take this the wrong way."

The old lady's calm gaze didn't change, but she did raise an eyebrow.

"If you need anything at all—for yourself or for Jack—I just want you to know that I would be happy to help. I did very well after I retired and started my new business."

Mrs. Pearson gave a faint smile. "Somehow I never imagined you behind a bar, dear."

"You should come in. Maybe not on football nights, but in the afternoon."

"Thank you for the invitation. Perhaps I will someday. I suppose I shouldn't have worn that shabby old coat the other day. I think you got the wrong impression. But I appreciate your kindness."

Mrs. Pearson set aside her plate. Annie noticed that she had barely touched her slice of cake.

"I haven't done anything yet," Nell reminded her.

"And you won't have to. We don't need help. Jack and I get by. There's not much that we need at this stage of our lives."

"That could change."

The old lady cleared her throat. "Everything changes," she said dryly. "Including who does what. Jack used to handle things like finances. I never had to worry. But he can't anymore. So I'm learning what I can."

"Oh?" Nell didn't rush into the void with a lot of chatter for once. Annie waited.

"I spoke with that Mr. Connally recently. He gave me some good advice. He may be able to give us the cash we need to stay in our home, but it's complicated. I couldn't say I understand every little detail of what he was proposing."

"Make sure that you do, Elsie," Nell said firmly.

"Oh, I will. First I have to find our copy of the deed."

Nell and Annie exchanged a look.

"Of course, I haven't signed anything yet."

"Will you talk to me before you do?" Nell said.

Mrs. Pearson looked up at the sound of a door opening elsewhere in the house. "Yes. But not now."

A tall, stoop-shouldered man came toward them and stopped in the doorway of the sunny room. Though his rugged face was lined and weathered, he was still handsome. But his gaze lacked focus. He looked at each of them in turn, smiling at his wife and staring hard at Nell.

"Hello, Jack," Nell said cheerfully.

"Hello." His deep voice sounded polite but blank, as if he had no idea who the woman who'd just greeted him might be.

"This is Annie," his wife said. "And you know Nell."

It was heartbreakingly clear that he didn't.

Elsie gave her visitors a speaking look that said it all. The conversation was effectively over. Jack sat down and got up again.

"He has good days and bad days," his wife murmured when her husband had left the room. "I just wish I had a name for what exactly is wrong." She paused, collecting herself, holding her head high. "It could be so many things."

Annie got the same impression of unshakable dignity. She would add silent courage to that.

"I'm sorry he didn't remember you, Nell. He never was too good with names. And now, well . . ." The old lady didn't finish the sentence.

"Elsie. You don't have to explain."

"There isn't anything more I can say. But he's still my Jack. And he always will be."

"I understand," Nell said finally. "I didn't know about this. But you don't have to deal with it alone, Elsie."

"I can't talk about it now." The old lady seemed to have withdrawn from them, her attention focused on the man moving about in the adjoining rooms. "I think you'd better go, in fact."

Nell rose reluctantly and Annie followed her lead. "I hope you can forgive me for not staying in touch," Nell said.

Elsie gave her a wry look. "Oh, of course. It's not entirely your fault. I never called you. And I do hope you'll come back."

"Of course I will."

It seemed best not to linger. They were outside in a few minutes.

"I almost don't know where to start," Nell said. "But I'm not going to forget about her. Not with Christmas right around the corner."

Annie took the white cardboard box of treats from the front seat and went in the side door of the house. Her mother never would have forgiven her for not bringing something home from her favorite bakery.

She set the Jelly Jam box down on the pine table in the kitchen and looked around. The winter sun poured through the windows. There was no sign of her mother, other than the immaculate counters and general air of tidiness. Lou Bennett had a place for everything and put everything in its place.

Tyrell had built the kitchen himself, putting in cabinets and shelves to his wife's specifications. All of it had been made to last.

Good storage beat hearts and flowers, her mom liked to say. But her husband made sure to remember those too.

Some day, some way, Annie was going to have a marriage like theirs. If a couple wasn't committed to love by deeds and not just words, she didn't see the point of it.

"Mom?" she called. "I'm home."

A faint hello echoed from somewhere.

Annie filled the electric kettle with water and looked through the cupboards for tea bags. She made two cups just in case her mother wanted one.

A few minutes went by before Lou appeared.

Annie couldn't actually see her. Her petite mother was invisible behind the lightweight boxes she carried. They were all neatly labeled in her bouncy handwriting.

Ornaments. Garlands. Tree Topper. There were more. Annie was glad to see her personal favorite in the stack. *Glass Birds.* They were heirlooms, hand-painted with showy tails, and spindly feet that had to be wound around Christmas tree branches.

"Is that you?" Annie asked, laughing as she went to her mother and removed the top boxes.

Lou set the rest of them on the kitchen table. "Seemed like high time I got all these down."

"We don't even have a Christmas tree yet."

"Oh, your father will take care of that. I just

wanted to make sure nothing's broken and see if we needed anything new."

"I understand there's a sale on elf-related merchandise at the hobby store."

"Is there? Do you have a coupon?"

"Would I lie to you? Yes to the first question. No to the second. I made you some tea. Let's look through the boxes."

They spent the better part of an hour taking a sentimental inventory before Annie brought up the subject of Mrs. Pearson.

"Elsie Pearson? Yes, I know who she is," Lou said absentmindedly. "But I couldn't say I know her personally."

Annie recounted the story from the beginning, including their accidental meeting and subsequent visit with Nell, without adding a word about how vulnerable the old lady had seemed to her. With her dad on the verge of turning seventy, getting old was the last thing he wanted to talk about, and she suspected that her mother thought the same way, even though she was nearly a decade younger than her husband.

Annie wrapped it up with her thoughts on Shep Connally.

"Oh. The blowhard from the town meeting." Her mother held up a glass bird and smoothed its flyaway tail. "I didn't think too much of him either."

"But would you say he's trying to con her and maybe some of the other old people?"

"I honestly don't know, dear."

Annie sighed. "I just want to help Mrs. Pearson."

Lou set the bird into its niche in the ornament box. "You can't help people who don't want to be helped, honey. She has a right to make her own decisions. And I think Nell is going to be better at dealing with the particular problems involved."

"What are you saying?"

"That you're young yet and you don't know everything."

"I never said I did," Annie replied indignantly.

Her mother seemed not to have heard her protest. "Above all, don't pry. If Mrs. Pearson wants your assistance with something, I'm sure she'll ask you. It does sound like you made a friend."

"I hope so."

Annie was quiet for a little while, fiddling with the ornaments. Lou Bennett finally stopped what she was doing long enough to sip her tea.

"Want me to heat that up for you?"

"I like it lukewarm."

"No, you don't." Annie took the cup from her and put it in the microwave, timing it for thirty seconds. She didn't turn to look at her mother when she asked another question.

"Mom, are you volunteering at the senior center this year?"

It wasn't exactly a center, just a spare room provided gratis at the town hall for seniors to meet in occasionally.

"Yes. Which reminds me. The president of the Groaners and Grumblers Club left me a message last night."

"What did you call them? That's not nice."

"Groaners and Grumblers. That's what they call themselves," Lou pointed out. "At least they have a sense of humor. It's not easy being old."

"You're not there yet, Mom." Annie took out the reheated cup of tea when the microwave beeped, and brought it over.

"Says you. I officially qualified as a senior this year."

"That bunch thinks you're fresh out of high school." Annie picked a mini box of raisins out of the fruit bowl and munched on a few. "So do you think you could keep an ear open? See if they have any shared concerns?"

"What are you getting at?"

Annie polished off the raisins. "Like if anyone complains about Shep Connally. Or mentions reverse mortgages. Or anything else relating to real estate that sounds fishy to you."

"If there's going to be an investigation, call the police."

"They need evidence."

Lou frowned and wiped off an imaginary spot on the counter with a folded dish towel. "Did they ask you to get it?"

"No. But I might as well start somewhere."

"Annie." Her mother stopped wiping and set aside the dish towel. "I think you're taking this too seriously. You're up in arms about something that hasn't happened and may never happen. I'm sure Nell knows who to contact at social services to help Mrs. Pearson."

"She did say she was going to."

"Good. I know you mean well, but you can't take

on a situation like that. Besides, you should be spending more time with people your own age."

"I am. I called Darla," Annie said. "We hung out at the ski lodge for a couple of hours."

"When was that?"

"Several days ago."

"That would be my point. 'Tis the season to be jolly." Lou went and got her purse and pulled out a flyer. "Did you know there's a dance coming up?"

"No." Annie glanced at the flyer her mother set in front of her.

"The first annual Snow Ball. Doesn't that sound romantic?" Lou sighed.

"Not particularly."

Her mother read aloud from the flyer. " 'Come one, come all, for a night of magic. Enjoy three live bands that will tickle your ears and get your toes tapping with country swing, rockabilly, and your favorite sweet serenades.' "

Annie wasn't about to admit that it sounded wonderful. "I don't want my ears tickled."

"Sourpuss," her mother chided. "You don't have to have a date to attend, you know."

"Okay," Annie said. "Because I can't get one."

"Does that mean you might go?" her mother asked slyly.

"I'm not promising anything."

"It's next Friday. Come to think of it, Helen Skerrit was going to come over that same night to play cards. She's bringing her stepson Alan. You know, the genius. Right now he has nothing to do. She said he just got kicked out of graduate school for some reason. Maybe what he needs is love and understanding."

Annie knew her mom was teasing her. "Count me out. Isn't he the one who sleeps all day and only eats corn chips?"

"Yes. And I'm prepared. There are five jumbo bags in the pantry."

Annie laughed at the wicked gleam in her mother's eye. "You're awful. All right. I'll think about the damn dance. I might even go. By myself. Just hide that flyer where Alan will never find it."

Lou folded it neatly in half and handed it to her daughter. "It's all yours. But promise me you'll go. You might meet someone."

Annie made a face. "What if I don't feel sociable?"

"Go anyway. You could change your mind."

Chapter 11

Annie was out at the barn, checking the siding in preparation for the first big storm of winter. There hadn't been much snow so far and it was already December. But it would come.

Her phone chirped in the pocket of her down vest. Annie took it out and looked at the screen.

It was a text message from Marshall Stone. Annie tapped the screen.

Rowdy's missing. Have u seen him?

That wasn't good news. She texted back. No.

She counted to ten. Against her better judgment, she typed another text. Want to meet up to look for him?

Sure.

Annie took a deep breath and let it out slowly. Seeing Marshall Stone again might not be the best idea. But she did care about the dog.

An hour or so later, they were driving around, looking for a flash of black-and-white fur. Rowdy was nowhere in sight.

"I let him out this morning and went back to get his leash. So it's my fault," Stone admitted. "When I got outside, he was gone. I whistled and whistled, but he didn't come back. I sure hope he didn't get hit by a car."

"It happens."

"I made a couple of calls. No one's reported a lost dog." He kept scanning the sides of the road and looking into the distance.

"If he did get hit and he's injured, he might stay away from anyone trying to help."

"True."

"Or maybe his real owner came back for him."

Marshall scowled. She guessed he was thinking about the Dumpster and whoever had abandoned the dog there in the first place. "I doubt that," he muttered.

There was a distant sound of barking. He listened carefully.

"Is that him?"

"I think so." His expression brightened considerably.

He kept the windows rolled down as he zeroed in on the barking. Soon enough, they spotted Rowdy, playing ring-toss in an open field with several young women. They looked like college students. Had winter break already begun? Annie guessed that it had.

"What an operator." Stone laughed.

Takes after you. Annie didn't want to say it. Marshall Stone wasn't her boyfriend. Just a good-looking guy women noticed. That wasn't a sin, per se.

"How am I going to persuade him to go home with me?" he asked as he got out of the truck.

Annie was irked by the way Stone's intent gaze moved from his dog to the girls, who squealed and giggled, amused by the antics of the happy-go-lucky stray.

"Hi there! Is this your dog?"

It was impossible to tell who'd asked the question.

"Yes." Laconic as ever. But Marshall had a huge, annoying grin on his face.

The girls were all pretty, without a care in the world, a mix of blondes and brunettes, their long hair tousled by the breeze despite their headbands. Annie couldn't help noticing the expensive ski jackets they wore, new for the season, thinking that she hadn't been able to afford even closeout items for some time.

"Do you have any dog treats?" she asked tightly from inside the truck.

"Look in the glove compartment. I think I stashed some CrunChees in there."

Annie pushed the button in the center of the molded door and opened it. There was a plastic bag with a couple of orange-cheese-colored dog biscuits stuffed next to the owner's manual.

"Yup. Here." She handed them over and shut the compartment.

Apparently Rowdy's new best friends were thinking along the same lines.

"Can we give him a snack?" one called, trying unsuccessfully to catch the playful animal. "He looks hungry."

"No, he doesn't," Annie muttered. Rowdy had filled out fast. She knew perfectly well that the playful young women were more interested in the dog's owner than the dog.

Stone opened the driver's side door without responding to her sarcastic comment. Or maybe he hadn't heard it.

"He has you fooled, ladies." He held up the treat bag. "That dog eats more than I do."

Stone grinned again in response to a wave of feminine laughter. Annie scowled.

Rowdy shook off the snow in his fur and trotted toward the truck.

"That can't be true," one said.

"He stole half the Thanksgiving turkey right off the counter," he informed them.

Annie shot Stone a look. She hadn't asked him how he'd spent the traditional holiday, figuring at the time that he'd probably zoomed up overnight to Wyoming on the interstate and returned by Sunday.

"Gosh. He looks so innocent."

About as innocent as his ruggedly good-looking master, Annie thought.

"And he's so friendly," someone else said. She was having trouble keeping track, what with all the gushing.

"We figured he had to belong to someone. But he didn't have a tag."

Again, it was kind of hard to tell which girl had said it. They tended to talk over each other and laugh a lot. Annie saw Marshall bend down and examine the dog.

"Hmm. Guess he managed to lose that. But it could've fallen off." Rowdy sat before he was asked to and got a CrunChee for his trouble. "Well, thanks for taking care of him."

"No problem." They kept on chattering like happy birds in the sunshine, ignoring Annie, who was still in the truck. Maybe they just didn't see her, what with the glare off the windshield. Or maybe it was the blinding brilliance of Marshall Stone's sexy smile.

She narrowed her gaze when one young woman approached the truck. *Oh, please,* she thought. She wasn't in the mood to chat with anyone.

The girl ran her mittened hand over the gleaming fender. "Ooh, nice truck. Is it new?"

Masculine pride tinged Stone's reply. "Yup."

The sun went behind a cloud and the reflective glare on the windshield vanished. The girl suddenly saw Annie and stepped back, her mascaraed eyes widening for a second. "Um, hello."

Annie managed a thin smile. "Hi."

The other girl effectively dismissed her by addressing her next remark exclusively to Marshall. "I didn't know you were with someone."

He barely glanced sideways at her, to her further annoyance. "That's Annie. She's a friend. I'm Marshall Stone."

"Oh, okay. Well, I'm Jill."

She didn't offer a last name and he didn't supply any additional clarification as to who Annie was to him.

Not really anyone, she thought crossly. There was no other term besides *friend* for their relationship so far. It was difficult to define and probably didn't even technically qualify as a relationship, but even so, it seemed to Annie that he could have been more enthusiastic about introducing her.

Marshall looked a little nervous, as if he'd been caught playing the field. Or maybe a guilty look would be more accurate. She wondered, if she were just a friend and nothing more, if he kissed all his female acquaintances the way he kissed her. She looked out the side window at nothing and sighed inwardly.

Rowdy jumped in when his master whistled, giving Annie an enthusiastic greeting despite his betrayal.

"Quit it," she told him. But she patted him, even though he was getting snow all over the seat. He panted with happy tiredness, letting his tongue loll out as Marshall got back in, leaving the window rolled down to give a final wave.

More squeals and giggles.

Now they all seemed to be admiring the truck, egged on by Jill. They probably took Stone for a rich young rancher. They had no way of knowing that he wasn't from around the area because they weren't local either.

A redhead joined the group. Where had she come from? Annie sat bolt upright when the redhead slipped off her jacket. She was wearing a hot pink sweater. Annie thought, uncharitably, that it clashed with her hair, which looked dyed.

The color of the sweater wasn't proof of anything. Annie hated herself for jumping to conclusions. There had to be a hundred million pink sweaters in the US, and Colorado could probably lay claim to about ten million of the total. It didn't mean a damn thing. But she had to admit that the visual connection had jolted her for a second.

Then she realized that Marshall was waving to that one in particular.

"What are you doing here?" the redhead called.

"Picking up my dog," he called back. "I'm not sure he wants to leave, though. Tough luck. I have things to do and places to go. You know how it is."

It sounded like he expected the newcomer to understand what he meant. Annie's jealousy—she had to admit to it—notched up.

"Got it. By the way, thanks for the ride the other day," the redhead added with a wink. "Bye, Rowdy!"

Okay. That was proof enough. The redhead had to have been the person who'd opened the truck door when Annie had spotted the flash of pink from up on the mountain.

Stone nodded and rolled up the window before he drove away.

"Funny how she knew the dog's name when you didn't say it and he didn't have a tag."

A minute or so passed. She didn't like how she felt or how she was acting, but she couldn't help the reaction. *Some people have real problems,* she reminded herself sternly.

"Let me guess," Stone finally spoke. "You don't think it's funny at all. You'd like to hit me with a brick, but we could end up in a ditch."

"That's about right. Also, I don't have a brick. Remind me to bring one next time I help you find your poor little lost doggy."

Rowdy gave her a soulful look. Annie half thought that Stone had put him up to this. Was it possible to train a dog to get lost? More to the point, could a man be trained to do the same thing?

"Nice girls, don't you think?"

That was at the top of the list of Questions She Had No Intention of Ever Answering.

"I'm glad he found them. Or vice versa." She could feel his quick sideways look at her. "Something on your mind?" he asked.

"Not really."

"I take it you didn't know any of them."

She gave an indifferent shrug. "They're not from Velde."

He pondered that for a moment. "Probably just passing through. Like me."

Annie had no comment.

"Okay, spit it out. Something is bugging you."

"Why do you want to know?"

"Because you're obviously upset."

"Aww. Next you'll be telling me that you care."

Stone cleared his throat. But he didn't say anything more. The tension between them stretched to the breaking point.

"Did I marry you and not remember it?" he asked in a low voice. "Because if I didn't, I believe I have the right to do what I want."

Annie stared straight ahead, fuming. "Who is that redhead?"

"I think her name is Bunny."

"You think." Annie didn't need one more reason to be suspicious. Of course, he didn't need to know a redhead's full name to spend an afternoon with her. Or even her real name, which probably wasn't Bunny.

"Her car broke down out at the subdivision. I gave her a lift to the service station. So what?"

He slowed down at an intersection of several country roads. They were in the middle of nowhere, but Annie reached for the door handle. She heard a click as he pushed a button that locked it.

"Don't. It's much too cold to walk by the side of the road. I'll drop you off wherever you like."

"In town. Anywhere on Main Street."

"Will do."

A headache-inducing silence prevailed until he pulled up into the first parking spot he saw. Annie got out and slammed the door hard enough to hurt her own eardrums. It rankled the hell out of her when she saw his handsome face through the windshield. She bent down to scoop up a handful of snow, which she packed into a ball and threw at him.

Stone turned on the wipers for a few seconds and grinned at her.

There hadn't been any car out at the subdivision. Just his goddamned truck. The worst of it was, there wasn't anyone she could tell about him being a heel. Even Darla would think she was stupid for believing him in the first place.

Annie headed away from his truck, not looking when she heard him drive past. She wasn't sure where she wanted to go or what she ought to do with the rest of her day.

A misspelled cardboard sign outside the church social hall caught her eye.

XMAS PAJUNT REEHERSUL AT 4.

Annie looked at her watch. It was 3:30. She walked up to the sign and read the fine print.

P.S. WE NEED HEY FOR THE MANGER.

It looked like a kid had done the lettering. Annie's bad mood started to fizzle out. She'd missed the pageant when she'd been working in Aspen and Vail. Not this year. And she wasn't just going to watch it. She was going to volunteer. Right now. There were several bales of hay in the Bennetts' barn that she could bring over later.

Just thinking about Stone's self-satisfied grin made her do an especially good job of stomping the snow off her boots in the entryway to the social hall. She was somewhat calmer when she went in.

Kids were running around everywhere, doing more laughing than rehearsing. The chorus director, Opal Lawson, was trying to keep order, without too much success.

"Need some help?"

"Annie, how nice to see you! Yes. If you could get the shepherds on stage, that would be great."

"Which ones are they?"

Opal looked around distractedly at the scampering kids. "Oh no. They took off their burlap robes. I only see two of them."

Annie hollered so loudly the rafters rang. "Shepherds! Front and center!"

Seven little boys separated themselves from the pack and ran over to her.

"Line up, please."

They obeyed. Opal collapsed in a chair. "How did you do that? Never mind. Thank you, Annie. I need all the help I can get."

"I can see that. Let's go, boys." Annie brought up the rear as the shepherds marched up the rickety wooden stairs and, jostling each other, stopped under a painted canvas sky filled with stars.

"Are you in charge now?" a fair-haired boy asked.

"Only of you guys. I bet you don't have any lines to rehearse. Shepherds usually don't say anything."

"I do," said an older boy with a bristling brown crew cut. "But it's just one word." He stepped forward and made the most of it. "Behold!"

Annie was impressed. The kid would be heard in the back row.

"Then we all point to the Star of Wonder when Miss Opal gives us our cue."

"That's a very important part of the show."

"We only have one wooden sheep. She said there might be real sheep for the parade, though," another boy said.

"There's going to be a parade?"

He nodded eagerly. "The stores on Main Street sponsor it. They give out candy and stuff to all the kids and we get to ride on the floats."

"That's something new," Annie said. "When I was a kid it was just the pageant."

"Were you ever in it?" The seven boys looked at her with interest.

"Yes. I stood in the back. I didn't have any lines either."

"Why not?"

Annie ruffled the hair of the boy who'd asked the question. "Because I could never remember them. But I loved being on stage. Until I looked out and saw my parents and my brothers in the front row."

"Miss Opal told us not to stare at our folks."

"Good idea. When I saw my mom and dad, I froze. One of the shepherds used his crook to get me to move. Say, do you guys have crooks?"

"Yeah." The crew-cut boy scrambled to his feet. "I know where they are."

By the time he returned with the props, Annie had found the sheep, a plywood cutout with a plank in back to keep it standing up. The other six boys clustered around it, patting its soft side.

"We glued on the cotton puffs last week," the smallest boy told her proudly. "It looks pretty real."

"It looks great," she reassured him. "Okay, everything seems to be under control. You might as well take a short break."

"Can we run around again?" the oldest boy asked hopefully.

"Just don't bump into people. And keep the noise down. And tell me your names before you go—no, wait. I have a better idea. Let's see if we can find stick-on badges for all of you so I don't forget who's who."

Boys did better when they had something useful

to do. They scattered and came back with peel-and-stick labels.

"Good enough." Annie lined them up and badged them one by one. The task was completed in less than half an hour. "Don't leave the social hall," she told them.

"They won't. I'll make sure of it," said her crew-cut lieutenant.

She smiled at him. "Okay. Thanks."

Annie moved away, spotting Jenny and Zoe amid the town kids. They were heading for Cilla and Ed Rivers. By the time Annie reached them, all four were clustered around an open laptop.

"What's up?"

"Shh," Zoe whispered. "We're going to talk to Mommy."

As the older of the two, Jenny got to hold the laptop, gazing into the screen as her baby sister leaned against her.

Annie looked at the screen and caught a glimpse of a woman with dark curly hair tucked under a white cap that concealed most of it. She was doing her best to be heard over the racket of an industrial-style kitchen going full tilt behind her.

"It's so good to see you girls," their mother said brightly. "I can't chat too long tonight, though. I only have a fifteen-minute break. The swing shift is coming in."

The girls either knew what a swing shift was or they didn't care.

"Can you read us a story later?" Jenny begged.

"I sure wish I could. But I have to work late."

"I'll do it, Bree," Cilla quickly assured her.

Though she was young, the careworn expression on Bree's face was a poignant reminder of what some parents had to do to provide for their kids. Taking a temporary job far away was part of the deal for this young mom.

Jenny looked up at Annie as if seeing her for the first time. She rotated the laptop to introduce her. "Mommy, this is Annie. She took us to the movies."

"Right. The lollipop one. Hi, Annie. Thanks so much."

"My pleasure. Your girls are a delight."

"Good to know. I can't wait to take them to the movies myself." There wasn't anything competitive in the statement, just the resignation of a mother who had to be away from those she loved most. "I really do appreciate it. They seem very happy in Velde."

"Mommy, when are you coming to get us?" Zoe's plaintive question was from the heart.

"As soon as I can, baby."

The moment was too personal. Annie stepped back, well out of range of the camera lens in the laptop's frame.

She headed toward a new source of commotion: There was scenery being banged together in a roped-off section of the hall. Power tools were in use or waiting to be used.

Annie shooed away a few curious kids who got too close. "You can watch if you want," she told them. "But stay over here." She dragged over a few folding chairs to set a boundary. "And don't distract the carpenters."

The children seemed inclined to cooperate, but

she stayed with them just in case. A church aide came along and took over guard duty, freeing Annie to be with her seven shepherds, who came barreling toward her. The oldest held a tablet with the glowing graphics of a video game.

"I got to Level Nine," he boasted. "I slew a dragon and stuck a troll lord in the dungeon."

"Yeah, but I got to Level Ten," the youngest bragged. "It's way harder than Nine."

"You cheated."

"Stop it," Annie said, and laughed.

"It's only a game," another boy protested.

"I grew up with two older brothers," she informed him. "There was never any such thing as *only a game.*"

They handed her the tablet. "Okay. You play it."

"Some other time. Here comes Miss Opal."

The chorus director gave her a weary smile. "I still have to rehearse the leads. They disappeared on me."

Annie looked over her head and saw a sweet-faced young girl and an older boy who hadn't taken off their rustic costumes. They walked side by side with solemn expressions. "There they are."

"Oh, thank goodness. All right, children." Opal waved all the participants onto the stage. "Let's take it from the top."

There was a piano in the shadows beyond the stage. Annie just made out a white-haired old lady waiting for a signal from Opal. At the downward motion of the chorus director's hand, she began to play the opening bars of "Silent Night."

It was Mrs. Pearson. Annie realized that she must have found someone to stay with Jack.

She caught Annie's eye and gave her a nod and a tiny smile.

When the cast had rehearsed the song twice, Opal dismissed them all, telling them to wait where she could see them until their parents arrived. The kids were too tuckered out to run around the way they had when Annie entered. Most found their jackets and flopped on top of them in various places on the varnished floor. A few took out books and sat cross-legged to read.

The chorus director took the opportunity to check her list. "Oh. I almost forgot. Can you keep an eye on the herd for a second?"

"You bet."

The kids lolled around, looking at the ceiling or talking to each other, but they stayed where they were. Opal returned, holding a white-wire lawn reindeer, the kind that nodded, in her arms.

"Would you mind taking this thing back to Nell? I don't think we'll be able to use it for the pageant." She handed it over.

Annie took the reindeer from her a little awkwardly. "What should I tell her? Is it broken?"

"No. It nods just fine. But it gets me off the beat."

"Oh. I guess you have enough to worry about." Annie glanced sideways when her seven shepherds thundered by.

Opal clapped her hands. "Line up, please."

They slowed their pace, but ran into each other nonetheless, shrieking with laughter. The choir director put a finger to her lips and they miraculously fell silent.

"Be good now," Annie told them. "And, Opal, let me know if you need help with anything else."

"I most certainly will," Opal said fervently. "Thanks for stopping in."

"Bye, Annie." The crew-cut boy made a scout's salute, which she returned with a smile, doing her best to hang on to the reindeer.

"Bye, guys. Be good."

Chapter 12

Once inside the saloon, Annie set the reindeer down in a booth, propping its front legs on the table as if it were waiting to be served.

She moved to the boxes Nell had hauled out of the closet and looked into a few. There were still a lot of decorations left. Someone else had helped her hang most of the colored lights, somewhat haphazardly. But that was how Nell liked to do things.

Whatever. Annie wasn't going to volunteer to do it perfectly, not if it meant risking a fall off a stepladder. The doctor's advice had stuck with her.

The empty boxes were stacked in size order, the small box with the question mark on it on top again. Annie picked it up, about to open it, when Nell appeared.

"What's in this one?" Annie asked.

"Nothing."

"Then why are you keeping it?"

"Well, it used to have something in it; I forget what. But I can't throw it away. What if the something shows up? Then I wouldn't have anything to put it in."

Annie laughed. "I see."

"Do you think you could help me get these tinsel garlands around the jukebox?" Nell asked. "You wouldn't have to get up on a chair or anything."

"Believe me, I wasn't planning to."

Nell searched through a glittering heap of garlands piled onto a booth table. "I only need you to hold one end. If I can find it."

Annie came over. "There it is." She reached in and held up a red tab.

"Excellent. Hold on to that." Nell located the other end and began to walk away, pulling one of the garlands free of the others. On her way to the jukebox she grabbed a roll of duct tape and slid it over her wrist like a bracelet.

Annie followed slowly.

Nell draped her end of the garland around her neck while she stopped to rip off pieces of tape, positioning them around the back of the jukebox. It only took a few minutes for her to do the job once the tape was in place. Nell took the red tab from Annie and let it dangle, stepping back to admire the effect. "Let's make magic," she said thoughtfully. She slipped a metal disc into the slot and punched the big plastic keys.

The first notes of a country-style Christmas carol

triggered a display of light and color from the old-fashioned console that bounced off the tinsel and brightened the darkened saloon.

"Now isn't that pretty?" Nell sighed with happiness as she turned to Annie.

"It sure is. Good idea."

Nell removed the duct tape bracelet and went behind the bar. "So can I get you anything?"

"No. Thanks though."

"Why'd you come in, anyway?" Nell used a glass to scoop up ice cubes from the reservoir below the bar and pumped club soda into it from the bar nozzle. "Not that I mind seeing you."

"Opal asked me to return Rudolph." Annie pointed to the white-wire critter. "She said he nods the wrong way."

"Oh. Well, I don't suppose there were lawn reindeer in Bethlehem anyway. He looks right at home in that booth. Maybe I'll leave him there."

Annie shrugged. She went back to the other booth and untangled the rest of the tinsel garlands, looping them around her arm before she set them down in a loose circle.

"So how did you convince Mrs. Pearson to play piano for the Christmas pageant? I'm assuming that was your doing."

"Yes, it was. I tell you, she was glad to get out when I promised to stay with Jack. She's only been leaving him to run quick errands, and not often. It's not good for her to be in the house so much. Or to have sole responsibility for his care."

Annie gave her an inquiring look.

"I put in a call to social services about getting a home health-care aide for Jack. She was overwhelmed."

"Did she say anything about her financial problems?"

"No. And I didn't ask. One thing at a time. You can't rush very old people."

Annie understood what Nell was getting at, but Mrs. Pearson was still vulnerable. However, if the Pearsons had Nell in their lives again, they would probably be okay.

"What are you going to do with the rest of these garlands?" Annie asked.

Nell finished her club soda and motioned toward the old staircase at the back of the saloon. "I was thinking of winding them around the banister."

"But no one goes up there. Didn't you tell me those rooms had been closed up for years?"

"Not anymore." Nell gave her a twinkly look. "I was feeling enterprising, so I cleaned out the two in front. There was some great old Victorian furniture under all the junk."

"And?"

Nell wiped down the bar with a clean white cloth until the mahogany gleamed. "I was thinking of fixing up a couple of private suites."

"You mean to rent out? Like the cabin?"

"No, there weren't any beds. And I don't have a hotel license or plan to get one. I mean suites for poker games. Penny poker." Nell waved away Annie's surprised look. "I'm not talking about serious gambling or hard drinking. But I'd make a mint on the beer and snacks. Plus the wives and girlfriends would know where their men were."

"I see," Annie said dryly. She thought of someone immediately. It was easy to imagine Marshall Stone at a card game, winning every hand, his expression never changing.

Nell left it at that. She bustled over to the bulletin board, removing old notices and putting up new ones with pushpins.

"You going to the Snow Ball, Annie?"

"Maybe."

"How about *yes*? It's a great word. I love the sound of it."

Annie eyed the saloon keeper with friendly suspicion. "If you don't mind my saying so, what's in it for you if I do say yes?"

"I'm on the planning committee." Nell had pretty much filled the available space on the bulletin board when she walked away. "We need an emcee. I thought of you."

Annie neatened up the garlands, just for something to do. "Why?"

"I can't do it. My ankles have been killing me. You'd have to stand, you know."

"That's no big deal, but I've never done any emceeing."

Nell gave a careless wave of her manicured hand. "You're so full of personality and pep, it doesn't matter. A stunner like you will get everyone's attention immediately."

Right now, Annie wasn't feeling particularly

stunning. In fact, she had avoided looking at her reflection in the mirror behind the display of liquor when she'd entered the saloon.

"I have a white Stetson you could wear," Nell said casually. She looked at the bulletin board, not at Annie.

"The dance isn't outdoors."

"No, but in a hat like that people will see you."

"What if I don't want to be seen?"

Nell ignored the question, sauntering back to the bulletin board.

"And," she went on, "I have a vintage western shirt that you'd probably like. Gorgeous. Also white." The older woman hummed as she repositioned a flyer.

"Bring it on." Annie actually was curious. She loved vintage duds.

"Wait until you get a load of this little number." Nell turned to face her, smiling. "It's a classic cowgirl style. Fancy yoke with fringe, silver embroidery, and curved arrow pockets."

"Sounds great."

"Would you like to see it? I just happen to have it right here."

Annie suppressed a smile as she nodded. Nell was obviously scheming up a storm. The older woman went over to a steamer trunk at the bottom of the back staircase and withdrew the shirt with a flourish.

"Wow," Annie said. "It really is gorgeous." The lavish embroidery had been expertly done by hand.

Nell held it against her. "I'm betting it'll be a perfect fit. Try it on."

Annie didn't need to be talked into it. "I hope so."

She'd seen shirts like it in a museum exhibit celebrating the era of the singing cowboys on TV. Nowadays there were plenty of reproductions, but nowhere near as well made. This one sported the label of a famous western designer from the 1950s.

"It's made for a woman, but somewhere there's a matching one for a lucky man," Nell trilled. "The sweethearts of the rodeo used a needle and silk thread to rope their cowboys, you know."

Annie almost didn't want to encourage her. But there was no stopping Nell when she was on a roll.

"Of course, a fancy shirt like that was intended for the parade around the ring before the bucking began," the saloon keeper added.

Annie admired the stitching. "Where did you get this?"

"Didn't I ever tell you that my big sister was a rodeo rider?"

"No. Are you making that up?"

"Don't make me take out the photo albums," Nell threatened. "Yes, she really was. Retired now. Bought a ranch in Arizona with her fifth husband."

"Five?" Annie would get the whole story out of Nell some other time. "Good for her."

"Sometimes it takes a while to figure out what you want in life, dear. Anyway, this was her favorite shirt. It's in perfect condition."

Annie headed for the bathroom and whipped

off her sweater, taking her time to put on the classic shirt and snap up the pearly snaps. She shot the cuffs as she gave a final shrug of her shoulders.

The shirt had been designed to do things for a girl. It clung to her curves in all the right places, but still looked ladylike. She turned to the side, noting the flirtatious flip of the fringe.

Incredible. She would have to go to the dance. There was no place else she could wear this and she didn't think for one minute that Nell would ever give it away.

She strolled out to show Nell.

"It does fit! Wonderful. You can take it home with you. So will you emcee?"

"Count on me."

Nell gave her a hug.

"Easy," Annie said with a laugh. "Don't wrinkle this."

"Oh, goodness, it's not a museum piece. Before you go, though, if you could help me with just one more thing?"

"Of course. But I can't get dirty."

Nell picked up the remaining garlands and nodded toward the staircase. "You won't. I swept and vacuumed every inch of that staircase. Let's get these wound around the banister."

"Sure."

"You go first. I guess we should see how long they are."

Annie took the end that Nell handed her and went up the creaking stairs without doing any winding. "The garlands should be at least double the length of the banister, right? Maybe even triple."

On the floor below, Nell frowned. "We might be a bit short. Oh dear. Just attach that tab, would you? There's a hook up there."

Annie found it and hung the tab on it, turning to look at the garland that slithered down the stairs to Nell. "I think there's enough," she began, resting a hand on the banister.

It gave way with a crack. Nell screamed.

Annie swayed on the landing, pressing her back against the wall to keep from falling. She didn't fall, but the banister did, toppling to the floor and breaking into pieces. Some of the side spindles went down with it and some stayed in place, sticking out at odd angles.

Nell swore and dropped the garlands. "Stay there."

"Okay." Annie was feeling a little shaky, but she knew the feeling would pass. "But don't come up. There's no telling what might give way next."

"Can you get down?" Nell asked anxiously.

"Of course. Give me a sec. I want to be sure of my leg. I twisted it a little and these stairs are steep."

"I'm so sorry, Annie. And after I've been up and down those stairs so many times too," Nell fretted. "Want me to call someone?"

"No. I can always go down on my rear end, step by step. I used to do that when I was a kid. These jeans can take it."

The door to the saloon opened. Annie looked down at Marshall Stone. His dark eyes widened when he took in her predicament.

"Whoa," he said, his deep voice echoing in the sudden silence. Two or three long strides and he was standing directly beneath her. "What happened?"

"It's an old staircase. I guess it was an accident waiting to happen." Nell put a hand on his arm to restrain him. "Don't go up. I think she'd better come down. Then we can rope it off. It's my fault. I should have known. It was so creaky. Oh, goodness."

Marshall looked up at Annie. "What do you want to do?"

She really didn't have a choice. "I'll come down now." She did it the undignified way, on her rump. To his credit, he didn't crack a smile or tease her.

About halfway down, he reached out to take her hand and made sure she was safe. Near the bottom, she extended her legs and let him help her up.

She rose somewhat unsteadily. His strong hand clasped hers firmly as he led her to a table. "You okay?"

"Yes. For a black diamond staircase."

Annie felt heat tint her cheeks under Marshall's steady gaze. If he liked the way she looked in the fitted cowgirl shirt, he seemed to know it wasn't the moment for a gentlemanly compliment. But she'd seen that smoldering look in his eyes before.

She just hadn't needed rescuing then.

"Nell, how about a cup of coffee?" Stone asked. "Make that two."

"Coming up." Nell fretted some more as she dashed about, clinking cups and saucers on a tray.

Annie thanked her when she came over to the table.

"Least I can do. Those oatmeal raisin cookies are from Jelly Jam. Sure cure for everything. Now how's that leg doing, young lady?"

"I think it's going to be fine." It ached. That was about all.

"Shouldn't you have the doc take a look at it?"

Annie groaned. "I just went in. He'll give me a lecture. If I stay off it for a day or so, that oughta be enough."

Nell seemed about to insist, but something made her stop. "Well, you two can discuss it. I'm going down to the cellar to get some rope and cordon off the area."

Marshall nodded as he picked up his coffee cup. "There's no harm done and nothing much left to fall down."

"Let's hope so," Nell said dramatically.

"It'll give the customers something to talk about."

She gave him a mock glare. "A collapsing staircase is the last thing you want people talking about. I wish I could shove the jukebox in front and cover up the sight. Want to be my hero and move it?"

Stone eyed the jukebox and shook his head. "Nope. I have to save my strength for the dance."

"Oh, are you going to the Snow Ball?" Nell crowed. "I'm so glad. I'm on the planning committee, you know. And Annie just volunteered to be our emcee."

Sort of, Annie thought. The bribe had worked.

"I loaned her that rodeo shirt just for the occasion. Doesn't she look pretty in it?"

Annie winced. Nell's compliment didn't need to be confirmed by Stone, who apparently could attract all the feminine company any man might want at any time.

"She sure does," he said calmly.

He probably thought the fancy shirt was a little silly. And since he hadn't made the original compliment, Annie didn't see a compelling need to thank him.

"Which reminds me. I forgot to give you the Stetson, Annie. Be right back."

Annie ripped open three packets of sugar and dumped them into her coffee, adding a healthy dose of cream. More than her usual, much more, because she still felt shaky, but for a different reason. Sitting up straight with her knees only inches away from Marshall Stone's made her nervous. She eased her chair back and crossed her legs at the ankles.

"Haven't seen you around for a while," he said. Like most of his conversation, it wasn't about him.

"Um, no. We've been busy at the ranch. Christmas plans, getting ready, that kind of thing."

"I see." He kept on his jacket but took off his

ball cap. The same one he'd been wearing the first time she'd seen him, Annie noticed.

They didn't say much else until Nell came back, holding a brand-new Stetson with a silver band. She showed it off with a flourish before she placed it on Annie's head, tipping the brim back slightly with one finger and fussing with Annie's hair.

"However do you get your hair so shiny?" Nell asked. "There. Oh my. You could be a model. I think I have a hand mirror somewhere around here if you'd like to look at yourself."

Annie blushed. She felt like a doll being dressed, although Stone's face barely changed expression as he watched.

"Don't bother, Nell," Annie said politely. "I have a Stetson like this, but not white."

"How's the fit?"

"Feels just right. Thanks, Nell."

Nell headed for the cellar. "Okay. You two are all set. I'll leave you alone. Now for that rope. And I should start making a list for the insurance claim. And . . ." Her voice trailed off as she reached the bottom of the stairs and moved away into the part of the cellar that wasn't underneath them.

Annie took off the hat and set it on the table next to theirs.

"It does look good on you." For a man as close-mouthed as Stone, that counted as a rave review.

"Thanks."

A short silence fell. "I'd be happy to take you to

the dance if you think you'll be up to it by then," he said softly.

Annie hadn't expected that. She uncrossed her legs, feeling a twinge in the healing one. She had an excuse.

"I don't know if I'd be doing any dancing. Maybe I should have Dr. Lyon look at my leg again. It's hard to tell right now if I really did twist it. I could be fine by tomorrow or I might need to wear a brace for a while. Besides, I have to be up on stage to introduce the bands and do whatever else Nell needs me to do."

"What about what you want to do?" The question was even softer than his invitation to attend the dance with him.

Annie had no idea how to answer it. "You should take someone else," she said finally, keeping her tone brisk.

"I don't have anyone else I want to go with."

"I'm sure you can find someone." She wasn't about to name any names. Like brunette Jill. Or redheaded Bunny.

Nell made more noise than necessary as she returned to the bottom of the cellar stairs and began to climb them. "Found the rope," she called. "And a KEEP OUT sign and a WET PAINT sign too. Neither one exactly applies, but they should do the trick."

She set the items down as she came closer.

"Marshall, I never did ask why you came in. Is everything okay up at the cabin?" Nell winked at Annie. "My paying guest."

"Everything's fine. A knob fell off one of the doors, but I fixed it."

"I wish every renter was like you," the older woman sighed. "I don't know what I'll do when you're gone."

"Winter break just started, Nell," Annie informed her. "You should do all right when the snow hits. I've seen some new faces around. You know, college girls."

Stone didn't even blink.

Stone took Rowdy out as soon as he got back to the cabin, craving fresh air even though the temperature had dropped at least ten degrees by nightfall.

The dog had tree trunks to sniff and snow hills to plunge into. Stone didn't pay much attention to the tugs on the leash as Rowdy investigated this and that fascinating thing.

Stone was thinking.

About Annie Bennett, of course. At the saloon, his heart had just about stopped when he'd thought she was about to fall from on high. Seeing her teetering on the edge made him feel sick inside. He'd gone straight to her, so fast he didn't remember doing it, and he would've caught her with ease.

But she hadn't needed a hero. Well, hell. It'd be nice if he ever got the chance, but she was as self-reliant and smart as a woman could be.

And so damn beautiful it was making him crazy.

That embroidered white shirt had fit her as closely as he wanted to hold her himself. She didn't seem to have noticed that a couple of pearl snaps had come open after the mishap. He had, for a fraction of a second—and then kept his gaze firmly on hers for the entire rest of the time they'd spent together. With the brim of the fine new Stetson framing her beautiful face, her shining dark hair spilling over her shoulders, and that high color in her cheeks, Annie had looked like a cowgirl angel with a white halo.

If only Nell hadn't been there. But Stone supposed that the older woman's well-meaning chatter might have made Annie feel a little safer around him. It wasn't just her near fall that had made her so nervous.

He knew Annie Bennett didn't think too highly of him. He still couldn't tell her exactly what it was he was doing in Velde, although his side of the investigation was progressing reasonably well.

But the interminable wait for Shep Connally to zero in on a mark was getting to him. And Stone had almost blown the new agent's cover by giving her a stupid fake name. Kerry Cox was going to give him serious hell when she found out he'd referred to her as Bunny. *If* she found out, he corrected himself. She was supposed to hang out with other girls, pretend to be passing through just like them and blend in, until the right moment. Shep Connally was a boozer and boaster. A pretty young thing on a bar stool next to him was likely to hear more than any male agent.

Marshall knew he would have to bide his time to catch the con man and anyone else in Velde who might be in on his schemes. But that was the least of his problems. He couldn't rest tonight for a whole other reason. Annie Bennett troubled his sleep. His wildest and sweetest dreams were all about her—and they never lasted long enough.

Chapter 13

The night of the dance came soon enough. Annie got dressed up in the white shirt and her best jeans. A lot of people were looking forward to the occasion and she owed it to them to help out with the show, whether or not she was raring to go.

Her parents had decided to stay in and watch their favorite TV programs. She half wondered if they were thinking she wouldn't have quite so good a time if her mom and dad were there. But Lou and Tyrell were mum on that subject.

If they only knew, she thought, sliding her hands over the steering wheel as she turned her red truck away from the ranch and onto the county road.

The white Stetson was beside her on the seat in an improvised hatbox. She would return it to Nell tonight. The drive to town didn't take long. She tried her best not to think about Stone or what girl he might bring to the dance.

She parked in the lot of a restaurant with an at-

tached dance hall that had once been a barn.
There weren't many spaces left. Couples of all ages
and families were streaming toward the entrance.
Annie peered through the windshield as she turned
off the ignition. She didn't see Stone. With a crowd
like this, she might not even have to speak with
him.

Annie decided to hold the Stetson in her hand
so as not to be too conspicuous, and zipped up her
jacket over the fancy shirt for the same reason. She
intended to disappear behind the curtain of the
low stage to one side of the hall and not talk to
anyone but Nell and the musicians until the moment she stepped out and took the mike to emcee.

She moved quickly through the crowd in the
front area that was serving as a lobby of sorts
tonight, nodding to the folks she knew and waving
to Darla without stopping to talk to her. People
were clustered around a glass cabinet set up on a
cloth-draped table that displayed a belt and a
handbag and a placard bearing the familiar logo
of Velde's saddlery shop.

"I'm buying five tickets," a man said. "It's for a
good cause."

Annie paused just long enough to read the sign.
The items would be raffled off to benefit the youth
group. Several teenagers were selling tickets from
a large roll and writing down each buyer's name
on every one.

She passed by, moving through the restaurant,
which had been converted to an informal buffet
serving simple food. Long tables held pots of chili

and pans of cornbread. Soft drinks and beer were nestled in tubs of ice.

Annie inhaled appreciatively. There was just about nothing sweeter than the aroma of freshly baked cornbread, and the spicy chili added a hearty note. Unfortunately, a whiff was all she could have. Most likely she wouldn't have time to eat and she had to keep the white shirt in pristine condition.

She looked ahead, not wanting to be tempted, and walked faster. Some of the musicians—not local bands; she didn't recognize any of them— were already setting up on the low stage and the curtain had been drawn back.

So much for hiding. But the crowd of people hadn't gotten this far yet and someone had set up a rope decorated with bandannas as a visual barrier that would stand until the dance began.

The rest of the decorations were, predictably, white. Foam snowballs had been glue-tacked to the walls and cardboard snowmen smiled in every corner. She spotted the white-wire reindeer in a corner, nodding away.

Annie set down the Stetson and slipped off her jacket, looking around for Nell. She was distracted by a low, appreciative whistle from a lanky, good-looking musician.

"Hey, beautiful," he said. He lifted his fiddle to his shoulder and played several bars of a reel, his eyes dancing with admiration.

Annie smiled at him. It was nice to be noticed, just so long as Marshall Stone wasn't doing the noticing.

"There you are, Annie." Nell bustled over. "Bret, this is our emcee," she said to the fiddler, who stopped playing, holding his instrument and bow upright in one hand.

"Nice to meet you." The lanky musician extended the other hand to shake hers. The other members of his band clambered onto the stage, including a female singer in a ruffled dress who eyed Annie with annoyance, as if she hadn't expected anyone to steal her thunder.

Annie turned to Nell. "Whose idea was the raffle?"

"Mine," Nell said proudly. "The churchwomen sponsored the buffet and did the cooking. That should bring in plenty of money too. Did you see the display? I wangled a couple of fabulous prizes."

"I saw the glass case. But I didn't get a chance to take a close look at what was inside."

"There's a custom-made belt with an inlaid buckle for the gents and a hand-tooled pocketbook in Spanish leather for the ladies. I just heard that we sold hundreds of tickets. Lots of folks are buying five or ten at a clip."

"That's great. So when are we drawing for the winners?"

"We could do the raffle after the opening dances, right about when the musicians take their first break. Is that okay with you, Bret?"

The musician nodded, preoccupied with tuning his fiddle.

"There's a lot of families," Nell continued. "You know how it is—some might have to leave early if kids get cranky. Anyway, here come the tickets now."

A teenage girl in a bright blue sweater went under the rope with the ticket box. She came up to the stage. "Here you go, Mrs. Dighton."

"Thanks, honey. How's the crowd?"

"Getting bigger. Kinda restless."

Nell nodded. "I think it's time to start letting people in. Could you tell the front door crew to see to that?"

"Sure." The girl in the blue sweater walked off, ducking under the rope again.

Nell shifted the box she held. "Hope they separated these into gents and ladies." She peered inside. "Yes, they did. Two bags, marked. Good." She set the box on a nearby chair.

In minutes, the dance hall was filled with what seemed to be everyone in Velde and the surrounding towns. Annie felt relieved not to spot Marshall in the crowd. Only a few of the men matched him for height and he was nowhere to be seen.

"Aren't you going to wear the Stetson?" Nell asked as an audio tech tested the mike clipped to a stand positioned to the right of the stage.

"Yes, of course. I forgot." Annie realized that she'd forgotten hairpins. She'd make do. She coiled her hair around one hand and held it on top of her head, swiftly clapping the white hat over it.

"I can't believe you're going to cover up all that glorious shiny hair," Nell said indignantly.

"It's already warm in here," Annie replied. "When everyone's in and the dancing starts, I'm going to be roasting. Especially with that—ouch—spotlight on me."

A blinding white light from overhead caught her. Annie had to close her eyes for a second before she could walk out of it.

"I suppose you're right," Nell said. She waved to the mingling crowd and got a few friendly hollers in return. "Let's go over the lineup. I made you a cheat sheet." She pulled out a long piece of paper and walked into the wings with Annie.

Nell held up the sheet in front of her. There were thumbnail-size pictures of each musician in every band next to their names. "Photos. Thanks." Annie scanned the rest curiously, which was mostly text.

"You don't have to say any of that," Nell reassured her. "I just threw in a few cute jokes in case you got stage fright."

"I don't think I will. I won't be able to see anybody when that spotlight's on."

"It is bright," Nell said. "Okay. I'm glad you're not nervous. It'll be just you and whatever band is playing during each set, and they'll have your back. If your mind goes blank, they'll start up a riff or tell a little story. I'll come on for the raffle, of course. You ready?"

"Ready as I'll ever be."

The glowing white light made a circle around the stand and the folds of the curtain behind it.

Nell handed over the cheat sheet. "Here you go. I'll introduce you."

Annie hesitated.

"Best foot forward," Nell encouraged her. "You

never know. This could be the start of a new career for you."

"I don't think so." She laughed, though. "Come on. Let's get it over with."

Nell did the honors to wild applause and Annie got the hang of emceeing very fast. She really couldn't see anyone beyond the very front of the stage. And the first band, a skilled bluegrass group, got just about everyone dancing to a lively jig, from the littlest kids to the seniors.

Annie relaxed, keeping time with her cowboy boots to the infectious rhythm. She saw Darla whirl near the stage and away again with her date, having a grand old time. The tiny flash of envy Annie felt didn't last longer than it took for Bret to wrap it up and launch into the next tune.

On it went. The band finally signaled her for a break and Annie announced it. She saw Nell out of the corner of her eye approaching her with the two bags of tickets.

Annie tipped the mike toward Nell as she reached the stand and set the bags on the flat top.

"Hello and welcome to the Snow Ball! Is everyone having a good time?"

The question almost didn't need to be asked. They certainly were.

Nell held up the bags. "We sold every one of the raffle tickets and I want to thank you all for your generosity!"

Cheers. Clapping.

"Each ticket has a name; our volunteers made sure of that. There will be two winners. Two."

The crowd echoed the word.

Nell held up the paper bags and shook them. "Ready for a raffle?"

Shouted yeses.

"Then here we go. Miss Annie, if you would please hand me your hat. . . ."

"What?"

Annie realized her startled response had been picked up by the mike when the crowd laughed. They seemed to think the two women were having fun, drawing out the suspense. It wasn't scripted on the cheat sheet, but Annie had to play along.

With a mischievous grin, Nell plucked the Stetson from Annie's head. Her long hair came down in shining waves, tumbling over her shoulders.

There were whoops of appreciation from the men. "Now calm down, cowboys!" Nell's ladylike taps on the mike got amped up to deafening thuds. "Attention, please!"

The older woman set one paper bag inside the hat and held it high.

All eyes were on her. And Annie, who knew she was blushing.

"There will be a bonus drawing," Nell announced in a low, breathy voice. That hadn't been on the cheat sheet either, Annie thought nervously. The crowd got quieter.

"Our lovely emcee has agreed to dance with the first gentleman whose ticket comes up!"

"No, I didn't." Annie managed to say the words out of the corner of her smiling mouth.

A few guys heard her and hooted. Everyone still thought they were kidding around, keeping the moment going.

"Oh yes, you did, Annie Bennett. In fact, I believe it was your idea. You're just bashful."

Annie's eyes widened. "Nell!"

"What?" Nell beamed at the crowd without turning to look at Annie.

Just in time, Annie remembered to shut off the microphone before she replied in a furious whisper. "I didn't agree to get raffled off. What were you thinking?"

"That it would be fun."

"You should have asked me."

"Oh, don't get your britches in a twist."

Annie was truly steamed. "I'm going to kill you. I really am."

Nell waved away the comment with maddening cheerfulness. "Don't. I'm leaving you the saloon in my will. It'd look bad if you did me in."

"Huh? Have you lost your mind? What has your will got to do with—"

"Yes!" Nell hollered, switching on the mike again. "Annie changed her mind! She says she will!"

Hoorays. Annie smiled weakly at the people out front.

Then Nell put a hand to her cheek as if she were thinking it over. But somehow Annie knew she wasn't off the hook.

"I'm forgetting my manners. Ladies first," Nell said decisively. "Let's draw for that Spanish leather pocketbook!"

She set aside the white Stetson and picked up the bag of women's tickets, reaching inside to stir them up vigorously.

With a final flourish, Nell pulled out a ticket

and read the name of the winner. A young woman made her way to the stage to claim a certificate for her prize, which she held up triumphantly before jumping down and disappearing into the crowd again.

"And now . . ." Nell plunked the white Stetson down in front of the mike.

There was no chance of pulling it away from her. God only knew if the saloon keeper had any other surprises planned.

Nell stuck a hand into the bag and stirred the tickets. She made a big show of looking into the bag. The crowd booed, going along with the joke.

"Oh, I know I'm not supposed to do that. All right. I'll behave myself. If you insist."

She signaled the band to play a few bars as she switched off the mike and cast a worried look at Annie.

"Looks like Marshall Stone bought an awful lot of the tickets," Nell murmured.

"He isn't even here."

"Yes, he is. I saw him in the back."

"While I was blinded by the light. You set me up."

"I did not." Nell made a motion to quiet the band and switched the mike back on. Ostentatiously, she closed her eyes. "Here we go."

Annie sent up a prayer. With any luck, the winner of the dance would be eight years old. She wouldn't mind getting her feet stepped on by a half-pint cowboy.

"And the winner is . . . the winner is . . . Jim Nickels! You out there, Jim?" Nell shielded her eyes from the spotlight and peered around.

There was a commotion over at the side of the dance hall as Jim got up.

Annie breathed a sigh of relief. Jim was someone she'd known in high school. He rose with the aid of his wife. He was on crutches, his lower leg encased in the kind of brace used for a badly sprained ankle.

"Can't dance worth a damn right now, Nell, but I'll take that belt!" he called.

"Sounds fair to me. Everyone okay with that?"

Seemed so.

"You stay right there, Jim," Nell instructed him. "Annie will bring you the certificate."

Jim held up his winning ticket. "So which one of you buckaroos would like to dance with Annie?"

The chorus of loud masculine yeses got a reluctant smile from Annie as she made her way to the man on crutches. She still didn't see Marshall anywhere, no matter what Nell said.

"You gotta be smooth," Jim added. "No stepping on her feet or hugging her too hard."

"That's right." Annie laughed, trying to get into the spirit of things.

She'd almost reached the man and his wife when a tall figure took the raffle ticket from Jim's hand. He replaced it with a hundred-dollar bill, first making sure that the crowd saw the bill as he held it up high.

"That's an additional donation," Marshall Stone called to Nell.

"Mercy me! And after you bought so many tickets too," Nell exclaimed. "Thank you, Mr. Stone!"

Annie fumed.

Stone grinned at her. He seemed awfully pleased with himself. She couldn't very well say no and reject a cash donation of that size.

Jim took the certificate from her. For a few seconds, she'd forgotten about it.

Then Jim tucked the hundred-dollar bill into her hand. "Looks like you got yourself a partner, Annie." He eased back down into his seat, being congratulated by his wife.

Everyone seemed to think it was hilarious. She didn't.

For the people in attendance, it was only a passing moment. But Annie couldn't help feeling like she'd just been bought and paid for in front of the entire town.

Marshall Stone extended a hand. "Miss Bennett. May I have this dance?"

"Guess so," she gritted out.

The music had begun again, a much slower number meant for couples to sway together, barely moving. Annie thought bitterly that Nell had to have planned that part.

So she had ended up with Stone. Annie would just have to make the best of it. At least now that she was off the stage, she could see.

He was wearing what appeared to be his Saturday-night best, dark new jeans and a crisp western-cut shirt. His hair was freshly cut and his smile conveyed pride at his recent ploy to get her to dance.

Pride and something else. Possessiveness.

Stone moved toward her and Annie almost stepped back. Then she remembered she had to be a good sport. She went to him with her arms slightly lifted, accepting him as her partner as the onlookers in their immediate vicinity applauded.

His strong hand slid around her waist and rested on the small of her back. With a jolt, she remembered where his hands had been before, when they'd kissed in the doorway.

He pulled her discreetly closer. There were a few inches of distance between them, but the tips of her breasts just barely touched his muscular chest for a second. Maybe it was two seconds. The sensation was extraordinary, all the more so because she couldn't pull away or make a fuss. And he hadn't done anything that was remotely wrong.

Smooth just so happened to be the right word to describe him.

Their first few steps together told Annie that he was just as skilled at dancing as he was at kissing. With sensual ease, he guided her to the dance floor. She was aware of the other couples around them, but not for long.

In Stone's embrace, the rest of the world faded away. There was only him. The warmth of the powerful arms that held her so lightly made her want to rest her cheek against his chest, just as if they were lovers.

She looked up unwillingly. Dark eyes gazed into hers. The fire in their depths was unmistakable. Annie couldn't break away.

Chapter 14

Stone danced with her as if they'd been dancing together forever. He didn't talk and neither did she. His body language said what he didn't, conveying his ardent desire for her with the gentle pressure of his body. His long legs moved against and sometimes between her own, making her want to just climb up him and claim another kiss, if they were only someplace where no one was watching.

The constantly shifting crowd kept them hemmed in and close together. The other couples were just as lost in the sensual slowness of the melody. But no other woman had the privilege of a first dance with Marshall. He was exclusively hers. Every move he made underscored that inescapable fact—and brought back the memory of that incendiary first kiss. And the second and third.

It would take all her self-control not to go for a fourth. She knew in her soul that his possessive closeness was partly to get back at her for refusing his invitation at Nell's saloon and partly for show.

Not all of the men were as friendly to him as Jim, and several had cast envious looks their way.

He didn't seem to notice them at all. The possibility that he might actually not be showing off crept into her mind. Tired of trying to figure it out, Annie rested her cheek just below his shoulder for an unthinking moment.

She drew in a breath when Stone caressed her hair, cupping her head for a few seconds, then letting his hand drift down to her upper back.

Instinctively, she leaned away, and her lower body arched against his. Oh my. He was all man and then some.

Even with her mixed feelings about him, she didn't see any reason not to enjoy the purely physical contact. He seemed to be of the same mind.

And then the tune changed.

Some requested a popular country song and the boot-scootin' got started. So much for the magic, although the livelier dancing was fun. And exhilarating.

Stone knew how to dance fast too. His steps anticipated hers. His hold was close but never confining. He led assertively without making her feel rushed.

Her heart was racing as they moved in tandem, barely aware of the other dancers spinning around the polished floor.

It just felt so damn good to be with him. Was she fooling herself?

Annie didn't have time to think about it before a young ranch hand cut in. He had a raw look to him, with shave-scraped cheeks and an overbite.

"She's all yours," Stone said with a smile and a wink at Annie. He whispered in her ear just before he handed her over to the competition, "Save the last dance for me, girl."

Had he really said that? Her new partner grabbed her hand, swung her out and brought her back before she could think.

"Hey there. My name's Eddy."

He was athletic and a little rough in contrast to Stone's smooth strength, rushed and careless where Stone had taken his time.

Hell. Annie kept up. She couldn't dance with the same man all night. And eventually she had to get back up on stage and give Nell a break. She was going through the motions with Eddy and both of them were sweating.

Gasping for air as the song concluded, she quickly thanked him and made her escape.

Annie clambered back up on stage, not missing Nell's wary look or the manicured hand on the mike switch.

Click. It was off.

"Are you still mad at me?" Nell inquired. "I really didn't plan for Stone to show off like that."

"No, I'm not mad. Just interested to know why you think he was showing off."

"Um. Well, maybe that was an unkind thing to say, under the circumstances. And the hundred dollars was a nice gesture, don't you think?"

"Yes. Here it is. I almost forgot about it." Annie took it out of the arrowed pocket of the cowgirl shirt. She'd hoped for a more enlightening answer. But it wasn't the time or place for a heart-to-heart talk with Nell or anyone else. She checked the cheat sheet. "Who's on next?"

Nell pointed to the band. "The Banjo Brothers. You will not believe how well they play. Then there's an intermission. Then we start up again with the Cowcatchers. They're a novelty band and they're pretty funny. You all set?"

"Yes. Thanks for covering for me. Hey, do you think you could ask someone on the crew to ease up on the spotlight?"

"I sure will."

Annie stood at the stand, watching Nell wend her way to the man at the light board. She breathed with relief when the spot on her dimmed down. She could see the dancers now.

There was Marshall, with a new partner, a petite girl in a crop top who had trouble keeping in step with him, though he was doing his best. She stopped and started up again several times.

Just watching him be so nice to someone else was even more frustrating. From every angle, he moved like the real deal. Annie would have loved to take the girl's place. But she had to stay where she was. Another, bolder woman elbowed his partner aside and got her claws into Marshall, tossing her hair around and smiling extravagantly.

The shameless hussies were out in force tonight. Annie thought ruefully that she had definitely qualified as one herself. It bothered her a little to watch, but she couldn't take her eyes off him.

No matter who Stone was partnering, he danced like a dream.

There was something unique about the way he

held a woman. As if he had her safe and could get her all excited at the same damn time. The one he was with now was flushed and laughing.

He was so close to her and yet his expression seemed far away, watchful and remote. He guided his partner into a turn and looked over her head, straight at Annie.

Even at this distance, his gaze burned into hers. Annie was transfixed. The drummer ended the song with a crash of cymbals and she jumped a little. As the band left the stage and the Banjo Brothers came on, she studied the cheat sheet. When she looked up, Marshall had left the dance floor. She spotted his flirty partner with someone else. Easy come, easy go.

Annie cleared her throat and switched the mike back on. "And now . . ."

She got through the introductions without a hitch, even as her gaze swept the hall for some sign of Marshall. Not there. Maybe he'd left. At least he hadn't left with Miss Teeth & Claws.

The Banjo Brothers began a dazzling set, building up melodies and breaking them down again with not one wrong note. The music was almost too complicated to dance to and a lot of people seemed happy to take a break and listen intently.

Annie did the same, carrying out a high stool from the wings so she could man her post and still watch the band on stage. The banjo players slowed it down and played tunes from mountains far away, softer songs that sounded lonely.

She felt a hand on her shoulder and looked up. Marshall Stone had gotten onto the stage without her being aware. He could move with the stealth of a cat when he wanted to. A very big cat.

Annie shrugged off his hand. He made no comment on her response. "Hey," he whispered. "I was wondering if you wanted to get together after this wraps up."

"Um—I don't know," she whispered back. "I probably should stay late and help Nell."

"Is that something you have to do or are you just avoiding me?"

"Why would I avoid you?" she asked innocently.

"I wish I knew." The deep grooves around his mouth tightened.

She relented when she saw that. "Check with me later, okay? I really do have to stay here. There's an intermission after these guys. Maybe Nell can take over after that."

The band played even more softly and he made no response beyond a nod. Stone left the stage with a silent jump down to the dance floor.

The leader of the banjo band nodded to one of his brothers and they picked up the pace with an upbeat tune for four. Annie cheered up some and hummed along as the men sang in close harmony. She turned around on the stool to make sure everything on the dance floor was as it should be and realized that she had another visitor.

The redhead in the pink sweater was in front of the stand. Only tonight she was wearing an interesting shade of green that brought out the color of her eyes. Annie didn't know what to say. The redhead took the initiative.

"Hi. We met the other day when you were with Marshall. You're Annie, right?"

She must have arrived too late to hear Nell's introduction.

"Yes, I am."

Annie really didn't want to ask if she was Bunny. But she didn't have to.

The redhead volunteered her name. "I'm Kerry."

Annie swallowed hard. "Hi."

"How's Rowdy?"

Save me, someone. Annie looked around. No one else was near the stage. She would have to be nice and not say anything sarcastic. "Fine, I guess. He's not my dog."

"Oh. Just asking."

Maybe, Annie thought, *Kerry doesn't know Marshall Stone much better than I do.*

"Well, nice to see you again. Just thought I'd say hi. Great dance."

"I'm glad you're having a good time." That line barely got out of her mouth. But in more ways than one, Annie Bennett was a co-hostess of the dance. There were no scheduled catfights and she wasn't going to start one.

"One more thing. Have you seen Marshall?" The redhead's green eyes sparkled.

Annie shrugged. "He came up and said hi too. That was about five minutes ago. I don't know where he is now."

Something in her tone served as a warning to the other girl, who actually backed away, giving a tentative wave. "Thanks. I'll look for him."

Annie waved back. "You do that."

She pleaded a headache to Nell during intermission.

"Oh dear. I'm so sorry. It is awfully loud up here."

Annie nodded. She hadn't thought of that as an excuse, but it would do.

She handed back the hat before she went to find her jacket. "I'll bring the shirt back tomorrow, if that's okay."

"That'll be fine," Nell said. "And you can hang on to the hat for now. Are you sure you're okay to drive home?"

"It's only a headache. Don't worry."

Annie zipped up her jacket and put the Stetson on her head again.

"You look darling," Nell said. One of the musicians called to her and she said a hasty good-bye to Annie, bustling past the drum set and knocking over the hi-hat, which clanged as it hit the floor.

Annie grinned, then remembered her alibi and kept a straight face. She headed directly for a side exit to avoid the people milling around in the front area. The heavy door was unlocked per fire regulations as she'd known it would be. She stepped outside into bracingly cold air and breathed in gratefully. The sky overhead was crowded with thousands of stars that sparkled in the frigid air.

She'd be fine once she got back to the ranch.

Annie looked for her truck, not seeing it at first. But then she'd come in through the front, not the side. She spotted it and walked that way. A deep voice stopped her.

"Going somewhere?"

Marshall. She turned around. Alone. Thank goodness for that. Clearly, Bunny didn't hop fast enough.

"Yes. Home."

"I thought you wanted me to check back with you."

It was no use wasting a sweet-as-pie smile on him when he couldn't see it. A plain reply would do. "I changed my mind."

"Thanks for letting me know."

Annie flipped up the collar of her jacket and turned to walk away. She could hear his footsteps crunching in the light snow as he followed behind her.

"You're welcome."

Stone caught up to her. "Can I ask what's on your mind?"

"Sure. Nothing."

"You got pretty close on the dance floor. Why so distant now?"

"I don't feel well."

He fell silent. But he stayed with her. "I'm a big girl," she said. "I don't need to be walked to my truck. Besides, we're here. This is it."

"No, it isn't. Red, yes. Yours, no."

Annie swore under her breath. He was right.

"I'll help you find it. Did you park to the east or west of the entrance?"

"I don't know," she mumbled ungratefully, walking on. "Did you bring your surveying equipment? We could use the telescope thing."

"I don't need it. I happen to know exactly where your truck is because I took the space right by it."

"Why didn't you say that in the first place?"

He stopped her with a firm hold on her arm. "Look, Annie, I don't want to argue with you. I just want to get you safely to your vehicle, if you're heading home. Can we agree on that much?"

She heard a clear feminine voice calling his name. Stone's expression didn't change and he didn't answer. She spotted her truck at last, looking small next to his big black shiny monster.

The voice rang out again. "Marshall? You in the parking lot?"

He didn't answer.

"Friend of yours?" she asked icily.

"I don't know the voice. I danced with a lot of women." He didn't budge.

"Tell me about it. See you around." She pulled away from him and opened the cab door with the remote on her key ring, zooming off as soon as the engine roared to life.

Annie made a stop at a convenience store just outside town, needing to calm down before she hit the road. She could leaf through a couple of magazines, pretend to read for a half hour. Annie hated to admit to being upset. She wanted to walk in through the ranch house door with a smile on her face and not deal with curious looks or tactful questions from her parents.

The selection of reading material on the rack was a little limited, but Annie made do with *New*

Potluck Suppers and even peeked into *Auto Repair Monthly* before she picked up a quart of milk and some off-brand cookies that were probably stale. She tossed a packet of beef jerky onto the counter for her dad and bought the potluck magazine for her mother, paid for all of it with a twenty, then walked back to her truck.

She clicked open the door and put the bagged items on the seat before she got in, turning at the sound of an engine humming by. A new, high-powered engine that belonged to a big shiny black truck.

Annie just glimpsed Marshall's rugged profile. He didn't look to the side and didn't see her. A semi came over the rise in the road and bore down on his truck, going well over the speed limit, honking its horn. The driver swerved dangerously to pass him. Annie realized she'd been holding her breath when she saw his taillights continuing on not too far down the road. She guessed he was okay.

And not only him.

He wasn't alone in the cab. There were two heads silhouetted in the glare from the headlights of a smaller, oncoming truck. He drove away too fast for her to tell whether his passenger was male or female.

Annie told herself that she didn't care.

Chapter 15

"That was close." Kerry leaned forward to try and see the semi around the next bend. "You don't think he was following us, do you?"

Stone shot her a disbelieving look. "He just passed us. Try a little deductive reasoning. He's probably trying to make it over the mountain before a storm hits. Happens all the time at higher elevations."

"Yeah. I knew that."

"So what the hell happened to your phone? I've been trying to reach you."

"Stolen."

Stone glanced over at his colleague. "Anything sensitive on it?"

"No. I upload my notes into the agency cloud and clear the memory every day."

"Where was it when they took it?"

"In my car," the redhead answered. "That's the last place I had it. My best guess is that it slipped out of my pocket and fell under the seat before I knew it was gone. Please don't give me a lecture."

"I wasn't going to." He kept his hands on the wheel as the grade got steeper, listening absently as the engine kicked up a notch to handle it. "Someone was prowling around my truck the other day."

"Did you catch him? Or should I assume it was a bad guy?" she asked dryly. "Could have been one of your many female fans."

"Give me a break. I can't help it if the ladies love me. And no. Nothing was taken. I didn't really see the person."

"Rowdy didn't bark?"

"He sniffed the door latch, so I guessed someone tried it to see if I'd left it unlocked and ran when I showed up with Annie."

"Ah," the redhead said. "Your new girlfriend. Is she staying in that cute little cabin you rented?"

"No. And she's not my girlfriend."

"You danced with her like she was," Kerry teased.

His jaw set in a stern line as he managed not to react. "So what?" Stone said finally. "I like dancing."

"Don't we all." Kerry snapped on the radio and hummed along with a forgettable song. "Looked to me as if you really liked *her*. But maybe *like* is not the operative word."

"What are you getting at?"

Kerry leaned her head back. "Mind if I play life coach?"

"Yes. You're a junior agent and I outrank you.

Also, and don't take this too personally, you're a kid. I don't need advice from someone who graduated from college a year ago."

Kerry seemed unruffled by his sharp retort. "Don't you ever get tired of ricocheting from state to state on all these boring assignments? Real estate fraud isn't exactly thrilling."

"It could get rough. This is a multistate investigation and the racket is making millions. You think these guys are going to be writing us thank-you notes after we slap cuffs on them?"

Kerry hummed some more. "Nope. I'm just trying to point out the obvious. You've been on the road too long."

"I appreciate your concern. So where do you want me to leave you?" He nodded toward the lights of the town ahead.

"My car is by the movie theater next to the motel."

"Is that where you're staying?"

"Yup. When I'm not pretending to be a ski bunny."

Marshall slapped the steering wheel. "Which reminds me. I told Annie your name was Bunny. You didn't happen to talk to her at the dance, did you?"

A strained silence fell. "I not only talked to her, I introduced myself. As Kerry. I wondered about the look she gave me. Other than that, I would say that she seems like a nice person."

"She is."

"And she's really beautiful. You blew it, Stone," Kerry said gleefully.

"Yeah. Big time." Marshall groaned. "Goddamn it. No wonder she suddenly hates my guts."

His partner in crime fighting began to laugh. "You're not going to be able to dance your way out of this one."

He cursed a blue streak as he made a right turn into the alley that ran between the movie theater and the motel.

"Are you still sure you don't want my advice?" Kerry needled him.

"Not right now. Who is that inside your car?"

Kerry sat straight up. "I don't know."

Marshall reached down and touched a finger-print to a hidden biometric lock. He took a gun out of the custom-made compartment next to his seat. "Want me to find out?"

"Not worth the risk. There's nothing in my car worth stealing, either."

He killed the headlights and stayed where he was. The man in the car clambered out of the passenger side and stood, catching his breath. For a second his jowly face showed clearly as he turned to look up at the fine snow drifting down under the streetlight.

"Shep Connally," Marshall muttered. "How about that."

"I suggest we let him go," Kerry offered. "I mean, get the plates, call them in to the county sheriff and the division office in Denver, and make sure he's followed when he's out of your area. But that's it."

"I know, I know. Shep is low level. But he's all we have to get to the others."

Stone didn't release the safety on the gun. They

both watched Connally get into a car parked close to Kerry's and drive away—but not before Stone pushed another button to take an infrared photo with the microcamera hidden in the truck's grille.

"Did you get it?" Kerry asked.

He pushed another button and a small laptop lifted up out of the dash, ready to use. Kerry tapped the screen to zoom in. "There you go. Arizona plates."

"That's where he got his start as a con man." Stone put the gun away and locked the compartment with his fingerprint. "He was a take-the-money-and-run type. An expert at fleecing little old ladies who hid cash in their mattresses."

"Anyone like that in Velde?"

"Every town has old folks." He thought of the town meeting that Kerry hadn't attended. "But our intel had him moving up to bigger and better scams. I've been concentrating on greedy guys looking to cut shady property deals."

"Like the new development with imaginary houses. Discounts for first buyers, lots of promises, and nothing gets built."

"That area is the most obvious," Marshall admitted. "But Connally could have decided to work his former hustle in the meantime. You know, my landlady could help me out with the old folks. She knows everyone in town."

"So check it out. She doesn't know me from Adam. Even though one of my new best friends tried to rent the cabin before you nabbed it."

"Really? I didn't know that."

"Jill's credit rating was crap. I guess yours was

solid gold. Does Nell think you're a surveyor or does she know who you really are?"

"She likes me," he answered flatly. "Not sure why. I know she ran a background check, but the agency ID wouldn't come up for that."

"Whatever. Back we go. I'm not getting in that car and I'm not sleeping here," Kerry said firmly. "Thanks in advance for inviting me to stay at the cabin, by the way. You're the best."

"No way."

"Why not?"

"Listen up, kid. Because I said so."

Kerry stopped by the next day with several bulging plastic bags stuffed with new clothes. Stone opened the cabin door she had just kicked to let him know she was there.

"Hello," he said. "The answer is still no."

"I figured." She hoisted the bags and studied his at-home attire. His holey football jersey and baggy sweatpants didn't seem to impress her. "Are you alone?"

"Yes. And don't give me grief about it."

Kerry peered past him all the same.

"Practicing your investigative skills?" he asked. Stone hated to be rude, but he wasn't going to invite her in for coffee.

"Just checking. Can you at least keep most of this until I find someplace else to stay?"

"You bet." He relieved her of the biggest bags.

Rowdy, who'd been treated to a long, late run last night, lifted his head from inside his padded dog bed and thumped his tail. Then he went back to sleep.

"Hi, pooch. Thanks so much, Stone. You're all heart. See you around. Maybe. I requested a transfer last night to a town in the next county. I'm supposed to hear by tomorrow. Seems like the investigation is widening its scope."

She seemed excited by the prospect. He felt a professional interest. That was about it. She didn't have to know that he'd been informed of her request and given his approval. If it really did get rough, he didn't want her there. And after all these months he wanted nothing more than to be done with crooks and sneaks once and for all.

"Sounds like a real opportunity, Kerry. Go for it."

"That's the plan."

"Let me know where you bunk down until then."

"I will."

He watched her get back into her rental car and drive off in the direction of Velde's main street. Then he tossed the bags on the bed and tied them closed with double-knotted surveyor's tags, stashing them quickly in the cabin's one small closet. For good measure, he pulled down the extra blankets from the top shelf and set them over the bags.

He'd made a stupid mistake once by offering up an alias for Kerry instead of her real name. With luck and a little patience on Annie's part, he could probably explain it well enough to get her to forgive. He wasn't going to make a second mistake by being careless with those bags.

He made himself a cup of black coffee and headed for the love seat, which was still turned toward the woodstove in the corner. It was a little early in the day for manly brooding and staring into the flames, but he might as well get it over with.

Stone stretched out as best he could, propping his socked feet on the armrest and wrangling a pillow behind his head. The antique love seat had been built when men were shorter and women were tiny.

But it had been cozy squeezing onto it with Annie. She'd stayed on his mind from the day he'd first seen her face.

He knew it was crazy, thinking about her so much. He had come to Colorado to get a job done. Romancing a girl who was as skittish as a wild horse wasn't in his job description. But when it came right down to it, he didn't plan to walk away from this town without her.

But she had her folks, and that ranch, and a life of her own he knew almost nothing about. What exactly did he have to offer her?

Stone sipped his coffee, lost in thought. He loved it here. The area around Velde had a wide-open feel that was timeless. The rugged land looked a lot like where he'd grown up in Wyoming.

His family's ranch was much smaller than the Bennetts' spread, though. And it had long since been sold to pay the bank and other creditors. He'd never really had a place he could call home.

Kerry was right. Jumping from state to state on random assignments was getting old. He'd spent too much of his life on endless stakeouts, staring through dark-tinted windows, waiting for something to happen.

It made a man only see the worst in people.

Something had to change.

He knew Annie was the reason he wanted to. Marshall set his cold coffee aside and folded his arms across his chest. He had to figure out a way to tell her the truth. And soon.

Chapter 16

Tyrell Bennett unfolded the note his wife had left for him on the kitchen table before he started in on the late breakfast his daughter had prepared for both of them. He read the note aloud.

" 'Gone to Cilla's. Baking cookies with her and the little girls.' "

"Sounds like fun," Annie said, buttering her toast.

Her father did the same, adding jam. "Now why on earth would Lou want to have fun when she can stay right here and wait on me hand and foot?"

"I know you're kidding."

"Of course I am. She knows you'll take care of me."

Annie gave him a mock glare and Tyrell laughed.

When they were done eating, he glanced through the local newspaper, then spread it out to show her the photos in the middle. "Bet you she went to see the Christmas decorations on Main Street. It's twinkle time."

"The Chamber of Commerce went all out. The lights are best at night, though." She poured herself a cup of coffee.

Tyrell nodded. "So how was the Snow Ball? Weren't you the emcee?"

"Yes, I was. After a while Nell took over." Annie didn't want to get into the details. "It was fun."

Her terse answer didn't keep Tyrell from being a dad. "You came back sooner than we expected. Not that we were waiting up for you," he added hastily.

"Yes, I did. I was feeling kinda tired. Guess that's why I slept late."

Annie usually got up just after her mom did and they shared an early breakfast, a habit they'd acquired in the last months. Now that her brothers didn't live on the ranch, Lou didn't have as much to do and they both welcomed the chance to spend time together without the men.

"Well then, you must be nice and rested," her dad said.

Annie gave him a sideways look. She still wasn't inclined to discuss Stone with her father. Although anyone who knew Tyrell and who'd seen her dancing with the surveyor would probably mention it eventually.

"Is that a hint? Nothing needs painting," she said. "And the barn isn't going to fall down. I checked."

Her dad folded the paper and put it to one side. "I was thinking you and me could walk the lines."

"Really?"

"Since that surveyor fella started poking around, I thought it'd be a good idea to check the boundary markers, make sure there's no weak spots in the fence—especially the part where the cow got through that one time. One of the hands fixed it. I'd like to see how it's holding up."

That surveyor fella was a step up from *that trespassing son-of-a-gun who tagged my fences.* Annie wondered why her dad had changed his tune. Maybe he'd already heard about her dancing with Stone last night and didn't want to give her a hard time about it.

"All right," she said with a smile. She would actually enjoy being out in the open on a cold, bright day. The memory of being in Stone's arms had been too sweet a dream to wake up from. She rose from the kitchen table and poured herself a cup of coffee, drinking it quickly.

They took her truck and Annie drove, jolting over tracks in the land that couldn't really be called roads. Tyrell braced himself against the dashboard.

"Take it easy, girl. When did the ruts get this deep, anyway?"

"Dunno. The snow will fill them in soon enough."

"Don't remind me." He gestured to a nearby section of fence. "Stop here. Let's walk a while."

She put the gearshift into park, and they both got out. Tyrell tugged at the brim of his Stetson to keep the sun out of his eyes and turned up his collar. Annie had a knit cap stuffed into her pocket, but she didn't bother with it. The wind coming down from the mountains was exhilarating.

Tyrell gave a nod. "Let's start over there. That's probably the oldest section of fence on the ranch. Still holding up."

She slipped her arm through his. "Like you."

Tyrell made a scoffing sound. "More or less."

From where they were, the old split rails and wood posts looked sturdy enough, but she knew there was a second, much more recent fence of metal and wire directly behind them. Her dad was sentimental about this stretch, the last remnant of her great-grandfather's hard work on the land he'd claimed.

"Now then. Bet you forgot why split rails are eleven feet long," he began.

She let go of his arm, amused by his teaching tone, a familiar echo of her childhood. "Tell me again."

"Eleven feet minus the ends that go in the post holes means each rail is actually ten feet. Helps you measure acres real quick, especially on horseback."

"Right. And an acre was how much an ox could plow in a day."

"You get a gold star for remembering that. Hell, I can remember my dad plowing with oxen. Did I ever tell you about that? We had to save gas, what with the shortages right after the war. He taught me how, just so I'd know it. He never did want to give up the team."

"They were something."

She'd only seen pictures. Annie couldn't recollect much of anything about her grandfather, who'd died when she was just a baby.

"Before your time," Tyrell mused. "Long before. You have a real feeling for the land, though."

She was touched to hear him say it.

"Different when you're on foot, isn't it?" he said. "You get to know its secrets and hidden places."

"Yes." They had almost reached a corner of the property, judging by the right angle of the fence only yards away. It had been left in its natural state. Annie's roping boots crunched over stubbly brown grass. Beneath the thin crust of snow, its tough roots sank deep into the dry soil, dormant until spring.

The subdued hues of the winter landscape were brightened by evergreen juniper. By it was a low thicket of rabbitbrush, its yellow blossoms turned into fluffy seedpods long since picked over by migrating birds.

They reached the corner. Annie rested a hand on a top rail for a few moments while her father had a look-see.

"Still standing," he said with satisfaction. "You could knock a fence like this down and reset it in a day if you had to. Of course, sometimes a tornado did the knocking down for you."

"When was the last one?"

"Couldn't say." He rubbed his chin thoughtfully. "Not in my lifetime."

Nestled in the foothills of the mountains, the ranch was spared some of the wild weather that hit the plains to the east. And they'd made out all right during the recent floods. But when it came to snow, they generally got the brunt of it.

Tyrell turned away from the fence and looked out over the rolling ranch land toward dark blue mountains dashed and streaked with snow.

He didn't quite smile, but the way his eyes crinkled up conveyed deep contentment. "Your great-grandfather picked good land."

"He sure did," Annie said softly. "I don't want the ranch to ever change. I love it the way it is. Wide open. You can breathe."

He looked at her fondly. "You're a true Bennett."

"Sam and Zach love it here too."

Her father jammed his hands into the pockets of his jean jacket. "I know. But they have lives of their own now."

"They'll be back."

His expression was pensive. "Maybe."

"Don't say that. They will."

"You know, I should have brought you along back in the day when I took the boys to walk the lines," Tyrell said. "Don't know why I never did. Tradition, I guess. It was more of a father-son thing to do."

"We're doing it now. That's good enough for me."

"All right then." He smiled down at her. "Let's keep on."

His long strides kept him slightly ahead of her. "Now where is that *monument?*"

"What?"

"Surveyor's term. All it means is a marker on the land. Could be a stone post or an old pipe."

He seemed to have regained his energy. She had trouble keeping up. "So which is it?"

Tyrell chuckled. "My money's on an old pipe. Bennetts wouldn't waste good money on a fancy cut stone."

"Is that it?"

Her father squatted down and cleared away a few handfuls of frozen brush to reveal a length of rusted pipe set into the earth. "Yep. Good eye." He straightened up and eyed the corner angle of the fence. "But if it's here, then it means the fence isn't on the property line. Dagnabbit. I may have to get a professional to do a real survey."

Annie held her breath.

"Not that guy who was working for Chuck Pfeffer either. I heard in town he's still around."

"I guess so. He was at the dance. His name is Stone, by the way. Marshall Stone. Nell introduced us."

That was true. Just not at the dance. Annie's comment was meant to deflect suspicion if her dad heard more about the Snow Ball. She couldn't very well pretend that she knew absolutely nothing about the surveyor.

"Oh?" Her father seemed more interested in the fence, although she could be wrong about that. The line of the newer fence extended ahead. Tyrell frowned when he saw several small neon tags tied to the wire, fluttering in the wind.

"Hmph. So he got out this way too." He tugged at one.

"Don't take them off."

"Why not?"

"Surveyors have to review their measurements, don't they?"

"Yes, but—" He looked at her quizzically. "Sounds like you've been learning a little about the subject."

Annie cleared her throat. "Um, I looked some things up online after you and Stone got into it."

"Wasn't an argument."

"It wasn't a friendly chat either. Look on the bright side. Maybe he won't have to come back more than once if he can still find those tags."

Tyrell left off fooling with them. "All right. Let's see what he comes up with then. He has to file his survey with the town. If he's honest."

"And what if he's crooked?" Annie actually did want to know.

"We'll find out. Of course, I'd have to pay someone else to prove him wrong."

There was exasperation in Annie's faint sigh. "Dad, with all the new development being planned, you should get a survey done."

"I suppose you're right," he muttered. "Which reminds me. I pulled over by the lookout at the top of the ridge and I saw that so-called development. Nothing but plots. No one working on anything. No lumber. No construction trailer."

"I know what you mean. I wondered about it myself."

"The candy canes on the street lamps were a nice touch. There goes the neighborhood, I guess,"

Tyrell said wryly. "It's hard to stop progress. If it is progress."

Annie was grateful for the change of subject. "Hey, I don't know if Mom told you, but I went to talk to the town clerk. I was kinda concerned about some of the old people after that town meeting."

"Anyone specific?"

"Elsie and Jack Pearson. Do you know them?"

The last name clearly registered. Tyrell nodded. "I remember Jack from back in the day. He's older than I am. But I don't know his wife too well. Haven't talked to him for years."

Annie hesitated, then offered an account of her visit to the Pearson home with Nell, starting with the reason why: the unopened letter from the tax assessor. Her father listened carefully.

"Mom told me to stay out of it and let Nell take charge," Annie finished. "She's known Mrs. Pearson for a long time, even though they hadn't talked for quite a while."

"I'd say your mother got it right," her father advised. "I'm sure that old lady has her own way of doing things. If I know Nell, she'll keep you posted."

"That's true." Annie gave a reluctant smile.

"You ready to head back?"

"Yeah. It's getting cold." She pulled the knit cap out of her pocket and put it on.

"Thanks for coming along. That long walk did me good. You too, girl. You got roses in your cheeks. Haven't seen you this bright eyed in a long time."

Annie looked up at her dad. "I just realized my leg didn't hurt the whole time."

"That's a good sign. Especially after a big dance. Oops." He stopped suddenly. "Sorry, little fella."

Some small creature that hadn't crept into its winter burrow scurried away through the undergrowth. "Was that a chipmunk?"

"Didn't see. Coulda been; he was quick. I almost stepped on him." Tyrell grinned at her. "Don't tell your mother."

"Why would I?"

"Well, you might. But listen. When we first met, I thought she was so pretty I asked her to dance even though I barely knew how. I stepped on her feet so many times she wouldn't give me her phone number."

"Really?"

"I'm surprised she never mentioned it. That's my Lou. Loyal as they come." Tyrell looked ahead, seeing the red truck at last. "So did you meet anyone at the dance?"

"Everyone in Velde was there. Plus a lot of new faces."

"And?"

"I had a good time, Dad."

"But not with anyone in particular."

"Nope," she said cheerfully.

"Just thought I'd ask," he said vaguely. "If you are seeing someone, you can tell me and Mom. You don't have to, of course."

"Thanks. Good to know."

Tyrell gave her a sheepish smile. "Well, at least you're getting back in the swing of things."

"I'm trying to."

"After all these months at home, your mom and I—well, we hope you still like being here."

"More than ever, Dad."

"We wouldn't mind a bit if you stayed for as long as you like. But maybe you want to get back to Aspen, start working again."

"I honestly don't know what I want to do. And I'm not making any decisions until after Christmas."

Tyrell slung a lean arm around her shoulders and gave her a squeeze. "That'll do. No more questions."

Annie shook her head. "Good. 'Cause I don't have answers. To anything."

Chapter 17

Elsie Pearson pushed aside a stack of opened bills. There simply wasn't the money to pay more than half of them. People had been kind, but the Pearsons had never taken a handout or asked for charity. They made do or went without. She set down her pen and folded her hands in her lap. Then she picked up the phone and set it in front of her, ready to call Connally. Something made her hesitate.

She wasn't a fool. He didn't seem entirely honest. She was sure he'd deliberately let her catch a glimpse of the bundles of cash in his briefcase when he'd come over to talk to her.

As if she would pay her taxes with cash if she took his offer. The town clerk would think she, Elsie Pearson, had robbed a bank. No, Connally would have to make a legitimate deal of some sort if she decided that there was no other way to keep their house.

Jack needed care above and beyond what their income would cover. She could swallow her pride for him.

But she had promised Nell that she would talk to her about things like this.

Elsie looked up the number in the address book by the phone and dialed.

"Elsie! Oh, goodness. I'm so sorry. I was going to call you, haven't had a free minute. The carpenter just got here. The back staircase at the saloon collapsed. . . ."

Mrs. Pearson listened politely to Nell's chatter without interrupting.

"And then there was the Snow Ball, which was a roaring success, and this weekend there's the parade. Do you think you can come?"

"Not if you're going."

The slight frostiness in her tone seemed to be lost on Nell at first. But the saloon keeper caught herself. "Maybe someone else could stay with Jack," she said worriedly.

The old lady cast a glance at her husband, who was looking absently out the window. "Never mind, dear. It's supposed to be awfully cold. The newspaper will have photos of it."

Awkwardly, Nell tried to make amends for not remembering that Jack couldn't be left alone, but the carpenter eventually commanded her attention. "I'm coming over later."

The two women agreed on a time and Mrs. Pearson hung up. She set Connally's business card to the right of the phone and got up to start dinner. Calling him didn't mean anything. It would be a simple request for more information, that was all.

Connally showed up after Elsie called him, full of ideas. Mrs. Pearson was courteous, but that was all. She couldn't go through with what he was suggesting and dodged his questions until he took the hint and left. She and Jack might never be able to pay him back. There had to be another way.

Jack came into the kitchen as she was washing the few dishes they'd used. She looked up, startled by how quietly he could still move for such a big man.

"I don't like him, Elsie." He said nothing more.

"I thought you were watching television."

"I was listening."

She slipped off her rubber gloves and hung them up. "Connally's a big talker, that's all. Nothing's going to change. We're staying right here. In our own house."

"All right." He stood there for a moment and then smiled.

His wife reached up and patted his cheek. "Don't worry, Jack. We'll manage somehow."

By the time Annie got into Velde again, the parade was imminent. She drove through the center of town just as the deputies were setting up blockades at the side street.

The main thoroughfare was oddly empty.

She rolled down her window to ask a deputy with a Santa-style vest over his khaki uniform, "Where is everybody?"

"Out by Nell's rental cabin. She told the organizers they could park the floats there."

"Okay. Thanks."

She swung the red truck in that general direction, wondering what Stone thought of that idea. In another minute, she slowed down and brought up the rear of a vaguely biblical exodus. Adults were swarmed with excited kids in costumes.

Annie spotted a few of her seven shepherds, wearing burlap robes with hoods over their colorful winter jackets and swinging their crooks importantly. She turned off, laughing, and went around the back way to get out of the path of the stream of participants.

She heard Rowdy barking before she saw him. There were several real sheep standing in the trampled snow in front of the cabin. Rowdy was doing his best to keep them together.

He circled the small herd, nipped at a black ankle or two, then sat down, staring balefully at the big ewe in front, who met his gaze with a wary one of her own.

"Live sheep? Whose idea was that?" Annie called to Stone, who came out the front door, bundled up for the cold day in a scarf and his cowboy hat.

"Nell's."

"Figures." She made a point of acting as if nothing had happened between them. As if she'd never spoken to Kerry at the dance.

Rowdy sprang into action to get a would-be stray back into position.

"Now we know what Rowdy used to do for a living," Stone observed.

"For sure." Annie parked and got out. The first of the floats was rolling forward. She saw the rest of the boys she'd supervised at the church hall. The crew-cut one came running up to her.

"Annie! Hi! Guess what. Miss Opal said we could ride on the float. We'll be the shepherds who watch by night during the day, I guess."

A ramp was being lowered from the back of the float, which was a flatbed with fencing all around a pastoral scene made of cardboard.

Nell popped out of the passenger side of the cab and got the kids in line.

"What do you think?" she asked the driver. "Sheep in first or kids?"

"Sheep," he said.

Stone whistled to Rowdy. "Move 'em out," he added. The dog herded like a pro. As for the sheep, they were used to being bossed around by self-important canines. Rowdy got them up the ramp without a hitch.

The excited kids were shoving each other until Nell told them sternly to behave.

"I don't think they had a stock dog at Bethlehem," she told the driver, who shrugged. "Children, are you ready?"

The boys and girls lined up. Chaos ensued, with

several stragglers adding to the confusion. Rowdy raced down the ramp and got to work.

The children screamed with laughter as he bumped and nosed at them. No nipping. But he meant business.

"Nell, he's herding us!" one yelled.

"And doing a darn good job of it, I'd say. Now get on up there. You know your places."

Between Nell and Rowdy, the shepherds and assorted other young Bethlehemites were loaded and good to go. The second float rolled up. Nell turned and saw Annie.

"This is going to be so much fun."

"Want me to drive you back to town?" Annie asked.

"No, but thanks. I'm going to stop by Mrs. Pearson's house first. I have been remiss," Nell said, looking a little ashamed of herself. "I said I'd stop by and what with everything, I didn't."

"You did reach social services, though."

"Yes. But you know how it is with a bureaucracy. You have to follow up. Oh, here come the singing elves. Aren't they adorable?"

The kids on the second float were decked out in peaked caps of red and green felt, and motley-colored costumes, also of felt.

Annie spotted Jenny and Zoe, sitting together on a giant wrapped present, holding hands. They weren't smiling.

"Oh dear. Those two little sweethearts are having a tough time," Nell whispered. "Cilla told me that everyone's doing the best they can to cheer them up, but they really, really miss their mom."

"Wish we could get her back home sooner."

Nell sighed with concern, looking after the second float as it rolled slowly past. "Maybe I'll think of something."

"You always do."

Chapter 18

Annie was exhausted. She'd watched the parade, pitched in at the hot-cocoa stand to pass out cups, helped kids find their parents and grandparents, and taken innumerable photos for everyone who asked her to.

Afterward, she caught up with Cilla and Ed Rivers, swinging the girls in the little park by the town square. Jenny and Zoe seemed to have cheered up.

Ed gave a big push and sent the older girl up in the air, squealing with glee.

"Hi, everyone. Did you enjoy the parade?"

"It was fun," the children chorused.

"You two looked very cute."

"We took about a million pictures of them," Cilla said, a little breathless from exertion.

"That's great." Annie remembered just in time not to say anything like *I bet their mom will love those.* "You know, I was just wondering what happens to the stuff on the floats. Do they store all that for next year?"

"Some of it," Cilla said. "But the giant presents on the elf float are supposed to go under the town Christmas tree. It's not up yet."

Annie looked toward the tree's usual spot in the small square. There were a couple of ladders and rigging equipment and what seemed to be boxes of outdoor lights, but no tree.

"I seem to remember your dad volunteering to cut one from your ranch," Ed said.

"He didn't tell me about it. But we do have a grove of blue spruces."

"Really?" Jenny was slowing down. "My teacher says that's Colorado's state tree."

"That's right."

"It would be neat if it was a Bennett tree." When her swing stopped completely, Jenny slid out of it and headed for a bench. "Do you have a picture of it on your phone?"

"Ah—no. I'm not sure my dad picked one to cut yet," Annie told her, sitting down herself, happy to rest. "He likes to take his time with things like that."

Zoe didn't seem as interested in the tree, delighted to have the attention of both Cilla and Ed all to herself for a little while.

"Oh. Well, I hope we can put some decorations on it," Jenny said. "We made paper-plate snowmen last week."

"I always loved doing crafts at school." Annie smiled. She'd never minded getting her fingers gluey, not if glitter was involved.

"I hope it's a big tree." Jenny's eyes sparkled.

"Oh, it will be. Did you know that one of our trees made it all the way to New York City?"

"Really?"

"That was a few years ago. My big brother Sam drove it across the country with my dad. But I'm sure we have a perfect one for here. It just wanted to finish growing first."

Jenny slipped her mittened hand into Annie's and rose from the bench. "Would you swing me some more?"

"Just for a little while," Ed cautioned. "It's late in the day and I'm sure Annie wants to get home."

"Hop on," Annie told her. She and Cilla swung the girls at exactly the same time. The children leaned back and laughed at the sky, kicking their booted feet.

Annie stopped by Nell's saloon to see how the staircase repairs were coming along. The carpenter had left a stack of lumber, including new spindles to replace the cracked ones, on a workbench, but not his tools.

There were no customers, but that was because Nell hadn't turned the CLOSED sign to the OPEN side. She must have just gotten back from the parade.

Nell came out from the back when she heard the clinking of the jingle-bell wreath on the door.

"Looks like he's making progress," Annie said.

"He had to stop." Frowning, the saloon keeper put her hands on her hips and surveyed the area, which was still roped off. "He said something about a high-maintenance girlfriend and not canceling the vacation he promised her. So I guess the poker suite won't be available until next year."

"You have plenty to do as it is," Annie replied. "Did you see Mrs. Pearson, by the way?"

Nell nodded, looking a little troubled. "I'm trying to be tactful, but I'm just itching to ask her if Shep Connally's been around. I saw his business card by her phone."

"My parents keep telling me to let you handle it."

"Well, that's probably best. And Elsie did promise to talk to me before she agreed to any sort of arrangement in the future."

"How about getting her some help?"

Nell beamed. "Now *that's* under way. I filled out the paperwork for a health-care aide for Jack. They should hear very soon."

The jingle-bell wreath rattled and clinked again.

"Mrs. Dighton?" A deputy stepped inside the bar.

"Deputy Keene! What can I do for you?"

The young officer came inside, his hat in his hand. "Just came in to let you know that the roads out of town might not be drivable by late tonight. In case you have any customers who wait too long to get home."

"None so far." She gestured to the empty booths and tables. "I did hear that there was a storm system blowing in. But I thought that was happening tomorrow."

"Tonight and tomorrow," Keene clarified.

"Oh my. I'll close by nine."

"All right then. Thank you, ladies." The deputy included Annie in his good-bye nod. "I'll be on my way."

Keene went out again. Nell headed for the refrigerator and pulled out a plastic container. "Want me to microwave some lasagna for you? I made it yesterday so I wouldn't have to cook after the parade."

"Okay. Thanks."

The portions weren't that big, but the lasagna was so hearty that Annie felt a little sleepy after they'd finished. "That was delicious, Nell."

"How about dessert?"

"Nope. I probably should be getting home."

"I understand."

She helped Nell clean up behind the bar, not that there was much to do, and said good-bye.

Outside, the town looked completely different. The snow had already begun, softening the angles of the old brick commercial buildings on Main Street and beginning to turn the parked cars into enormous marshmallows. Annie's truck was more white than red.

She cleared snow from the windshield before she got in, and batted it off the door handles and locks. Sliding into the cab, she turned on the wipers to get rid of the rest.

Deputy Keene was driving slowly down the street with another officer in a cruiser. The tires sprayed snow as he made a U-turn and rolled down the window to talk to a bunch of teenagers horsing around near the town square.

"You kids need to get on home. This is going to get worse."

"Five minutes more?" a girl pleaded.

"That's all. I'll drive you home myself if I have to."

They went back to playing and throwing sloppy snowballs while Annie turned the key in the ignition. Her tires spun.

"Not good," she muttered. The snow was coming down harder now, in big wet flakes that the wipers couldn't brush away in one go.

The defroster wasn't working too well either. She rolled down the window on the opposite side to get rid of the blurring mist on the inside. The snow blew in and got all over the seat.

It wasn't a blizzard, just a pretty good storm, puffy and soft as a down comforter. A few vehicles crawled by, avoiding the parts of the street with swerve marks.

The teenagers scattered, running and sliding, and were soon gone. So was the cop cruiser.

Annie got out to look at the back wheels. The problem was the mix of melting snow and the fresh, much colder snow on top of it. She doubted her tires were even touching the surface of the street when they spun. Essentially, the truck was floating.

Deputy Keene came back, driving even more slowly.

"Wouldn't try it," he called to her. "Do you have somewhere to stay in town?"

"Of course. Don't worry about me." She waved him on as she got back in the cab. There were several options, starting with Nell.

She called the saloon directly and got no answer. Nell must have closed right after Annie had left. She frowned when she realized that she didn't have any other number for Nell.

All right. There was Darla.

No answer there either. She looked at the screen. An icon indicating a problem with her service popped up. Cell phones didn't do too well during storms up here. She put the phone in her pocket, wanting to save the battery.

Annie kept the wipers going, waiting for the deputies to drive back around.

"Hey," she called to Keene and his partner. "I can't get a call out."

"Want me to radio the dispatcher and tell her to contact your folks?"

"Could you? They still have a landline. Works better than a cell in these conditions." She gave him the information he needed and watched him type it into the laptop attached to the dashboard. The dispatcher replied in seconds.

"What do you want her to tell them?"

"That I'm staying with a friend."

"Which friend?"

"They won't care once they know I'm all right for the night."

The officers seemed to assume that she had temporary accommodations all figured out, Annie realized when they drove away again.

She could knock on a few doors. Someone had to be home.

The streets were still walkable. Barely. She would have to slog through the snow. Good thing she had on high waterproof boots and a heavy jacket with a hood. Annie switched off the engine and considered her next move.

It took her a few seconds to realize that a large, gleaming black truck had pulled up next to hers, its powerful engine muffled by the heavy snowfall.

She rolled down her window and so did Stone.

"You all right?"

"I'm stuck," she admitted. "I can't get home and my cell phone service conked out. The deputy's been by a few times. He's going to have the dispatcher contact my mom and dad, so I don't have to worry about that. What I need right now is a place to stay for the night."

He pulled up ahead of her and double-parked to stay out of the icy slush by the curb, turning on the emergency blinkers. Then he got out and tromped back.

"You can use my phone." He handed it over.

"Thanks. Want to get in?"

"Okay." She heard him walking around as she consulted her otherwise useless phone to get her friends' numbers from her contacts. Stone got in, staying quiet as she tried several.

Every call went straight to voice mail.

"Shoot. Guess they don't have cell service either." Annie handed back his phone. "How come yours works so well?"

"Different model," he said, as if that was enough of an explanation.

"Oh. Thanks anyway."

The deputies pulled up again. "Dispatcher

reached your folks. They said to hunker down." Keene glanced at Stone without concern. "Glad you're not alone. We gotta get out to the main road."

"Not a problem. Thanks for checking on me." She settled back. "Now what?"

"You really don't have any place to stay?"

"Not yet. I was about to get out and start walking, knock on a few doors."

Stone gazed out through the snow-clogged windshield. "Probably not a good idea at this point. Want to call your parents from my phone and tell them you're with me?"

"They think I'm going to stay with a friend."

"And I don't fit that definition."

"Um, no. Look, let me try Nell again. You're her tenant—do you have her cell number?"

"Yes, I do." He scrolled through his contacts, found the number and tapped it, and gave her the phone again.

The call rang through. "How about that. She must have the same type of phone you do," Annie said.

"Wouldn't know."

The ringing stopped. "Hellooo," Nell trilled.

"Hey, it's Annie. How are you making out? Are you okay?"

"Never better."

Sounded like Nell had been indulging in her favorite peach brandy. Annie wished she could have a shot herself. "That's great. Ah, I was wondering—with this snow—"

"It's fabulous, isn't it?"

Annie heard a muffled sound as if Nell was covering the receiver and speaking to someone else.

"Sorry. I have company."

Annie checked the clock in the truck, surprised to see that over an hour had passed since she'd left Nell.

"We're going to make hot toddies and get snuggled up."

Annie made out a male voice, but not the words.

"The rum is in the other cabinet, Chester." Nell spoke to Annie again. "I have to go. See you after the snowstorm."

"Okay. Thanks." Annie ended the call and gave Stone a puzzled look. "I don't want to be a third wheel. Apparently Nell has company. Someone named Chester. For some reason, I know that name. Just can't put a face to it."

"Good for Nell. Look, we can't stay out here all night. It sounds like you really have no other place to go. Why don't you stay with me?"

"I wouldn't want to impose," she said, a faint edge to her voice. She wondered if Bunny—no, Kerry—stayed there sometimes too.

"It's not a problem. Leave your truck here," he instructed. "We'll take mine."

For a few seconds, Annie contemplated telling him that she would rather freeze, but she decided against it. The deputies would come back eventually and she would end up sleeping in a jail cell for the night if she didn't go with Stone.

* * *

Rowdy burst out the door, did his business, barked at the snow, and ran back in again, going in crazy circles on the rug.

"He likes the snow," Stone said.

"I can see that."

He took her jacket from her and hung it over a chair, pushing it near a baseboard heater. She was glad there was backup for the little woodstove in the corner.

Stone offered her a glass of wine, which she accepted. She wasn't very hungry after the lasagna, but she nibbled at the snack plate he put together for both of them, perching on a bar stool at the kitchenette counter. They chatted for a while. Not about the dance. It was as if they had never kissed, never held each other.

And there was that giddy redhead. That was still on her mind. She couldn't guess what Stone was thinking, though.

He kept a careful distance from her. Tired as she was, Annie was fine with that. She kept up the neutral small talk, twirling a lock of hair in her fingers as he got through the rest of his household routine in silence, feeding the dog and putting things away.

She moved to the love seat.

"Would you like another glass of wine?"

Annie yawned. She was feeling sleepy. And safe. Being in such a cozy space while a storm raged outside was great.

"Sure." She held out her glass and he filled it

halfway, bringing over the snack plate and setting it down before turning away. Rowdy sneaked a chunk of cheese off it before either of them could stop him.

Annie laughed, finishing the glass of wine so that she could rest her head on the back of the love seat. The cabin was blissfully warm. Before she knew it she had dozed off.

Her eyes opened. Rowdy was beside her, flopped on the folds of an afghan that she guessed Stone had thrown over her. Annie focused on the face of a clock across the room. She'd drifted off for no more than half an hour.

Stone was busy. Putting up a clothesline. Unless she was dreaming it.

"What are you doing?"

He made sure it was tight. "Guarding your virtue."

"What? I can do that myself," she said. She watched him throw a blanket over the clothesline.

"You can take the bed," he offered. "I have a sleeping bag and a pad for the floor. This is a wall."

"Is that really necessary?"

A smile played at the corners of his sensual mouth. "I don't have anyone to guard my virtue."

Annie reached out and ruffled Rowdy's black and white fur. "What about your faithful dog?"

"Not in his job description." Stone kept on with his task. "This blanket is going up and it's staying up, just in case you're suddenly overcome by flaming lust."

Annie rolled her eyes, knowing he wasn't looking at her. He was pulling out the wrinkles in the blanket by dragging it along the clothesline.

"Just wanted to give you some privacy."

She didn't know what to say. But it was gentlemanly of him to rig something up. Her dad, who would never know that she'd been here, would have appreciated it. Annie wasn't entirely sure that she did.

"Okay." He stood back and looked at the makeshift wall. "You can get ready for bed."

"What about you?"

"I changed while you dozed off."

Annie checked him out more closely. So he had. Stone was wearing sweatpants and a long-sleeved T-shirt and thick clean socks. She looked at the puffy white bed. Identical items were laid out on it for her, many sizes too big.

"Your pajamas. Best I could do under the circumstances."

"Thanks." She couldn't bring herself to tell him that she usually slept in nothing but her underwear and a tank top. The situation was charged enough as it was.

He dimmed the light by the bed and went over to his side of the Great Wall of Blanket, getting into the sleeping bag on the floor and turning his back to her.

Rowdy jumped down from the love seat and investigated, sniffing at his master with the intent concern of a search-and-rescue dog.

"Scram," Stone growled.

Rowdy obeyed the terse command and went back to Annie, wagging his tail.

Annie bit her lip to keep from laughing out loud and told him to lie down. She settled for the long-sleeved T-shirt and huge socks, and folded up the sweatpants at the bottom of the bed. Then she scrambled under the poufy comforter. She'd definitely gotten the better deal.

"Sweet dreams," she said softly.

There was a moment of silence.

"Yeah. Same to you," Stone muttered.

Annie didn't remember falling asleep. Daylight poured in the windows, brightening most of the cabin. But the blanket on the clothesline had kept the sun off the bed where she lay, utterly content. The storm had passed.

Stone was in the kitchen making noise.

"Are you up?" she called.

"Obviously."

She guessed by the irritable edge in his voice that he hadn't been comfortable on the floor.

"I'll buy you breakfast," she said coaxingly.

"No. I mean, there isn't any coffee or eggs or bread, and we do need to go out, but I'm buying."

"If you insist." She sat up and reached for the folded sweatpants, pulling them on and hanging on to the waistband so they didn't fall off. Then she came out, pushing the blanket aside.

Stone hadn't shaved. His jaw was shadowed with attractive dark stubble and his hair was tousled. He ran a hand through it, not looking at her.

"Gotta find my boots. Gotta get the snow off the truck. You can shower. Plenty of time."

Out he went.

Annie shrugged, looking at his back as he closed

the cabin door behind him. She might as well take him up on that. Two glasses of wine had her feeling just a tiny bit woozy this morning. A hot, pounding spray all over her body would take care of that. But she didn't want to wash her hair.

She scrabbled through her jacket pockets for a hairpin, finding a long one that would hold up her mane for a few minutes. When she came out, she dressed quickly and joined Stone outside. He glanced at her, frowning as if she looked different.

"Nice hairdo," he said gruffly. He seemed to mean it.

Annie had forgotten to take down the careless knot. A few damp tendrils of hair still clung to her cheeks. She pulled out the hairpin and let her hair tumble down to keep her neck warm.

Stone went past her, whistling to the dog to follow, and put Rowdy inside. Annie was already in his truck, enjoying the heat blasting from the sleek dashboard console. He soon joined her.

"Anyplace in particular you'd like to have breakfast?"

"Jelly Jam is always good."

He nodded and rolled out.

Main Street was virtually empty of people, although the town snowplow had cleared it. Her red truck was pretty much buried as a result.

"Looks like they're open," she said happily. Stone pulled his vehicle into a cleared spot and they went in.

He ordered the biggest breakfast on the menu, and finally smiled when a waitress brought over a huge jug of hot coffee. There were more people coming in. The town was waking up later than usual. Stone poured Annie's coffee first and then filled his own mug.

"Whew. I need this."

"Thanks for last night," she said, sipping her own. She looked over his shoulder, not really seeing the man who'd just come in.

But Tyrell Bennett saw her. He stared at Stone and at Annie, until she felt the force of his gaze and set down her cup.

"What's the matter?" Stone asked.

"My dad just walked in."

Marshall Stone turned around. But Tyrell had already gone.

"Annie. It's not like you're a teenager. And nothing happened. Just explain, okay? I can't."

She looked out the plate glass window of Jelly Jam, swallowing hard when her father's pickup roared by. There was a tall blue spruce tied inside the back.

He didn't look in her direction.

Annie sank her head into her hands and closed her eyes. "This isn't going to be easy."

Chapter 19

"**L**et's go," Stone said. He put several bills on the table to cover the meal and the tip. "I'll help you dig out the truck."

Annie shook her head. "I can do it."

Stone got up and put on his jacket. "Suit yourself. But I really don't think—"

With the barest nod, she indicated the other customers at tables a little distance away. No one was looking at them, but that didn't change the fact that Velde was a small town. "I'd rather not get into it here," she muttered.

Stone was silent as he escorted her through the doors of Jelly Jam out to the snowy pavement. "How about here?"

Annie walked ahead, knowing that he would quickly catch up to her. "No," she said when he did. "Just no."

"Mind if I ask if you talked to him about me? Like, after the dance?"

"Actually, I didn't." Annie stopped and turned

to face him. "I just told him that I had a good time, not with anyone special."

"Oh."

"Last night, when the deputy offered to contact my folks, I only told him to say that I was staying with a friend. I never gave a name. So for my dad, seeing me with you first thing in the morning—it just looks bad, that's all. I have to figure out how to tell him nothing happened."

"You sure that's the way to go?" His dark eyes held her gaze. He wasn't smiling. At least he didn't think it was funny.

"I have to be honest with him," Annie insisted.

"What if he thinks you're not telling the truth?"

"Please. Both my parents can read me like a book. Although I would say my mom's better at it than he is."

"That's unfortunate," Stone said, scuffing snow with his boot. "Because he already doesn't like me and I have yet to meet your mom."

"Whatever. They know I have my own life. I mean, I did until I broke my leg and had to move home."

"Then what happened?"

"I didn't date anyone from here, not when I was hobbling around, if that's what you mean. It's just that—well, he has to adjust to the fact that I can. When I was working in Vail and Aspen, I never had to deal with guys meeting my dad. But I was never serious about anyone, so it didn't matter."

He studied her for a few seconds, his strong jaw set and his mouth in a firm line. "And now it does. That's interesting."

Annie made a frustrated sound as she whirled away and strode on. Her emphatic steps began to slide on an icy stretch. She struggled for balance, about to slip. Stone caught her by the waist and set her down on a dry patch of sidewalk that someone had shoveled off.

"Sorry," he said flatly. "I didn't mean to get you in trouble."

"It's not like that. I have to talk to him, that's all. By myself."

They walked to her truck without saying anything more.

Stone looked it over. "Not too bad. I suppose you can do it yourself."

"Wouldn't be the first time."

She heard the muffled ringing of a cell phone and realized it was his. Stone took it from his pocket, looked at the number, and frowned. He put the phone away.

"Aren't you going to answer it?"

"Some other time," he said casually. "I'm with you."

That remark could be interpreted in more than one way. Annie didn't want to think about it too much. "You should go."

"All right." He stepped back as they said their good-byes, and she felt a pang of longing, realizing that she had been unconsciously expecting some sort of touch or kiss. Stone's nod was all he would offer as they parted company. He went down the street, walking as briskly as the slippery sidewalks would allow.

Annie had an uneasy feeling about the call he

hadn't taken. It wasn't like anyone needed the services of a surveyor after a snowfall. Who had wanted to talk to him?

Hmm. If he'd wanted her to know, he would have told her. There were just too many things she still didn't know about Marshall Stone.

Annie climbed into the back of her truck and cleared off the tool chest that held a folding shovel. She straightened before she unlatched the tool chest, watching Stone stride around a corner. She figured he was going back to the restaurant. His truck was still there. Thank goodness Jelly Jam was nowhere near the town square, where her dad was probably helping to put up the blue spruce.

Annie clambered back out and got to work. The snow was nowhere near as fluffy as it looked. It had begun to melt, making it heavy, and a lot of it had turned to chunky ice where the sun didn't reach. She cut through the chunks with the edge of the shovel and smashed them into small bits. It didn't take her long to free the wheels. She opened the door and tossed the shovel into the passenger-side foot well and got in.

Time to face the music.

Annie circled the town square from a distance. Just as she'd thought, her dad was there, directing a two-man crew installing the blue spruce from the Bennett ranch. Tyrell was giving instructions and not doing any heavy lifting.

Annie found a parking space behind some evergreen shrubs, hoping he wouldn't see her until the installation was completed. She left the key in the ignition and kept the heat on, then switched on the radio, listening to the weather report and then the news. No more snow for a while. Peace on earth at the moment. Good enough.

She leaned her head back, closing her eyes for a little while that turned out to be longer than she thought.

A rap on the window snapped her out of her doze.

Tyrell chuckled as Annie rolled it down. "Did I wake you up?"

"No," she said defensively. "I was just tired, that's all." Annie wished she could take the words back the second they were out of her mouth. She didn't want him to think she'd been up all night. As if she wasn't in hot water already.

Her father nodded and made no reply. He moved away and she saw him go around the back of the truck in her side mirror. Soon enough, he'd reached the passenger-side door, which he opened, climbing in.

"The spruce looks good," Annie said.

"It's a fine tree." Her father paused for a moment. "Now then. We need to talk."

Annie braced herself. Tyrell had a way of getting to the point. And he did.

"It's none of my business where you were last night. You're not a child. And that's all I have to say about that."

No questions. No accusations. She quickly glanced at her father. He looked straight ahead through the truck's windshield.

"I just wish you trusted me enough to tell me the truth. But maybe you felt you couldn't." Tyrell looked at her steadily. "Unless there isn't anything to tell."

"I didn't plan to—it just sort of happened. Darla didn't answer and I couldn't reach anyone else and Nell had a friend over and the snow was really coming down, so . . . I ended up with him."

"Where?"

Her father's nonchalance didn't last long, no matter what he said. Annie suppressed a smile.

"Nell's rental cabin," she answered. "He insisted that I take the bed. He slept on the floor with the dog."

"Oh."

The younger man from the tree crew, a heavyset guy in a padded flannel jacket, was heading their way. He waved when he caught sight of them behind the windshield and called to Tyrell.

"Be right there," her father called back.

"Aren't you done with the installation?" she asked.

"Apparently not. Anyway, there's one more thing, Annie."

"What?"

"I knew you didn't pick up that information about surveying online. Our Internet's been down for a week."

Annie looked at him sideways, biting her lip. Busted. It was no use trying to act innocent. "Shoot. I never noticed."

"Next time keep your story straight." Tyrell

opened the door and got out. "From what I hear, Stone is quite the dancer."

"Dad—"

He shut the truck door before she could finish the sentence. So her father had guessed at some of what was going on even before this morning and had kept his mouth shut. Now, that she never would have expected.

She ventured a smile when he looked back at her. Tyrell made her wait for a few seconds before a faint smile creased his face. They understood each other. She couldn't ask for anything more.

The man in the flannel jacket gave her a polite nod, and commanded her father's attention as they walked back to the town square.

Relieved, Annie rested her hands on the wheel, thinking that the conversation could have gone very differently. She collected herself, and put the gearshift in drive, rolling away from the curb and turning down a different street.

Then she slammed on the brakes. A half block ahead, Stone's gleaming black truck shot through an intersection with no light or stop sign. She saw his passenger for only a second or two. The red-head.

There went her good mood. Annie reversed and went in the opposite direction.

Then she pulled over. She wasn't going to go back to the ranch or to the town square. No, she was going to stay on the side streets until she calmed down.

And do what? she asked herself.

Annie chastised herself for not thinking of Mrs.
Pearson sooner. She would go by and make sure
the old lady and her husband were all right. If they
needed shoveling out, Annie needed the exercise.
The frigid air might just cool off the heat of her
temper.

So Kerry had called Stone. Now she knew why
he hadn't answered. Annie felt like a fool.

There weren't many cars in the part of town
where the Pearsons lived. The houses were mostly
small and set on large lots, built back when land
was cheap. No wonder Shep Connally had been
trying to make friends with Mrs. Pearson. The area
was home to a lot of seniors whose children had
grown and gone decades ago.

Annie noticed the quiet. There were no kids
making snowmen or forts or having snowball
fights. No snowblowers, either, but then it hadn't
been a major storm and the bright sun would help
melt a lot of it. She parked and made her way
down the sidewalk, waving to a couple of hale-
looking old guys in trapper hats who were out with
big red shovels. Maybe Mrs. Pearson had hired
someone to do her walkway.

She stopped at their mailbox. There were footsteps in the undisturbed snow, only one set, going
to the door. Probably a woman's. They were neat
and narrow. Maybe a friend had stopped in.

Annie glimpsed the old lady through a window,
waving at her. She waved back and hurried up the
walkway to the porch. Mrs. Pearson had the door

open before she'd raised her gloved hand to knock on it.

"Good morning, Annie. How nice to see you. Would you like some coffee?"

"No, thanks. Just had some." Annie stepped into the small foyer and glanced toward the table, where a thirtyish woman with short, nut-brown hair was sitting, filling out forms. She looked up from her paperwork and gave a friendly nod.

"But you can stay for a bit, can't you?" Mrs. Pearson asked Annie.

"Sure."

"Then take off those warm things and come meet Jane Generosa. She's a visiting nurse from the county. Nell contacted her. We're finding out about some benefits and programs that could be very helpful."

"That's great. Hi, Jane." Annie unzipped her jacket, stuffing her gloves into a pocket before she hung the jacket up on a hook.

"I'll take a cup of coffee," Jane said. "Good morning, Annie."

It wasn't only the sun that brightened the interior of the little house. The visiting nurse's cheerful nature was clear from her broad smile and self-assurance. Nell had obviously forgotten to mention anything about this last night, but then Nell had been pretty cheerful herself. Annie made a mental note to stop by the saloon and catch up with her.

Jane returned her attention to the forms, obviously finishing up her morning's work.

Annie sensed immediately that the nurse was

thoroughly capable, exactly what both Pearsons needed right now.

"You can sit there, dear." Mrs. Pearson indicated a chair across the table for Annie and went into the kitchen.

Jack's rumbling voice issued from inside it. "I took care of the coffee, Elsie. You don't have to fuss."

"All right then."

The elderly couple reentered, Elsie behind Jack, who was holding a cup on a saucer. He set it down with care as Jane Generosa collected the papers and stacked them on one side. "Thank you, Mr. Pearson." She relaxed and leaned back a little, her plump shape filling the chair.

"Call me Jack."

Elsie put creamer and sugar on the table. She gave Annie a tiny, crinkly wink, no doubt noticing Annie's surprise at seeing her husband in such a good mood.

"Glad you could make it to Velde," Annie began, speaking to Jane. "No one was expecting this much snow."

Jane lightened her coffee and sipped it appreciatively. "The main roads got cleared pretty fast. Of course, I always check the highway report before I head out."

"Good idea." Now Annie understood her dad's early arrival in Velde. He must have cut and loaded the tree yesterday, and moved the truck into the garage when the snow started really coming down. She wondered who had helped him.

The four of them chatted for a little while. Then

Jane gathered up her papers and put them into a canvas briefcase, sorting them out into the right pockets. "Thanks for the coffee. Too bad I have to leave," she sighed. "This has been a really pleasant morning. If you have any more questions, please feel free to contact me."

"We will," Elsie said. "But I do have a question before you go. On the home health aide."

"There are several in this area, including one I've known for years. She just completed an assignment and I believe she's free. I'll let you know as soon as I can."

"Thanks so much," Elsie said, looking at her husband. He seemed agreeable to the idea, judging by his expression.

Jane Generosa located her business cards in a small pocket of the briefcase and put one on the table. Then she handed another to Annie. "It's good to know the Pearsons have friends to look in on them. You can call me too."

Annie nodded. She got the point.

"Where are you going?" Jack wanted to know.

The visiting nurse named a town that he seemed to remember. He nodded. "Drive carefully," he said. "The roads stay icy longer out that way."

"I'll keep that in mind. Annie, very nice to meet you."

She rose from the table when the nurse did. "Yes. Same here. I'll walk you out, since I stopped by to shovel the walk. Might as well get to it."

Elsie didn't protest or tell her to sit down, and neither did Jack. They were holding hands.

"I'll take care of that and come back in," she promised the couple. Annie had seen an old coal shovel, banged-up but serviceable, on the porch behind some wicker chairs. It would do.

She didn't bother with her jacket as she went outside with bundled-up Jane. Just the gloves. Clearing the walkway would get her warmed up fast.

Annie said good-bye to Jane as she adjusted the shoulder strap of the canvas briefcase and went down the porch stairs. "Thanks so much," Annie called after her.

"Just doing my job," Jane replied with the same cheerful smile.

Annie watched her go, thinking there was much more to it than that for Jane. *Satisfaction* was the word.

She moved the wicker chairs and dragged out the coal shovel by its rusted handle. When she was done, she would make a stop at the hardware store and buy the Pearsons a lightweight one.

Annie hoisted the old shovel and went down the steps. She had cleared them all completely before she realized that she'd accomplished another objective: working off her anger at Marshall Stone, which was pretty much gone.

But not forgotten. She shoveled and scraped the walkway in record time.

Sooner or later Annie would have to go back to the ranch. But she swung by the saloon first, pushing open the door to see that every booth was full.

Nell and her son, Harold, were running back

and forth between the bar and the beeping microwave, carrying snack items and sandwiches to the tables, along with pitchers of beer and canned soda.

Nell grinned at Annie, wiping her hands on her apron. "The whole town came in. What can I do for you?"

"Nothing. Just wanted to say hi. I went to the Pearsons' house to see if they needed shoveling out and I met the visiting nurse."

"Wonderful!" Nell beamed. "Wonderful. Did you like her?"

"Very much."

"I don't know her personally, but I do know the county official in charge of the program. He comes in here occasionally."

"I see. Well, you would like Jane Generosa. She was filling out about a hundred forms so the Pearsons didn't have to."

Harold went by her, balancing a heavy tray. "Hey, Annie."

"Oh dear. I have to get back to work." Nell stepped away from the bar and Annie noticed the new addition to it. The model of a covered wagon that they'd seen in the shop window took pride of place in the center of the bar.

"Holy cow. Did you buy that?" Annie went right up to it to enjoy the details. It was protected by a glass case, but she could get much closer than she could at the shop.

"Yes, I did," Nell said proudly. "I found out that the artist does the dioramas for a frontier museum in Telluride. And he is just the nicest man."

Annie straightened. "What was his name again?"

"Chester Byron Hamilton. He brought it over yesterday before it started snowing hard."

"Oh." So that was the owner of the male voice in the background when she'd called Nell, looking for a place to stay. Annie had half a mind to ask if Chester had enjoyed snuggling over hot toddies. But she didn't. The saloon was getting crowded and the jingle-bell wreath on the door was making a racket.

"Here come more customers," Nell said gleefully. A party of young women in skiwear breezed in, talking nonstop. Annie thought she recognized a few from Rowdy's fan club on the day he'd run away. But no redhead named Bunny or Kerry.

"I should go," Annie said, taking one last look at the covered wagon on the bar. "I'm glad you bought that. It looks great there. And good luck with Chester."

Nell sailed past her, the order pad in her hand fluttering. "I may be in love," she murmured.

"Really?" Annie gave her an amused look.

"When you're my age, you figure it out sooner. No time to waste, dear."

"Whatever you say, Nell."

Summoned by her son, who'd been besieged by the ski bunnies, Nell scurried away. Annie headed for the inner door, pulling on her gloves and pushing it open just as someone came through the swinging doors on the outside, a tall man who was silhouetted by the sun.

She nearly ran into Stone's broad chest.

"Oh—it's you. Hi."

"Nice to see you too," he said dryly. "You leaving?"

"Yes. Going home."

"How did it go with your dad?"

Annie hesitated, not wanting to give him the time of day, let alone a straight answer.

"He was actually okay about it. Teased me a little. That was all."

Stone nodded. "Good to hear. So I guess he's not going to come after me with a shotgun or anything."

"No. He didn't seem to think my honor needed defending."

Annie stepped to the side, about to go around him.

"Well, I have to go in," he said with a trace of reluctance. "I'm meeting someone. They could be here already."

Annie kept on going. "The place is packed."

"See you around."

She pretended she didn't hear him say that and she didn't answer. Annie didn't plan to return to town until the night of the Christmas pageant. And that was several days away.

Chapter 20

Annie was backstage, fielding complaints as she helped her little shepherds get into their burlap costumes.

"I'm hot."

"This itches."

"When do we go on?"

She responded to all of them simultaneously. "Go stand by the fan until the curtain opens. Stop scratching. You're on right after the star."

The choir director had decided on having Tina, a girl with a sweet soprano voice, play the Star of Wonder. She would climb a ladder to the painted sky, where there was a platform for her to sit on and sing a solo.

Tina stood in front of a mirror, tucking a few stray locks of her hair inside the silver-paper star that circled her face. Her mom tightened the elastic strap that held it on. The rest of her was draped in dark cloth the same color as the sky.

"Tina has a neat costume," one of the boys said,

a touch of envy in his voice. "I wish we could be stars too."

"There's only room for one on the platform. Now don't forget to look up at her when Opal gives you your cue," Annie advised them.

"We will," they promised.

"Where's that sheep?" she asked, looking around.

"Some of the high school kids made extras. We have a whole bunch now."

"We do?" Annie looked around again, not seeing even one cotton-puff sheep. Then Nell's son appeared, pushing a hand truck loaded with the new critters. "Oh. There they are."

She waved Harold over so he could unload them. "They're on skateboard wheels," he explained. "And each one has a handle in back, so the kids can roll them along. Worked fine at the dress rehearsal."

Something Annie had missed after not marking it on her calendar. "I'll take your word for it."

The boys did seem to know how to manage the prop sheep. They rolled them back and forth, working off a little nervous energy before the performance. The crew-cut kid who had stayed more or less in charge of the others set his sheep aside and went to peek through the curtain.

"Don't do that," Annie said. They didn't have to whisper, what with the recorded carols playing over the sound system.

"Nobody saw me," he reassured her. "There's tons of people out there. And more coming in."

"Good. I hope we sell out. More money for the youth group."

"Can I go see?" asked the littlest boy.

"Nope. Everyone line up with their sheep. Miss Opal is here."

The choir director had hurried into the backstage area, dressed in wine-red velvet, her hair beautifully styled.

Annie looked down at her jeans and plain sweater. Nothing special, but her clothes were comfortable and no one was going to see her.

Opal rehearsed Tina for a minute or so, then moved to the other young performers. She smoothed Jenny's hair and bent down to pat little Zoe's cheek. The sisters didn't have speaking parts, but they had insisted on participating. The shepherds quit horsing around when Opal reached them.

"Hello, boys. How's the flock? Are the new sheep cooperating?"

"Yes, ma'am," they chorused.

"Well, they look great and so do you," the choir director said approvingly. "Oh, I wish we could've had a camel," she whispered to Annie. "Maybe next year."

The children fidgeted as Opal made sure all was in readiness. They grew quiet when the lights on the other side of the curtains dimmed and the audience noise died down.

Opal stepped through and welcomed the audience. An unseen hand pulled the curtains apart and the pageant began.

The star entered and went up the ladder, sitting down on the platform atop it for her solo. Annie waited until Tina had sung the first few bars, then gave the first shepherd a little push. He was staring at the audience from the wings, transfixed, completely missing the choir director's repeated cues.

"Go," she whispered urgently. He got over his stage fright at the sound of her voice and led the others on without a hitch.

They rolled their sheep and stopped on a strip of colored tape as one, gazing up at the Star of Wonder. Tina was warbling away, obviously enjoying the spotlight. When she was done, the crew-cut shepherd held up his crook and said his line. "Behold!"

The word echoed to wild applause.

Annie was proud of them all. She peered out into the audience, seeing her parents and Nell, and Ed and Cilla Rivers, all sitting together. Ed had a mini video recorder up and running to get every minute of the performance, especially scenes that included Jenny and Zoe; she was sure of it. There were lots of other people she knew but hadn't caught up with in a while. It was great. Nothing could spoil this night.

Tina finished her song and climbed down. The shepherds rolled on and out. Annie was supposed to meet them at the other side of the stage, but she didn't get there in time.

She'd spotted Marshall Stone in the last row. There was an empty seat beside him. It was the only one left. The show had sold out.

Never in a million years would she have expected him to attend a family event like this. At least he was alone. For now, she told herself crossly, tearing her gaze away from his tall form. She ran around the back of the stage to get to her little guys before they scattered.

"How'd we do?" they whispered excitedly.

"Shh. You did great. Now we have to go out the back way very quietly and then you can watch the rest of the pageant."

They peeled off the itchy burlap costumes they wore over their regular clothes and tossed them into the laundry sack Annie held out. "Stack the sheep over there," she murmured, pointing. "Then follow me."

They obeyed and trotted after her, not jostling each other too much and not making any noise. She led them outside the building through a narrow alley and in again, down a corridor that ran across the back of the hall. There was a low balustrade that separated the viewing area from the seats and they were happy to lean on it and watch their friends in action.

Annie watched Marshall. There was still no one in the seat next to him. One long arm was stretched over its back. She craned her neck. He'd put his Stetson on the empty seat, as if he was reserving it for whoever hadn't showed.

She felt a certain pleasure in the fact that he'd been stood up and she hoped the redhead had done it. Stone seemed relaxed, though. His attention was on the performance, which he seemed to be enjoying completely.

The first act concluded to even more wild applause and the ceiling lights went on. Many in the audience stood and stretched. Some headed out to the front of the hall, where candy and snacks were being sold to raise additional funds.

Annie sat back when Marshall rose. He looked around at the doors, and the people passing in and out. Then his hat went flying.

Her eyes widened. Rowdy, sporting a huge red bow, had jumped up on the empty seat to greet some kids.

They patted him while he wagged his tail. Annie couldn't help eavesdropping.

"Did he like the pageant?"

"He loved it. And thanks for the last-minute tickets, kids. Rowdy wasn't expecting to be treated to a show."

"How come he didn't sit in the seat?" a young boy wanted to know.

"He generally prefers the floor," was Stone's answer.

"We thought he'd sit in it because he's so famous," a girl insisted. "After he herded us onto the float, everyone was talking about him. That's why we stuck the red bow on him."

"You hear that, Rowdy?" Marshall looked down at him. "You're a VIP. I just get to hold your leash."

Rowdy barked, only once, but heads turned.

"I think I'd better get him outside for the rest of the intermission," Stone told the kids. They stepped back to let him proceed up the aisle. He turned sideways to ease out of the narrow space between seat rows and lifted his gaze.

"Hello, Annie."

She waggled her fingers at him. "Hi."

"We're going out to, uh, get some fresh air. Want to join us?" Marshall asked.

"I have to stay with my group."

"You can go with him," a boy solemnly assured. "We'll be good. We promise, right, guys?"

"Yeah." Seven times over.

Annie shook her head. "Miss Opal would never let me hear the end of it if I left you angels to your own devices."

"But we're not angels," the crew-cut boy protested.

"Exactly my point." She turned to speak to Marshall again, but Rowdy had tugged him away.

The lights had dimmed when he returned and took his seat again. The dog lay at his feet, where Annie couldn't see him.

The boys had joined their parents in the audience and she was alone in the same spot. He hadn't looked up at her when he'd come back with Rowdy and she hadn't really minded that much.

The pageant continued. Missed cues, forgotten lines, and kids stepping on each other's costumes—none of it mattered, compared to the good time they were having and the magic they were creating. It was a night to remember for Velde's youngsters.

And for Annie.

She moved back into the shadows and slouched way down in a different seat when she saw her mother and father get up after the finale, hoping they wouldn't see her as they headed up the aisle. Annie had no idea what, if anything, her dad had told her mom about where she'd been the other night—the subject hadn't come up. If they saw her in Stone's vicinity, it just might.

They were picking their way through a crowd of people and didn't look up. Annie could watch the scene without anyone seeing her. The same kids plus a few more of their friends were already clustered around Rowdy. Lou stopped and patted her husband's arm.

"Oh, Ty, will you look at that adorable pooch. What would you say he is?"

Her father's expert eye for animals got it right the first time. "Cattle dog, mixed breed. And I do believe that's the one who was helping out at the parade," Tyrell said. "Got his picture in the paper, herding kids."

So it wasn't just the Internet outage Annie had missed out on. The local news had been tossed into the kindling box before she'd read it.

Her mother seemed to want to speak to Stone. The Bennetts stood in the aisle, the departing audience members flowing around them, until most of the kids drifted away. Tyrell exchanged a few words with Stone, and then, to her amazement, clapped him on the shoulder.

"I coulda used a dog like that for my three back in the day. You train him yourself?"

Stone chuckled and looked down at his dog, who had scrambled up from under the seat. "No, sir. I only found him a few weeks ago. He'd run off from somewhere and been on his own for a while. No microchip or tag. He made it pretty clear that I needed a dog."

Tyrell smiled slightly.

"I knew from the looks of him that he was a herder," Stone continued, "but not that he could do what he did. He's the reason I got the last two tickets. The kids wanted to see him again."

"Oh. Well, he got his picture in the paper."

"Didn't see it."

"I'll ask the gal in the *Register* office to send you a copy. Where are you staying?"

Her father already knew the answer to that question. Maybe he just didn't want Stone to know *how* he knew.

"Nell Dighton's rental cabin."

Her father nodded. "Tell you what. I'll drop it off at the saloon. She'll make sure you get it."

"Thanks," Stone said. "I appreciate that. I don't know how much longer I'll be staying in Velde. Always a new assignment. I'm nearly done here."

"Ah. I did want to ask you about that."

Annie tensed. Her mother had let go of her husband's arm and turned to chat with a friend.

"As you know, Chuck Pfeffer and I disagree about the precise location of the boundary line between our ranches. I believe I'm entitled to a copy of the surveyor's report."

"You certainly are. And I'll make sure you get one."

Tyrell harrumphed, as if he hadn't anticipated instant cooperation. "Thank you. I look forward to reading it."

Stone's back was to her, but Annie guessed from the tone of his voice that he expected her father to be pleased with the results.

That was even more interesting than the fact

that her father had sought him out and talked to him.

Annie edged farther back into the darkness. She ought to be able to sneak out and get in her truck before the two men were done talking; she might even get home first and hole up in her room where she could think.

The empty seat beside Marshall had been meant for Rowdy. But she'd still seen him with the red-head a few days ago. And now she knew for sure that he was leaving town. Probably before Christmas.

So that was that. A new year would begin and he would be long gone. Annie told herself not to care. But the thought of him leaving still hurt.

Chapter 21

"That's a wicked cold wind out there. Just listen to it."

Marta, the line cook on the night shift, unbuttoned her white kitchen coat and slung it over the back of a metal chair across from Bree Rivers.

Bree shook her head and dumped another teaspoon of sugar in the mug of creamy coffee in front of her. "I'd rather not."

"No getting away from it," Marta said. "Any more brew on the burner?"

"Yes. I just made a fresh pot. I'll get you some."

The winter gale howled outside the cinderblock building. Listening to it, Bree frowned. She felt sometimes like the North Dakota wind could get in and find her. It blew into her dreams and troubled her sleep.

"Thanks," Marta said. "Black is fine." She was a stocky woman with gnarled hands that had done too much kitchen work to ever be smooth again. Her hair had never gone completely gray, but silver threads showed in the dark braids wound around her head.

Bree drank the rest of her coffee quickly, then brought the mug with her for a refill, taking another from the china cart that had just been rolled out of the industrial dishwasher. She cradled it in her palm. It was nice and warm and heavy. The mugs were nearly unbreakable, like practically everything else in the barracks-style cafeteria attached to the huge kitchen at the oil field base.

It never closed. Cooks and dishwashers and buffet servers worked around the clock. There was always another shift of riggers and roughnecks slamming through the metal doors, muttering about being half starved and colder than a dead cow.

At least they appreciated the food, so long as it was plentiful and hot.

"Here you go." Bree returned and set the filled mug in front of Marta.

The other cook wrapped both hands around it and inhaled the aroma. "I need this."

"Don't you go to bed right after your shift?" Bree asked.

"Not always. Sometimes I can't. I think this is going to be one of those times. They're stepping up production out there. More guys, longer chow lines, more stress. Everything aches."

"Put a nice fat paycheck on the spot where it hurts the most," Bree advised with a wry smile.

"You're right about that. I saved most of mine."

"I did too. Nothing up here to spend it on, right?"

"You got those two little girls to think about."

"I miss them so damn much." Bree's hazel eyes were suspiciously shiny. "My cousin Cilla keeps me posted on everything they do. She and her husband never had kids, but they treat them like grandchildren. She's my angel. I know they're safe with her."

"You wouldn't stick around here if they weren't," Marta said.

"No." Bree sighed. She took off her kitchen cap and smoothed her curly dark hair, then replaced the cap. "At least we can video chat, but it's not the same."

"I understand." Marta nodded glumly. "Even though I never had kids and never wanted any."

"It's not like Cilla had to take them in, either. She's a lot older than me and we're only cousins by marriage. But she made me promise I wouldn't stay here indefinitely."

"Fat chance. Take the money and run," Marta said, rubbing her lower back with one hand.

"I will. Soon as I have enough."

Marta stood up wearily. "Think about it. Maybe you do."

"Huh?"

"Go home for Christmas. You mean a lot more to those little sweethearts than the dough."

"They only have me, Marta. And I don't know when I'll get a chance to earn this much money again."

The other cook shook her head, not in the mood to argue.

"Want to see the Christmas pageant they were in?" Bree took out her smartphone and tapped the screen to bring up the video.

"Sure."

"Jenny and Zoe aren't in every scene, but—oh. There they are, rehearsing. And the young lady in back of them is Annie. They think the world of her. She's the daughter of my cousin's best friend—"

"Draw me a diagram," Marta said gruffly. But she listened patiently as Bree kept right on explaining. Then she got up.

"Wait. You can't go yet. There's more," Bree said. "A lot more."

Marta seemed resigned to her fate. After a while she even thawed. "Aww. Those kids are so cute I can hardly stand it. And your little girls are the cutest of all. How can you bear to be away from them for so long?"

"I'm counting the days," Bree replied. There was a stubborn set to her tired mouth. "I signed on through January in order to get the holiday bonus. That's two months' extra pay right there."

"I know," Marta said. "But I still think you should get home for Christmas. Come to think of it, I could cover for you. If I work twice as hard, the head cook won't even notice you're gone." She stretched and flinched when a muscle in her side caught. "Ouch."

"No way."

Marta scowled at her and walked off.

*　*　*

The tall blue spruce from the Bennett ranch had been strung with lights and outdoor decorations. Around it was most of the children's choir and nearly every other youngster and adult in Velde.

The afternoon light was fading fast and the kids were restless. Opal raised a gloved hand and the choir launched into a rousing rendition of "Jingle Bells," to get everyone singing along. Mrs. Pearson, a quavery but determined soprano, joined in too. Annie held the hands of Jenny and Zoe, who'd run to her when Ed and Cilla gave the okay. Then Nell, who'd supplied most of the decorations from her stash, did the honors and flipped the switch.

Bright eyes reflected the dazzling illumination as everyone clapped and cheered, with Annie and her parents joining in. Photos were snapped, invitations exchanged, and the tree-lighting ceremony was over.

Attendees wandered off with bigger kids in tow. The little ones insisted on being carried and more than one young head rested on a grown-up shoulder. Not to fall asleep, but for one last look at the magical beauty of the tree.

Cilla took charge of the little girls again. They seemed more wistful than wowed by the tree, and stayed close to her. Zoe, the younger of the two, hid inside the folds of Cilla's big warm poncho like a baby chick.

"Bye, Annie." Jenny waved to her as Ed led the way to their car.

"So long." Annie smiled. "See you around."

"Are you coming back with us or staying in town?" The question came from her mom. Lou Bennett turned away from her husband, who was digging in a pocket for the keys to his truck.

"Coming back," Annie said, as if they should have known that. "Let's get a roaring fire going and warm up, get started on the Christmas cookies."

"Okay," Tyrell said. "I was thinking we could talk to the boys on the laptop."

"Good idea. Us Bennetts have to stay in touch." Her mom sighed. "We get farther apart every year."

Annie slid her arm through her mother's. "I'm right here. So don't talk like that."

"Okay, honey."

Nell ushered Mrs. Pearson into the saloon. "There's my son, all grown up. He's not as cute as he used to be but he turned out fine."

Harold was tending bar. A new waitress had been hired for the season and was busy taking orders from several tables.

"My goodness. So this is your place," Mrs. Pearson said. "It's very cozy. I approve."

Nell guided her to a back booth. "We can have this all to ourselves. What would you like? A glass of sherry?"

"That would be very nice. You wouldn't happen to have a cookie to go with it, would you?"

"Annie Bennett brought me a box of her mom's Christmas cookies. You sit down and I'll bring everything." She helped the old lady with her coat and hung it on the hook by the booth, then bustled away.

She returned with two tiny glasses, a bottle of sherry, and the cookie box, setting everything down and sliding into the vinyl seat bench across from Elsie's.

"What a treat this is. Thank you for picking me up."

"Now that you have some help, you can get out more. It'll do you good." Nell uncorked the bottle and poured out a thimbleful of sherry for the old lady, who chose a fancy iced cookie to go with it. Mrs. Pearson took a sip and coughed a little. "I don't remember the last time I had a drink." A faint tinge of color reddened her cheeks.

The saloon keeper filled her own small glass and clinked it against Mrs. Pearson's. "Here's to the holidays."

They chatted for a while, not noticing who came and went.

Marshall Stone entered alone, heading for the bar. He glanced at the two women in the back booth, deciding not to go over and say hello. They were deep in conversation and seemed to be the best of friends, although the lady with Nell looked to be at least a generation older.

The saloon looked about the same as always, except for a model of a covered wagon displayed in a glass case on the bar. Even from across the room, the craftsmanship and detail were impressive.

He ordered a beer and drank it slowly, thinking about his dinner options, not inclined to bring takeout back to the cabin and not particularly wanting to dine solo in public. In this friendly little town, he was beginning to be recognized everywhere he went.

Another reason he needed to move on. But he still hadn't checked a single bad guy off his list. Stone reached into the bowl of peanuts and ate a few, listening absently to what he could hear of Nell's chitchat and the old lady's infrequent responses.

His mind was elsewhere. On Annie. He still couldn't figure out exactly why her dad had stopped to talk to him.

Yes, sir. No, sir. I'd be happy to provide you with a copy of the report, sir. And by the way, I think I'm falling in love with your daughter. Hope you don't mind.

Tyrell Bennett might not have minded her bunking down at the cabin, but he would hit the roof if he ever knew what Stone had been thinking during every minute Annie was there.

The way she moves. Those eyes. That smile.

He wanted to see her smile more. Annie worried about everyone else and not herself, it seemed to him. According to that fountain of information known as Nell, she was a dutiful daughter and a good friend, loyal and loving.

However, Annie stopped short of being too good to be true—there was something wild and sweetly enticing about her and she didn't strike him as innocent. Exactly what he'd been looking for, in fact, without his ever knowing it until the day he'd seen her face. Stone had never expected to meet a woman who was so damn close to perfect.

But she wasn't his. He would have to hit the road again when this assignment was over. It would be irresponsible and wrong to go one step further with beautiful Annie Bennett.

He forced himself to not think about her.

There was the report—he'd have to print out a hard copy somehow. He'd e-mailed the file to the town clerk, who was fine with that. But Tyrell Bennett would want something he could hold in his hand to read and reread.

The old man was absolutely right about being entitled to see the surveyor's report. All owners of abutting land were supposed to, whether or not there was a dispute going on. And Bennett would be very pleased to have proof that Chuck Pfeffer had most likely reset the old split rail fence and also moved the new one that backed it.

Stone took several swallows of beer. The peanuts were making him thirsty. The thought of someone trying to put something over on honorable people like the Bennetts was making him mad all over again.

Pfeffer must have assumed that Tyrell never got out that far and wouldn't notice. But Stone had compared his new, accurate measurements against the old ones on the original deed. Numbers didn't lie. This particular neighbor did.

The sneak would have to give back every inch of the land grab he'd hoped to get away with and pay for a new fence. If he tried to unload his ranch first, he wouldn't be able to. Stone had alerted the town clerk to the discrepancy, which meant Pfeffer didn't have a clear title and couldn't sell.

Tough luck.

If only Stone could resolve the fraud case that easily. All he needed was to nab one of the crooks to get him to rat out the others as part of a plea bargain. Shep Connally had been his choice. But the silver-haired con man had slipped away after giving that speech at the Velde town meeting, except for that one time they'd spotted him going through Kerry's car.

She hadn't been able to track him down either, not even after she'd been assigned to the next county as an undercover and started to look for him in different towns farther away. Their subsequent meetings added nothing to the Connally file.

Most likely Shep was using an alias. His MO was undoubtedly the same, starting with offering "free" financial and investment advice to senior citizens' groups. Shep and his kind preyed on the most vulnerable and they knew how to get old folks to trust them and believe their promises—before they cleaned out bank accounts and skipped town one step ahead of the law.

For Stone, the chase had lost its excitement. After this case got wrapped up, he would move on. But to what, he didn't exactly know.

Annie Bennett had thrown him for a loop. He'd

always made it a point not to get involved with anyone when he was on assignment. Especially not in small towns, or with a rancher's daughter.

Which meant she was all about family. It was clear to him that the Bennetts stuck together—and Annie was the youngest and the only girl to boot. Never mind her father. She had two older brothers he had yet to meet. Stone would have to prove himself to all three of the Bennett men if he wanted to claim her for his own.

Whatever it takes. The thought came into his mind unbidden. Stone wished there was a way to not want her.

Keeping a safe distance from her at the cabin had been hard. Real hard.

If Annie only knew how he had suffered, lying on the floor, struggling to get comfortable in that narrow sleeping bag, listening to her soft breathing, hearing her stir as she dreamed. He'd fallen asleep just before dawn and woken up to dog breath and a wet nose in his eye.

Yeah. If she'd known, she would have laughed at him and rightly so.

The noise level in the bar had risen as more customers came in. The two women talking in the nearby booth raised their voices slightly.

Stone was startled to hear the old lady with Nell mention Shep Connally. He hadn't been listening long enough to pick up the reason why. He paid close attention, continuing to look into the bar mirror and not directly at them.

"I finally told him that we had no plans to sell. Not to him or anyone else." The old lady leaned across the table part of the booth, but her whisper carried farther than that. "Did you know that he carries bundles of cash in a briefcase? He snapped it open and I just got a glimpse. I think he was trying to impress me." She sat back. "I still said no."

Stone stayed where he was. He set a buck under the empty beer mug, figuring that he would talk to Nell as soon as he got a chance. Maybe there was more. There had to be more.

"You mean you're planning to set up a sting?" Nell clapped her hands. "I've never been so excited in my life."

"You can't broadcast this all over town," Stone said firmly. "In fact, you can't tell anyone. In advance or afterward. We still have to catch the others."

"Goodness no. I won't breathe a word."

Mrs. Pearson laughed dryly. "I'm holding you to that, Nelly girl."

"Well, if I did, both of you would know it was me. So I can't."

"Right. And from what Mr. Stone has told us, you're not going to be actually involved."

"I could sit outside in my car and monitor the video feed from the scene."

"Two deputies in unmarkeds will do that before they station themselves at the doors," Stone said.

Nell visibly deflated. Then she brightened. "What if I take Jack out? He's not going to be there for this, I assume."

"One more time," Stone said patiently. "Mrs.

Pearson is going to ask the home health-care aide to drive Jack to the library and stay there with him for a couple of hours. He's been asking to go."

"That's correct," the old lady confirmed.

"Neither he nor the aide will know anything about this in advance or afterward."

Nell nodded. "Makes sense."

"My partner Kerry is going to pretend to be the aide in a wig and uniform, and she'll wear non-functional earbuds so he'll think she can't hear him and Mrs. Pearson. She'll sit with me in a darkened room, because Connally may know what Kerry looks like. He broke into her car. And I am going to be Jack. With the help of this."

Stone held up a can of white spray-on hair dye.

"I know what I can do." Nell cheered up again. "I'll style you. And Kerry too, if she likes."

"That should keep you out of trouble. We want this to go as smoothly as possible."

"I promise to vamoose and not come back until you call me or Elsie does. But is she going to be safe? How do you know what a cornered man might do?" Nell asked.

"We don't. Kerry and I both have guns for a reason. And we will have the advantage of surprise. I'm not that worried. Shep's never been violent and never even threatened anyone. He's not going to want to add twenty years or more to his sentence by assaulting federal officers. He might try to escape, though. But the deputies will be at the front and back doors by then."

"Besides," Mrs. Pearson said to Nell, gesturing at Stone, "look at the size of this man. He's taller

and stronger than Jack and fifty years younger.
Would you try to bust out if you were a perp? With
Stone packing serious heat? I don't think so."

They both stared at her.

"What's wrong? I enjoy a good cop show now
and then," the old lady said primly.

"Nothing." Stone suppressed a smile. "I just
never expected to hear you talk like that. This isn't
a show, though. It is a sting and it's the real deal. I
can't tell you how much I appreciate your cooperation, Mrs. Pearson."

"Connally called me right back. I suspect he hasn't
found any other takers. I'm looking forward to doing
my bit."

Nell sighed with admiration. Mrs. Pearson only
shrugged.

Stone set down the spray can of dye and Nell
peered at the instructions on the back. "Says it
washes right out."

"Good," Stone said.

"After five shampoos." Nell laughed at the concerned look on his face. "Not really. I was kidding."

"That's okay. I can take it. And, Nell, I want you
to know that I appreciate your help too. Real estate fraud is big business. Land in Colorado gets
more valuable every year."

"Don't I know it. My property taxes keep going up."

Stone acknowledged that with a nod.

"I think, Mrs. Pearson, that Connally won't do
more than try to obtain financial power of attorney by having you sign something and then forg-

ing your signature on real documents. All he wants to do is empty your bank account and skip town."

"I took out all the money just in case. I can't wait to see him arrested," the old lady said gently.

A few days later, they were ready to roll. Connally was due to arrive at the Pearson house in two hours.

Stone squeezed his eyes shut as Nell, wearing safety glasses and a huge scarf over her own hair, climbed onto a stool and sprayed his dark hair. She set down the can and quickly combed in the white dye for a pepper-and-salt look, heavy on the salt.

"That's believable," she said with satisfaction, climbing down. "I have a shirt of Jack's laid out if you want to change into it."

"I'll wear my own. A shirt is a shirt. Thanks. Go help Kerry."

Nell took off the glasses and scarf, and went into the other room.

At the appointed time, there was a knock at the door. "All set?" Mrs. Pearson whispered to Stone and Kerry.

"Yup. Kerry?"

"Yes."

They sat in semidarkness, watching Mrs. Pearson go to the door. "Mr. Connally, how nice to see you. I'm so happy you could come."

He offered her a smile and looked toward the

adjoining room. Stone and Kerry had turned away from the open door.

"Is that your husband?" Connally asked. "Who's with him?"

"The aide. Don't worry. He's much less restless when she sits with him quietly. And she's always wearing those darn earbuds. Can't hear a thing I say from the next room."

"All right then."

He followed her to the table, took a sheaf of papers out of his briefcase, and settled into a chair, refusing Mrs. Pearson's offer of a hot drink. Then he launched into his pitch. She listened carefully, asking a question now and then. Connally was smooth and fast. It only took him half an hour to explain the deal.

"All you have to do to keep the cash flowing is to sign right there on the dotted line," he said, uncapping a fountain pen.

"What a nice pen," Mrs. Pearson said. "I like the old ones with nibs and real ink."

"I'm a traditionalist myself, Mrs. P. I thought a lady like you might prefer a real pen to one of those cheap plastic things. It makes a document look more dignified, don't you think?"

"I do indeed." She squinted at the paper. "Just tell me one more time what I'll get."

He looked at his watch. "Everything we agreed on."

"So you will hold the deed to my house in trust and invest the profit for me if I should decide to sell—"

"Which is entirely up to you. No pressure, Mrs.

P. I do business the old-fashioned way. I trust you. And you trust me. So we are entering into a trust agreement by mutual consent. Go right ahead and sign."

Mrs. Pearson was still studying the document. "And if I sell the house and there is sufficient profit, I receive the income from that trust."

"Yes, yes." He tapped the dotted line. "If you would sign. I do have a bit of a time crunch."

She held the fountain pen poised above the paper, then scribbled her name. "Wait!" she cried. "How could I make a mistake like that?"

"I beg your pardon?"

"I used my maiden name instead of my married name. I don't think this is legal."

The last six words were what Stone and Kerry had been waiting to hear. Before Connally could turn around, they had him cuffed to the chair he was sitting in.

"Shepherd Connally, you are under arrest."

"What for?" The question sounded almost rhetorical. The man knew.

"For financial fraud. Right here and right now." Stone picked up the papers from the table, looking closely at the bottom one that Mrs. Pearson hadn't been able to see when she signed it. "She never agreed to give you power of attorney. So the DA will start with that. And you know good and goddamn well that you're suspected of fraud and under investigation for other crimes in several states."

Stone tested the cuffs, looking up when the deputies entered. He moved to face Connally and continued. "It is my duty to inform you that you have the right to remain silent. Anything you say can and will be used against you in a court of law. If you do not have an attorney . . ."

Nell came in the front door, her eyes bright with excitement. "I saw him being taken away in the unmarked car, but I waited to walk over. Are all of you okay? What happens now?"

She looked at Stone and Kerry, who were sitting at the table, filling out arrest reports. "Paperwork," they answered simultaneously. "They never do this on cop shows."

Nell averted her gaze. "I won't peek. Elsie, dear, I'm sure you need a cup of tea."

"Thank you, Nell. That would be very pleasant."

"My goodness. You're so calm."

"It's over. I don't want to think about it. But don't forget your vow of silence."

"My lips are zipped. Not one word to anyone. No need to remind me."

Mrs. Pearson gave her a shaky smile. "Nell. I just want to say thanks. For everything. You did more than you know."

Chapter 22

The day was cold and clear, with a stiff breeze that blew snow crystals off the remaining drifts. Annie's eyes teared up as she blinked and rubbed her stinging cheeks with her mittens. She should have put on lotion but she hadn't. Now she would look like a doll. Oh well. There were worse fates than having red cheeks and shining eyes.

She'd come into town to pick up hardware items for her dad. The cold snap was making his knees ache and he hadn't been up to the drive.

Ahead of her on the sidewalk was a wrought-iron bench and on it was Marshall Stone, absorbed in a newspaper that he held in gloved hands, his collar turned up against the cold and his Stetson pulled down to block the sun.

He didn't hear her coming. Annie stopped in front of him and he finally looked up.

"Hello. Haven't seen you in a few days." Annie kept her tone casual. Where he went and what he did really were none of her concern. Exactly why he was sitting on a bench outside the town laundromat wasn't, either. But she asked anyway. "What are you doing here?"

"Hey, Annie." He set aside the newspaper. "Rowdy's bed was getting doggy and this place has big machines. Too hot for me in there, though, so I came out. Just thought I'd do all my laundry before—oops."

Before what? Was he vacating the cabin? About to leave town?

The newspaper went flying. He stood and collected most of it, fighting the breeze to put it back together, more or less. Some of the pages were torn.

"There's an article I wanted to keep," he explained.

Annie tried to seem interested. "On what?"

"A real estate scam, a big one near Denver." He stuck the newspaper under his arm. "They used eminent domain to move long-term residents off property that was then condemned. It's complicated. Am I boring you yet?"

"Not really."

"Thanks for being tactful." He grinned at her. "Can I take you out for a cup of coffee or something?"

"Don't you have to watch your laundry?"

"I don't think anyone's going to steal it." He looked at her hopefully. "I'd like to talk to you."

Annie shrugged that off. If he was planning to make a big deal out of what should be an ordinary good-bye, she didn't feel like listening. "Um, thanks. But no. I really have to get back to the ranch. I just came in to pick up some screws and stuff for my dad."

He looked through the window of the Laundromat. It was a pleasant place, new, that attracted ski tourists and other people just passing through. There didn't seem to be any other customers. There were only two machines in use, side by side, sloshing away.

"Too bad. I have time."

How nice of him to fit her in between Soak and Spin. Annie frowned and stepped past him.

"Don't walk away."

Give me one good reason not to. She didn't say the words, just pulled out the list from her pocket and waved it at him. "Too many things to do. You know how it is."

Stone took two long strides to catch up to her. "Come on, Annie. Don't be like that. I meant to call you. I've been busy myself."

She stopped. The terse explanation didn't mollify her. "Of course. Fences and boundary markers just do not wait. If you weren't out there making sure everything lines up, they would uproot themselves and walk away."

A smile flickered around the corners of his mouth. "Interesting way to put it. Fences have been known to move. Rocks too. But it's usually people who do the moving."

"Uh-huh. What are you getting at?"

"I'll walk you to the hardware store," he said without answering the question. "In case you need help carrying anything."

She consulted the list. "Spring latch for bathroom cabinet. Picture hooks. Wood screws, small box. I can probably manage all that."

His gloved hand caught her arm above the elbow. Annie pulled, but he wouldn't let her go. It was broad daylight, but that darkly commanding look in his eyes didn't brighten.

"What's the matter?" His voice was low, though there was no one passing by.

"Nothing. I really am busy."

Stone let go of her arm and watched her walk away. He headed back to the Laundromat and went in, setting down the newspaper before he took off his jacket and hat. She'd really frosted his shorts. He needed to warm up.

After a while, the washing machines shuddered to a halt. Stone pulled out the wet wash and got everything into a dryer. Then he reread the article for something to do while he waited a second time.

He knew the Denver division office had paid for the public-service ad that ran next to the article. They'd also made sure that no mention of Shep Connally's arrest appeared in the newspapers or any other media outlets.

Connally hadn't talked much, and he probably wouldn't until he sat down for milk and cookies with the DA, who was on vacation until January. Extra weeks added to the waiting game.

At least it gave Stone more time with Annie. Or—he amended the thought—more time to figure out what was bugging Annie. He wished he could tell her the truth about who he was and what

he was doing. The twists and turns of the complicated case were getting in his way.

She didn't trust him. He could see it in her eyes.
And there was no way to reassure her. Stone tossed
the newspaper into the tall trash can by the window just before she walked by it, not looking in.

"We'll be seeing clear skies across the Rockies
and out over the Plains for the next few days," the
weatherman announced, "with scattered snow and
extreme cold to the east into North Dakota."

Bree reached for the remote and turned down
the volume on the kitchen TV. She went back to
the stew simmering on the multi-burner range in
several huge pots, lifting the lid of each and stir-
ring.

"That's us," a line cook muttered. "I can't stand
this weather."

Bree picked up a large bowl of chopped vegetables and put handfuls into each pot. "It's warm in
here," she said philosophically.

He only grunted.

She looked out beyond the pass-through window into the cafeteria. A shift of workers was just
finishing, rising to empty their trays and get back
to work. The clanging racket of cutlery and metal
was so familiar, she barely noticed it by now.

"I'm going on break," Bree told her coworker.

"Okay. Eat something."

The kitchen staff looked after each other in a
no-nonsense way. For the most part, there was no

time for small gestures of friendship. They worked practically round the clock. No slacking off allowed. The pace was relentless.

Bowls of rice pudding, each topped with a maraschino cherry, were lined up by the hundreds on rolling shelves. She took a bowl, wanting something bland at the moment.

Bree nibbled at the cherry as she went through the swinging doors into the echoing cafeteria. A heavyset field boss waved her over to sit with him and his crew. They'd been here the longest, earned the most, and were on friendly terms with a lot of people from the kitchen.

"Hi, Karl. Hi, guys."

A stern glare from Karl and the others slid down to make space for her on the bench.

"What is that?" Karl asked, looking at the creamy glop in the bowl she set down.

"Rice pudding."

He shook his graying, buzz-cut head. "Thought it was oatmeal. Either way, it's all yours."

"I wasn't planning to share it," she teased him. She ate a few spoonfuls, then put the spoon down.

"No appetite? Or does it taste as bad as it looks?" Karl asked. The other guys guffawed.

"I'm not hungry," Bree said. She really wasn't. She'd only helped herself to the pudding because the line cook had told her to eat something.

"Well, don't go away," Karl said. He moved the bowl to the center of the table. "Me and the boys want to make you a proposition."

Bree gave him a wary look, even though she knew Karl was married and had a daughter her age plus younger kids. Besides, he never let any of the roughnecks on his crew say a rude word to her.

"Really." The one word seemed like a safe enough reply.

"We heard—don't ask me how—that you aren't going home for Christmas."

"That's right."

"No. That's wrong," Karl growled.

"It's my business, not yours." Bree wasn't annoyed by his blunt comments, just drawing a line. Sometimes you had to with these guys.

Karl looked at the others. "You hear that? With all due respect to this nice lady, I don't agree."

"Me neither."

"Nope."

And so on, up and down the table.

Bree was puzzled. The older man understood something about what she was going through, though he was happily married. He had five boys at home in Kansas who were a lot younger than his grown daughter. "Don't tease me, Karl," she said quietly.

"This is no joke, Bree. We passed the hat last night. Give it here."

A man's upside-down hat went from hand to hand until it reached Karl. He placed it in front of her where the rice-pudding bowl had been.

Bree saw the cloth sack inside it. It seemed to be stuffed with bills.

"You may count it at your leisure," Karl said. "There's the gas money you need to get home, plus the bonus you woulda gotten."

"I can't take this."

Karl stared her down. "Oh, yes you can."

Bree looked up and saw Marta by the wall, giving her a smile of encouragement.

"Marta, did you tell them about me and the kids?"

The other cook nodded.

Bree pressed her lips together, her eyes wide and shining as she looked down the table and back at Karl.

"Don't cry," he whispered. "We'll take it all back if you do. Just can't stand it when women cry."

She lowered her head for a silent moment. Then, with a huge grin on her face, she lifted her chin and declared, "Okay! I can't say no!"

Karl confirmed that. "Damn straight. She's going home for the holidays, fellas!"

Bree held up the hat to loud cheers, saying thank you to every man at the table. A few workers on the incoming shift glanced curiously toward their table, until the usual commotion began as hard hats came off and trays were banged down and slid along on the counter railing.

"Guess I should go pack. Oh my. I'm not going to tell the girls. What a surprise."

"Then you have to call me from the road. What's your number? Just so your name comes up. I'll answer right away." He took a smartphone out of the pocket of his workshirt and peered at the screen.

"Ready? It's three-five-seven—"

Karl took a photo of Bree clutching the hat and turned the phone around to show her. "Never seen you look happier."

"That's a fact!" She hugged him to more cheers.

On second thought, Bree called Cilla and Ed Rivers after the girls had gone to bed to tell them she was coming. She promised to keep in touch during the drive. The forecast didn't predict any big storms. Her dented mom-mobile oughta make it.

"You're good to go. We just wanted to be sure." An oil field mechanic walked out from under her car and around the hydraulic lift, holding a lube gun.

"Thanks. I still can't believe I'm going. You've all been incredibly helpful."

He shrugged. "Didn't want you driving all that way to get to them kids without checking your car. I'm thorough, and the crews know it."

He pushed a button to lower the hydraulic lift as Bree watched. Once the tires touched the concrete floor, he patted the hood with a massive hand that looked like it could leave a dent in rolled steel. "Lots of miles on her, but she's still going strong."

"I always remember to have the oil changed and the tires rotated. There's a maintenance booklet in the glove compartment with the dates."

"Yes, ma'am. I took a look at that before I jacked the car," he said politely. "And the engine was in pretty good shape. But we're talking about driving through North Dakota, Wyoming, and Montana in winter. You need your vehicle to be in great shape.

I got it hummin' like a bumblebee now. You'll get to Colorado just fine."

"I can't thank you enough." She fumbled in her purse for a bill—she had a few fifties in there.

The mechanic shook his head, his thick brows drawing together. "Don't even think about paying me," he said. "Just drive safe. You got a long way to go."

Chapter 23

Annie was one of the last riders on the ski lift for the day. Still not cleared to swoop down slopes, she had decided to rattle up, if only for the view. She was solo this time.

She got off at the top and went toward the lodge to buy a cup of tea. It would keep her hands warm. She wanted to be outside, despite the frigid air. The sky was clear, but beginning to darken toward the west, when she brought the cup to a table placed away from the others and sat down.

The town of Velde lit up as the day began to fade away. Every street was strung with lights, every lamp decorated with giant candy canes and Christmas bows. Far below, the scene looked like something inside a snow globe, pretty and sparkling and unreal.

Tiny figures moved about on the sidewalks. Cars, not many, moved slowly down the streets. Some stopped between the traffic lights. Annie figured the people inside were calling to friends, wishing happy holidays to all.

She was going to spend every second of hers surrounded by family. Mother, father, brothers—and now, sisters-in-law she really wanted to know better. There would be plenty to talk about, wonderful food, and good cheer. She was infinitely grateful for all of it.

The aching loneliness she felt would soon pass, Annie told herself.

So would the annoyance known as Marshall Stone. A few kisses and a dance didn't add up to anything permanent.

She sipped the cooling tea, telling herself that she deserved a lot of credit for not getting emotional over Mr. Tall, Dark, and Uncommunicative.

Out in the distance, she saw a lone tree suddenly blaze with colored lights. It was topped with a star that shone golden against the dark blue drifts of snow. A ranch family's tree. Solitary and yet there for all to enjoy.

"Miss? We're closing in fifteen minutes."

Annie looked around. A teenage waitress stood near the lodge, holding a tray. She didn't have a jacket on and probably wasn't going to come over.

Time to go anyway. Annie rose and walked over to give her the empty cup. "Thanks. I was kind of lost in thought."

"No problem."

Back down on the streets, Annie realized that she was now one of the tiny figures in the snow globe. She smiled to herself. The thought sort of helped her get perspective on her situation.

Until she saw Marshall Stone opening the door of his big black truck. She heard static from a car radio inside, something she hadn't noticed when she was riding in it with him. Another one of his gizmos, no doubt.

An emergency call crackled in. She stopped a few feet away and listened, holding a tote with the few grocery items she'd picked up.

"Stone, stand by. We may need you to go rescue a lady. She went off the road into a snowdrift. No injuries. Shook up is all."

"Okay. Got everything but the keg of brandy."

"Seriously, dude." That had to be the new deputy, a former snowboarder. "They got her dug out, but her car's totaled. She needs a ride to town."

"What's going on up there?"

"The pass is a mess. A snow squall blew through. What's it look like in Velde?"

"Clear."

"Hope it lasts. The squall went the other way."

"Storms like that move out fast. How am I going to find you?"

"Look for the black and white. Roof lights are on. We're about ten miles to the west out on the old ridge road. I'll send the coordinates to your GPS app."

Stone took out his smartphone. "Okay." He waited.

Annie stepped back, but not quickly enough. He saw her.

"Annie. Did you hear all that?"

"Yes. How come they're calling you?"

Stone's phone beeped as the coordinates came through. "They need all the help they can get, obviously. Want to come along?"

"I guess I could," she said reluctantly. "But I don't want to drive my truck somewhere I might not be able to get out of."

"I meant come with me."

She hesitated, then nodded. "Okay."

He got behind the wheel as she went around the side, climbing in again. It wasn't a date, she told herself. It was a rescue.

The car radio filled the silence, crackling with news of more stranded drivers. Mountain weather was unpredictable this late in December.

"Any word on who the lady is? From Velde?"

"The deputy didn't say, so maybe. You all seem to know each other."

"We actually don't. The town's not that small."

A loud crackle from the car radio carried the deputy's voice to them. "Stone?"

"On my way."

"The lady says she has family in Velde."

Stone glanced toward Annie. "There you go."

"Her name is Bree Rivers."

Annie sat bolt upright within the confines of her shoulder belt. "That's Cilla's cousin. She's the mom of those two little girls. You saw them."

"I did?"

"At the pageant."

"There were a lot of kids there, Annie."

"Yeah, well—let's get going. I'm glad she's all

right. She took a job at a North Dakota oil field as a cook. Saving her money for a new start. I understood she wasn't coming back until January."

"Maybe she decided to drive down for Christmas."

"Good guess. I wonder if I should call my mother."

"Not yet. Let's go get Bree first."

Annie stared ahead. There was very little traffic. The sudden squall must have overtaken other vehicles besides Bree's. She looked up, realizing that the sky had disappeared behind thick clouds.

"Are we going to get caught in this?"

"He said it went thataway." Stone lifted a hand from the wheel and flipped back the cover on a globe-type compass.

"Look at that."

"It's the real deal. GPS isn't everything."

Red and blue flashes of light tinted the air above the rise in the road. Stone gunned the engine and slowed when he saw the accident scene.

As soon as he stopped Annie jumped out and went to the cruiser. Stone got out and talked to the deputy while Annie peered into the back window.

"Bree? It's me, Annie."

The woman wrapped in the silver heat blanket brightened. She cracked the door to say hello. "Hi. Are you an EMT too?"

"No. I just came along with my friend. We're going to bring you back to town."

"That would be wonderful. I think these guys are needed elsewhere. I guess you heard I went into a snowdrift."

"Yeah. Glad you're okay. Let's get you inside the truck."

She helped Bree out of the back. Bree took off the heat blanket and put it into the cruiser. "Someone else is going to need this."

"No doubt."

Stone was already at the wheel. He'd turned on the wipers to remove the light snow that had begun to fall. "Let's roll out."

"Thanks so much," Bree called to the deputy. The young man in the cruiser wasn't waiting around to chat. He took off, driving up into the pass.

"I'm Stone. You know Annie. Let's go. I don't want to get caught in any more snow."

Annie took a few seconds to make sure Bree was comfortable in the backseat and then got in quickly, putting the grocery tote between her feet.

They drove down the road as the snow began to fall harder. It wasn't long before the flakes were whirling in all directions.

Stone swore under his breath. "Looks like another squall. Not quite here yet. Think we could make a run for the ranch?"

Annie looked out the window, barely recognizing the landmarks. She spotted a wide gate she knew, not on Bennett land, but not far from it.

"Yes. It's up ahead."

Bree was awfully quiet in the backseat. Out of the frying pan, into the fire. "I'm okay," she said in response to Annie's glance over her shoulder.

"Go for it," she told Stone. "I'd rather we were off the road than stuck on it. Right here!"

She'd glimpsed the turnoff at the last second.

He swerved, keeping some control over the steering wheel, but they skidded into a wire fence. Three neon surveyor's tags swept against the window before the wire snapped with a piercing twang.

"Don't worry. Everything's under control," Stone said.

Annie rocked back in the seat, the breath knocked out of her. She heard Bree gasp. "Are you crazy?"

"I know exactly where we are."

"Yeah. So do I. In a whiteout."

"It's not that bad yet." Stone reversed a few feet and gunned the truck again. The wheels spun and grabbed the stubbly ground beneath the snow. "But it will be," he added as they roared forward.

"What are you doing?" Bree gasped.

"Going off-road. The truck is all-terrain. The ranch is due north of those three tags, less than half a mile if I remember right. Keep your eye on that compass."

Annie did, without knowing quite what she was supposed to look for.

The huge truck jolted over uneven ground below, sometimes swerving in and out of potholes they couldn't see.

Ahead were lights. The snow fell more heavily, obscuring them.

"Is that the ranch?"

"Hope so!"

"Hang on," Stone said grimly. They roared ahead. The lights flickered out. "We still going north?"

She clutched the dashboard and peered at the compass. "Yes."

"They may have lost power," Stone muttered.

"Now what do we do?" Annie asked.

"Drive in the dark," he answered with infuriating calm.

A huge gust of wind slammed into the struggling truck. Annie slid to the side. Bree screamed. Another gust from the opposite direction pushed the truck back up.

Even Stone seemed rattled by that. He caught his breath for a few seconds, then forged on.

Annie swore. "The compass fell off."

"Then find it."

"I can't. Not with a seat belt on."

"You have five seconds."

She unlatched it and scrabbled desperately in the foot well, feeling for the smooth globe. "Here."

"Give me that." He slapped it back on the dash and the ball glowed again. Stone revved the engine and maneuvered the truck until the needle hit due north. "Keep me on track. I can't drive through blinding snow and be a Boy Scout at the same time."

"No. Of course not. Didn't expect you to."

"Bree, you good?"

A weak "yes" from the back. Then Annie thought of something. She stared worriedly at the spinning compass.

"What if the directions got scrambled up?"

"It's a goddamn compass, Annie. The needle will always point north. Unless you stepped on it."

"I didn't," she snapped, buckling up again. "Keep going. I think we're okay."

She saw nothing but snow. Then the lights again. Much larger. Square. Very close. A gust blasted the snow off something huge and dark.

"That's the chimney!" she screamed. "Stop!"

Stone slammed on the brakes. Annie went forward and her hand hit a button on the glove compartment. A ton of stuff tumbled out over her lap. She stuck it all into the tote. God only knew what gizmo she might have to find next.

"Bree?" She looked over the seat.

The other woman had a dazed look. "Get me out of here." Annie heard her unbuckle her seat belt. She did the same and so did Stone.

He jumped out and yanked open the back door, dragging Bree toward him and scooping her up in his arms. Head down, Stone carried her through the ranch house door, which Annie's mom and dad had just opened.

Annie took the keys out of the ignition and grabbed everything she could—Bree's purse too. The truck might be buried by morning. It all went into the tote.

Chapter 24

The next hour faded into a daze for the three people who'd been in the truck.

Lou got everyone what they needed. Tyrell followed her lead. Bree was settled in an armchair, on the phone with Cilla and Ed.

"Yes. I made it. I'm fine. There was an accident, but I'm at the Bennetts'. Please don't worry. I'll be there tomorrow. And not a word to the girls."

"She needs to rest," Lou whispered to Annie. "Think of it, her driving all that way and then, wham, a snowstorm."

"*Wham* is the word," Annie said. She was exhausted. Her body ached. So did her head.

"That must have been one hell of a ride, Stone. What kind of truck is that?"

"Custom model. Tricked out to the max." He'd taken a plain wooden chair, seeming unable to relax.

"Well. I think the man at the wheel—you—is the reason everyone got here safe and sound."

"I knew where I was, once I saw the flags on the fence. Got my bearings, headed here."

Tyrell looked at his wife.

"And you were going to tear them off," Lou said, shaking her head.

"The lights helped," Stone said. "Until you lost power."

"Not for long, thank God," Lou said fervently. "Now, Ty, come help me get the bedrooms ready. We can talk in the morning."

Bree followed Annie's mother out of the room, and after a look at Stone and Annie, Tyrell did too.

"Made it. Told you," Stone said softly.

Was that a twinkle in his tired eyes or a reflection of the firelight? She looked at him, intensely grateful. Other, stronger feelings welled in her heart. For once, his arrogance didn't get a rise out of her.

"You're amazing."

"No, I'm not. I do what needs to be done and try not to think about it."

"Right. No big deal. You're still my hero. Thank you."

He leaned back in the chair, clasping his hands behind his head. "You're welcome."

Annie got up and bent over him. The tender kiss she pressed to his lips said everything she couldn't right then.

"Nice. But your folks are around."

"Yes. They live here. Let's go into the kitchen."

She took his hand and pulled him up. Stone encircled her waist and wrapped her up in a huge hug.

"I kinda like being a hero. Can we do that again sometime?"

"Hell no," she said vehemently.

She made two cups of cocoa and set them on the counter. "Better let that cool," she told Stone, pushing aside the tote she'd brought in. Then she looked inside again, lifting out Bree's purse. "She might need that."

Absently, Annie began to take out the things underneath, random items that had fallen out of the glove compartment.

There were papers, the owner's manual for the truck, a tire gauge, a pack of chewing gum, more papers, and a stapled report.

"What is this?"

She read it before Stone could stop her. Her eyes widened. There it was in black and white. An arrest report for Shep Connally. Mrs. Pearson's sworn statement. A photocopy of Marshall Stone's federal ID.

"Take a guess," he said laconically.

"Why didn't you tell me?"

He explained the reasons why in more detail and told her why she couldn't tell anyone for the time being.

Annie just stared at him.

"Did Nell know about this?"

"There is nothing that woman doesn't know or can't find out. I'm thinking of recruiting her for the bureau."

"Um. One more question. Who is the redhead?"

"A colleague. New hire. And her real name is Kerry, by the way."

Annie made a face. "Oh. Guess I could have given you the benefit of the doubt."

"But you didn't." Stone grinned, as if he was getting used to that. "Come here."

Annie started to—and stopped when Tyrell came into the kitchen. "Dad. Is Bree all right?"

"Your mom got her tucked up in bed. They're talking now. Thought I'd come down, see how you two were getting on."

"Mr. Bennett, I have something for you." Stone shuffled through the papers on the counter, gathering up most of them and sticking them back into the tote.

"What?"

"The survey report." Stone handed it over. "Pfeffer owes you a new fence. He tried to grab some of your land."

"That squattin' son-of-a-gun. Are you sure?"

"Yes."

"Stupid thing to do. He screwed up his title, that's for sure." Tyrell leafed through it. "Hmm. Maybe he'll sell to me cheap. Wouldn't mind adding some land to the spread. Never know when you'll need it."

He shot a meaningful look at Annie and then nodded at Stone. "I'll leave you two alone. I'm sure you don't mind."

They moved closer together when they heard his footsteps go down the hall. There was a brief moment of silence when her father stopped.

"You go right ahead and kiss her," he called in a low voice. "No one's looking."

Chapter 25

Several weeks later . . .

"**I**'m glad we got away."

Stone gave Annie's hand a squeeze as he helped her over a low fence. "We needed to, now that Christmas is over. Family is fine, but just you and me is even better."

"I know what you mean. Mom did too. Dad, well, he just has to get used to the idea."

They were staying at a lodge complex in the Wyoming backcountry, in their own private cabin, a big one close to hiking trails and cross-country skiing. They were out early to grab all the sunshine on offer during the short winter days.

"Rowdy would love it up here. I hope he's not missing us too much."

Stone chuckled. "I talked to Nell while you were in the shower. She dotes on that dog. Says he'll do until she gets a grandchild. Hey, did you hear from Bree?"

"Yes. She's doing great. The kids are still over the moon about her showing up on Christmas Eve. Cilla told them that Santa took care of that, per your request."

"Good."

"Bree's thinking about baking at Jelly Jam. She wants to settle down in Velde."

"You'd miss those little girls if they went away."

"I really would. Brothers aren't everything."

"I won't tell Sam or Zach you said that. Nice guys, both of them."

Annie laughed and squeezed his gloved hand. "They didn't give you too much of a hard time."

"Your dad let me know what to expect."

"And my mom refereed."

They walked on, plowing through the snow, following the blaze marks in the trees to stay on the trail. They'd finally had time to get to know each other better and the feelings between them ran deep.

They came out into a clearing. Annie tripped over a branch buried in the snow and fell headlong. She laughed as she rolled over. The snow was soft and feathery, almost dry.

"You okay?" Stone reached down, but she batted his hand away.

"Of course. I'm all bundled up." Annie stayed there. "I'm actually warm. It's true what they say about snow being good insulation."

"I wouldn't test that theory for too long if I were you."

She didn't get up.

"Okay. If you can't beat 'em, join 'em."

He went to his knees, then lay down next to her, turning his head. "You look beautiful in white. I will never forget you in that cowgirl shirt and the matching Stetson. Thought you looked like an angel."

"Hey, let's make some." She straightened her arms and moved them up and down to make wings. Then she moved her legs from side to side, in, then out, to create an angel dress. Annie sat up carefully. "Your turn."

"All right."

He made the same moves but skipped the dress part. Stone sat up and scrambled to stand. His angel turned out much taller than hers, with very large wings and long legs. "Not bad."

Then he pulled her up.

"Aww. They look like they love each other," Annie said. "They're holding hands—I mean, wings."

"So they are."

In the space between the two figures, the tips of her wing and his wing crossed.

Stone brushed the clinging snow off Annie's back and shoulders, then helped her shake it from the hood of her jacket. She did the same for him.

"Had enough?"

"I think so."

They took one more look at the silent angels and turned toward the lodge.

* * *

Their cabin was almost too big and comfortable to be called a cabin. But it shared some features with Nell's little hideaway.

The poufy bed was similar, just bigger, with an antique mahogany headboard-and-footboard set, and posts at each corner holding up drifts of white, filmy material. Stone took off his hiking boots and padded over to the bed in his socks, moving aside the sheer drape. He looked at it curiously.

"What do you call that stuff?"

"Chiffon."

"Oh. Like the cake."

"I would have said veils and gowns, but yes, there is chiffon cake."

She headed for the overstuffed sectional sofa, wishing it was a love seat but unwilling to complain. She tucked herself into one end and pulled an afghan over her feet while she watched Stone set up cordwood for a fire.

Crouched, he still looked tall. He was absorbed in the task, taking the time to do it right. At last he lit a long match and ignited the handful of dry pine needles he'd used for kindling. The seasoned wood caught. Flickering flames soon turned into a blaze that made his rugged face glow.

"Nice." He rose and turned to look at her, returning her smile. Then he moved to the sofa, choosing the other end.

"Comfortable, but too big," he said after a while. "Are you thinking what I'm thinking?"

Annie giggled and nodded. "Yes."

They both got up and dragged out the wide center section and moved it by the wall, then pushed the ends together. He sat down again and she did too.

"That's better," he said with satisfaction. "I like you next to me."

She moved into his lap. "Doesn't get any 'nexter' than this."

"Mmm." His voice rumbled in his throat, vibrating against her lips. She nuzzled his neck, letting her hand drift over the flannel shirt that covered his muscular chest.

Annie arched in his lap, sensually relaxed, cradled in his strong arms and held close. She murmured a protest when the jeans-clad thighs that warmed her rear shifted.

"We have to talk. Before this goes too far," he said.

"That's the idea. And I don't want to talk."

With a groan, he lifted her away from him and set her down on the cushion beside him. Annie took her revenge by thumping him with a pillow.

"We'll get back to what we were doing," he said. "I promise. Don't hit me."

She gave him a mock glare. "Why do we have to stop?"

Stone reached over and rummaged through the duffel bag he'd set by the sofa. "I have something to give you."

"I'd rather be kissed."

He didn't speak to that, just straightened up again, holding a box she recognized. It had a question mark on the side.

"Doesn't that belong to Nell?"

"She said I could have it."

"Oh. Well, what for? It's too small to be useful. She didn't even remember what she'd kept in it."

Stone chuckled. "That should be obvious."

"Not to me."

"It's marked with a question, so it's meant to hold a question."

She took it from his hand, going along with the joke, whatever it was. Something rattled inside. "Sounds like a big one."

"Look inside."

Annie lifted the lid. The small box held a box that was smaller still, covered in pure white velvet, with rounded corners. She took it out and turned it around in her fingers. "What is this?"

"A ring. Open it and see."

"In the shape of a question mark?"

"No."

"Is it . . . oh my." Her soft voice trailed off as she snapped open the box. A round diamond set in platinum caught the light of the fire. Stone turned toward her and caressed her cheek. The gentleness of his touch made her look at him.

"I know what I want, Annie. I'm ready for some changes in my life. The question is what you want."

"Are you asking me to marry you?" She gazed at him with wide eyes.

"Yes."

She was too stunned to say anything for a long moment.

"You don't have to answer right away," he assured her. He lifted the diamond ring from its white silk nest. "May I?"

Annie held out her left hand. There had never

been a ring on it. Until Stone, there hadn't been a man she would have wanted to put a ring on it.

He slid it onto her finger. "Take your time. Think it over. I can wait. You're worth waiting for. I love you."

"I—I love you too." Her voice was shaky. But she knew she did. "And you can have your answer right now. Yes."

He nodded. Then he kissed her again. Annie never wanted to stop. And now she would never have to.

If you enjoyed
CHRISTMAS IN COWBOY COUNTRY,
keep reading for a special preview of
TEXAS TRUE,
the first book in Janet Dailey's new series,
The Tylers of Texas,
available this April as a Zebra paperback!

When Virgil "Bull" Tyler left this life, it was said that his departing spirit roared like a norther across the yellowed spring pastureland, shrilled upward among the buttes and hoodoos of the Caprock Escarpment, and lost itself in the cry of a red-tailed hawk circling above the high Texas plain.

Later on, folks would claim they'd felt Bull's passing like a sudden chill on the March wind. But his son Will Tyler had felt nothing. Busy with morning chores, Will was unaware of his father's death until he heard the shouts of the husky male nurse who came in every morning to get the old man out of bed and into his wheelchair.

Will knew at once what had happened. By the time his long strides carried him to the rambling stone ranch house, he'd managed to brace for what he would find. All the same, the sight of that once-powerful body lying rigid under the patchwork quilt, the lifeless blue eyes staring up at the ceiling, hit him like a kick in the gut. He'd lived his whole thirty-nine years in his father's shadow. Now the old man was gone. But the shadow remained.

"Do you want me to call nine-one-one?" The young man was new to the ranch. Bull had gone through a parade of hired caregivers in the six years since a riding accident had shattered his spine, paralyzing his hips and legs.

"What for?" Will pulled the sheet over his father's face. In the movies somebody would've closed those eyes. In real life, Will knew for a fact that it didn't work.

"We'll need to call somebody," the nurse said. "The county coroner, maybe? They'll want to know what killed him."

Alcohol and pain pills, Will surmised. But what the hell, there were protocols to be followed. "Fine, go ahead and call," he said. "I'll be outside if you need me."

Bernice Crawford, the plump, graying widow who'd been the Tylers' cook and housekeeper since Will's boyhood, met him in the hall. Tears were streaming down her apple-cheeked face. "Oh, Will! I'm so sorry!"

"I know." Will searched for words of comfort for her. "Dad thought the world of you, Bernice."

"He was a miserable old man," she said. "You know that as well as I do. But he carried the burden God gave him, and now he's free of it."

Will gave her shoulder an awkward squeeze before he turned away and strode toward the front door. He needed to breathe fresh air. And he needed time to gather his thoughts.

He made it to the wide, covered porch before the raw reality slammed home. Setting his jaw, he gripped the rail and forced himself to breathe. His father was dead. He felt the void left by Bull's passing—and the weight of responsibility for this ranch and everyone in it that was now his to shoulder alone. The morning breeze carried the smells of spring—thawing manure, sprouting grass, and restless animals. Hammer blows rang from the hollow beyond the barn, where the hands were shoring up the calving pens for the pregnant heifers that had been bred a week ahead of the older cows. The rest of the cattle that had wintered in the canyon would soon need rounding up for the drive to spring pasture above the escarpment on the Llano Estacado—the Staked Plain, given that name by early Spaniards because the land was so flat and desolate that they had to drive stakes in the ground to keep from losing their way.

As he looked down from the low rise where the house stood, Will's gaze swept over the heart of the sprawling Rimrock Ranch—the vast complex of sheds, corrals, and barns, the hotel-like bunkhouse for unmarried hands, the adjoining cookhouse and commissary, and the line of neat brick bungalows for workers with families. To the east a shallow playa lake glittered pale aquamarine in the sunlight. It made a pretty sight, but the water was no good to drink. With the summer heat it would evaporate, leaving behind an ugly white patch of alkali where nothing would grow.

Will scowled up at the cloudless sky. Last summer's drought had been a nightmare. If no rain fell, the coming summer could be even worse, with the grass turning to dust and the cattle having to be sold off early, at a pittance on the plummeting beef market.

Will had managed the ranch for the past six years and done it as competently as his father ever had. But even from his wheelchair Bull had been the driving spirit behind Rimrock. Only now that he was gone did Will feel the full burden of his legacy.

"Looks like we'll be planning a funeral." The dry voice startled Will before he noticed the old man seated in one of the rocking chairs with Tag, the ranch border collie, sprawled at his feet. Jasper Platt had been foreman since before Will was born. Now that rheumatism kept him out of the saddle, he was semiretired. But Will still relied on him. No one understood the ranch and everything on it, including the people, the way Jasper did.

"When did you find out?" Will asked.

"About the same time you did." Jasper was whip spare and tough as an old saddle. His hair was an unruly white thatch, his skin burned dark as walnut below the pale line left by his hat. The joints of his fingers were knotted with arthritis.

"You'd best start phoning people," he said. "Some of them, like Beau, will need time to get here."

"I know." Will had already begun a mental list. His younger brother Beau was out on the East Coast and hadn't set foot on the ranch in more than a decade—not since he'd bolted to join the army after a big blowup with his father. The rest of the folks who mattered enough to call lived on neighboring ranches or twenty miles down the state highway in Blanco Springs, the county seat. Most of them could wait until after the date and time for the funeral had been set. But Will's ex-wife, Tori, who lived in Blanco with their twelve-year-old daughter, Erin, would need to know right away. Erin would take the news hard. Whatever Bull had been to others, he was her grandpa.

Neither call would be easy to make. Beau was out of the army now and working for the government in Washington. He had kept them informed of his whereabouts, but an address and a couple phone numbers were about all Will knew about his brother's life out East.

As for Tori—short for Victoria—she'd left Will eight years ago to practice law in town. Shared custody of their daughter had kept things civil between them. But the tension when they spoke was like thin ice on a winter pond, still likely to crack at the slightest shift.

The nearest mortuary was in Lubbock. He'd have to call them, too. They'd most likely want to pick up the body at the coroner's. *The body.* Hell, what a cold, unfeeling process. Too bad they couldn't just wrap the old man in a blanket and stash him in the Caprock like the Indians used to do. Bull would have liked that.

As if conjured by the thought of Indians, a solitary figure stepped out of the horse barn and stood for a moment, gazing across the muddy yard. Fourteen years ago, Sky Fletcher, the part-

Comanche assistant foreman, had wandered onto the ranch as a skinny teenage orphan and stayed to prove himself as a man known across the state for his skill with horses.

"Does Sky know?" Will asked Jasper.

"He knows. And he said to tell you that when you're ready, he'll crank up the backhoe and dig the grave next to your mother's."

"Sky's got better things to do."

Jasper gave him a sharp glance. "Bull was good to that boy. He wants to help. Let him."

"Fine. Tell him thanks." Will looked back toward the barn, but Sky was no longer in sight.

Squaring his shoulders, Will took a couple of deep breaths and crossed the porch to the front door. It was time to face the truth that awaited him inside the house.

His father was dead—and the void he'd left behind was as deep as the red Texas earth.

M

More from Bestselling Author
JANET DAILEY

Available Wherever Books Are Sold!